Out Lasted

SHERWOOD OUTLAWS
BOOK THREE

HAYLEY OSBORN

LEXITY INK
PUBLISHING

Lexity Ink Publishing
Christchurch, New Zealand

Publisher's Note: This is a work of fiction. Names,
characters, places, and incidents are a product of the
author's imagination. Locales and public names are
sometimes used for atmospheric purposes. Any resemblance
to actual people, living or dead, or to businesses, companies,
events, institutions, or locales is completely coincidental.

Book Layout ©2017 BookDesignTemplates.com
Cover Design by Covers by Combs
Editing by Melissa A Craven

Outlasted/ Hayley Osborn. -- 1st ed.
ISBN 978-0-473-49743-9
Also available as an eBook

For Mum and Dad

ONE

I WAS still.

I was silent.

I was shattered.

"We can't catch them on foot," puffed Tuck, his fingers pressed tight around my wrist to keep me sprinting deeper into the forest the way I wanted to.

The thundering of hooves quietened into the distance while I tried to catch my breath. Rob was gone. Thrown over the back of a horse with an arrow in his back, just like I'd seen in my dreams. I swiped at tears I didn't recall crying and ignored the ache in my throat from screaming words I didn't recall speaking.

Gone.

I'd been complacent. Or naïve. Probably both. For months, I'd seen warnings of this very moment, and I hadn't stopped it. Even now, I stood catching my breath on the forest trail while Gisborne stole Rob away, rather than actually doing anything. I struggled against Tuck's grasp. "Not when we stand still and don't try."

My boots and the bottom of my dress were damp from the early morning dew, but the cold barely registered against the ache in my chest. I'd watched the arrow sink into Rob's back, heard his scream of pain. I hadn't helped him. Each moment I continued to do nothing, Rob slipped farther away. He couldn't help himself. We had to help him. I had to. I pulled at Tuck's grip again. "Let me go! I need to save him."

His fingers tightened until his grip bordered on painful. "Maryanne. Stop. We will follow them. All of us. Whether we leave now, or stall for half an hour while we get our things together isn't going to make any difference."

Probably not in the grand scheme of things. But to me it already felt like I'd lost Rob, and standing around waiting wouldn't make that feeling go away.

Footsteps pounded against the dirt trail and we turned to find John sprinting toward us. He'd barely stopped running before I blurted, "Gisborne took Rob."

He gave a single nod, his jaw set but his gaze pained. "I saw. From up at the village."

"We'll go get Miller and Alan, pack up, then go after them." Tuck released my wrist and nodded, waiting until I started along the forest trail toward the village before following.

"Alan's missing." John spoke to our backs, hesitating between words like he didn't want to tell us. It wasn't hard to guess why. Alan was Rob's older brother. He had Down Syndrome and Rob had always thought Alan was safest if he didn't live in the forest with us. That was until I talked him into bringing Alan to live with us last week.

I spun to look at him. "What do you mean?" Alan couldn't be missing. We didn't have time for missing.

"He's not in the village. No one's seen him this morning." He glanced at me. "You were closer than me. Did Gisborne take him, too?"

"No." Gisborne had his eye on only one prize, and that was Rob. I could still see that arrow striking him in the back, the soldier throwing him over a horse. Tears again filled my eyes. "Only Rob." My voice wobbled and I pressed the heels of my hands into my eye sockets, forcing my tears away and making myself concentrate on John's voice. Pushing Rob down in my thoughts was an impossible task. "Where do you think Alan's gone?"

John glanced at the trees surrounding us as if that would give him the answers we so desperately needed. "No clue. But he can't have gone far. It's only just light."

True. I dragged a hand through my messy hair—I hadn't even had the chance to brush it this morning before my world turned upside down. I was torn. I wanted to go after Rob this minute. The urge to do so was a physical pull on my body. But Alan needed us, too. Possibly more than Rob. "We have to search the forest for Alan. Before we go after Rob." It wasn't that I didn't want to search for Alan, it was that I knew from bitter experience what Gisborne could do when he kidnapped someone, and the longer we took to find Rob, the more opportunity Gisborne had to hurt him. That was, if Rob wasn't dead already.

Tuck nodded, his eyes glued on the place where the soldiers had disappeared on the trail a few minutes earlier. "We do." Perhaps we all wanted to be in two places at once right now.

"Spread out." John turned in a circle. "I'll go this way. Tuck, you go that way. Maryanne, you search around here. If you find him, yell out, and then go back to the hut in the village."

I nodded and moved off the trail, calling Alan's name. *He can't have gone far.* John had voiced what we were all hoping.

In the distance, John and Tuck, and eventually Miller and some of the villagers, called his name, too. Their calls grew weaker as the distance stretched between us. No one yelled to say they'd found him.

I don't know how long we searched. An hour. Longer. Less. With each passing minute, I grew more frantic. Worried about Alan. Terrified for Rob. I heard it in my voice every time I shouted Alan's name. I didn't even know if I was doing a thorough search or not. I was walking fast, hoping my pace would help us find him sooner. Because, once we found him, we could go after Rob.

I clambered over a fallen tree and found Miller on the other side. He shook his head. "He's not here." Miller looked terrible. His eyes were blood-shot, his cheeks red and his tunic untucked. It was probably because of Rob but could just as easily be the remnants of a big night last night. We'd come to the village of Huxley yesterday for their Valentine's Day party and spent the night eating and dancing. I'd never been as happy as I was when I fell asleep last night. Now I felt the opposite. Miller had consumed a lot of whiskey at the party and was probably feeling pretty bad this morning anyway, and that was without everything else that had happened.

"He has to be." I pushed past him. The longer we stood around talking, the longer Rob was with Gisborne.

Miller moved in front of me, ducking to look in my eyes. "Lady Maryanne. He's not here. Maybe he's where John or Tuck are searching. But he's not here."

He was right. I'd walked back and forth, working in a grid to search between the edge of the path and the fallen oak. I might have moved fast as I searched, but I hadn't seen anything to suggest anyone had left the trails around the village recently. "Well, maybe we need to check in with them."

Miller shook his head, his eyes skimming my face as worry creased his forehead. "No. We should go back to the hut and wait there for the others."

I stared at him. Go back to the hut? Gisborne had kidnapped Rob, and Alan was lost in the forest. "How will that help anyone?"

"Maybe Alan's gone back there to wait for us?"

Of course. That had to be where he was. I should have considered it sooner. I started back toward the village at a run. Alan was probably already there, panicking because he couldn't find us. I needed to start thinking clearly if I was going to be any help to either of them.

Miller jogged beside me and was just a step behind when I threw open the door to the little hut we'd slept in last night. I stopped on the threshold.

Empty.

Miller pushed past me. His strawberry-blond hair duck-tailed in all directions and his face was pale. I had no idea what to do next. I didn't know why I was looking to a fourteen-year-old for help, except that I couldn't do this anymore. I couldn't see past the gaping hole that was Rob or make any sort of decision. Whereas, Miller seemed able to.

For a moment, he stood still, looking around the hut. Then he picked a blanket up from the floor and wrapped it around my shoulders before directing me to sit in front of the fire. I could barely keep the blanket secured over my body, I was shivering so hard. I didn't recall when that started. Or why.

I pulled my legs up to my chest and wrapped my arms around them while Miller built up the fire. In no time the hut—which contained nothing but a set of broken shelves, a few plates and mugs in various states of repair, and a heavy copper cooking pot—was warm. But all the warmth in the world couldn't heat my soul.

"Do you think they found Alan yet?" My voice was raspy from screaming Rob's name and then Alan's in the forest. Miller couldn't know any more than me, but it felt better to talk than to silently wade through my guilt. I should have stopped this happening.

"They will." He pressed a mug of tea I didn't want into my shaking hands and took a deep swig from his own mug, probably trying to rid himself of the effects of last night. Tears filled my eyes. Last night, when Rob and I had finally told each other how we felt. Last night, the best night of my entire life.

I placed my mug on the packed dirt floor near the fire and got to my feet. Now was not the time to feel sorry for myself. "I should help them. I should go back out there." Sitting around on my butt wasn't doing anyone any good. It certainly wouldn't make up for allowing Gisborne to take Rob.

Miller pulled me back down. "John and Tuck have it under control. I think you need to rest." His eyes fell on my shaking hands. "And you should be here when they bring Alan back."

"Where could he have gone?" Alan had never wandered away like this.

"Don't know, milady." Miller took another swig from his mug, then burst into silent, shaking tears. He leaned forward and put his head in his hands, his hair falling over top of them. "This is all my fault."

"Miller." I placed a hand on his shoulder. "It's not." There was no possible way Miller could take responsibility for any of this.

"It's nice of you to say, milady, but I know the truth. Both you and Rob tipped whiskey out of my mug last night, but I found a way to get more. We only stayed in the village because of me, because I couldn't walk in a straight line, because I couldn't stay awake. If we'd left the way we planned..."

"Gisborne would have found us somewhere else." Maybe not this morning, but eventually. Besides, I had a mortgage on guilt over today's events. "Rob and I were getting on better yesterday, maybe that distracted him and he didn't hear the soldiers coming."

Miller picked up his mug and stared miserably into it, about as willing to release his guilt as I was.

I gave his shoulder a squeeze. "You'll feel better about everything once your headache wears off." That was a stretch. None of us were going to feel better until we had Rob and Alan back with us.

But Miller, for all his attempts to act older, sometimes needed reassurance.

"You know I have a headache?" He lifted his eyes to meet mine.

"It's called a hangover. It's what happens when you don't listen to your elders and sneak too many mugs of whiskey." I tried to smile. I had the beginnings of a headache, too. The magic that helped me understand their twelfth century English seemed weaker this morning. Or I had to concentrate harder to use it. Or I was really stressed and everything was more difficult than usual, including breathing.

"I'll listen always from now on," he said gloomily.

Footsteps outside made both of us turn expectantly to the door. It opened and John strode in. He paused for a moment looking at the raging fireplace at the far end of the room, then threw off his cloak and pushed up his sleeves. It must be hotter in here than I'd thought. I still felt frozen to the core.

"Any luck?" I knew the answer. If he'd found Alan, he would have come bounding through the door right behind John.

John shook his head and poured himself some tea from the pot bubbling over the fire. "Might need to look farther afield. Need to talk to Tuck first to make sure we're not covering the same ground." Like Miller, he stared into his mug, and heaved out a huge sigh. If this was hard on me, it was wrecking them. They'd been family for almost four years now, longer for Rob and Tuck. I'd only known them all for a few months. "I don't know what we should do next. Follow Gisborne? Try to save Rob? Keep searching for Alan? What if Rob's dead already, and Alan isn't? Or the other way around? What if we spend time searching for the wrong one? What if...?" He ran his hand through his always messy hair, his jaw stiffening in an attempt to keep all emotion from his face.

His questions were an echo of those rushing through my mind. There were so many possibilities and if we made the wrong decision, someone might die. I had no more answers than he did. I patted John's knee. "Maybe Tuck will find him."

We watched the leaping flames of the fire in silence until the door of the hut opened and shut again. Tuck shrugged off his cloak and shook his head. Then he threw his cloak across the small room where it hit the wall and slid to the floor. "Dammit all to hell."

None of us spoke. Tuck never swore. Tuck showed his anger through snide comments. Throwing things, yelling and swearing weren't his style.

"I knew coming here was a bad idea." He looked at me as he spoke. Somehow, the decision to attend the party last night, the decision we'd all agreed on together, was suddenly my fault.

Tuck wanted a fight. It was how he worked through things, but he wasn't getting what he needed from me. We should be doing something constructive, and fighting wasn't it.

I looked from one face to the next in the dim light of the hut. Loss. Defeat. Misery. Every expression was the same. This was Gisborne's fault.

That man had already taken so much from so many; I would not allow him to steal any more from us. I stood and began packing the few things we'd brought with us into my pack. I'd already spent far too long sitting around feeling sorry for myself. That wasn't how I did things. At least, it wasn't since Rob came into my life.

"What are you doing?" Miller asked.

"Leaving. We can't stay here. We're sitting targets if Gisborne decides to return. And each moment we stay puts the entire village at risk. I don't think any of us want that on our conscience." Gisborne would be back. I was next on his list. He'd said so as his horse carried Rob away.

There was a chorus of murmured noes.

"I believe Rob is still alive and if he is, Gisborne will try to keep him that way for a while yet." The first part of that sentence was based on nothing more than hope. The second part was likely true. When I was at home in Christchurch, seeing Rob shot with an arrow wasn't the only dream I'd had. I'd also dreamed of Rob at Nottingham Castle with Gisborne. Plus, there was Gisborne's threat before he left. "He said something to that effect. I think Gisborne has taken Rob to Nottingham."

If one premonition could come true, so could another. It went totally against what Gisborne had done when he'd kidnapped John or Miller or me, but I'd seen Nottingham Castle in my dreams. I was certain that was where they'd gone. And no one else was offering up any other suggestions.

"We'll split up. John and Miller can go in search of Alan. Tuck and I will go to Nottingham for Rob." Tuck was the last person I wanted to spend days with alone, but I wanted Alan to feel safe and happy the moment we found him, and there was more chance of that happening if he was with John than Tuck.

As for my plan, it wasn't great. It wasn't even a good plan. However, it was something. And we all needed to be doing something.

John pushed himself to his feet. "I can't think of anything better, so I'm in."

"Me too," said Miller. He stood and picked up his cloak. "Tell us where you searched Tuck, so we don't go over the same area again."

Tuck's back was to us, his hands in his hair. Other than turning to glare at me, he'd barely moved since throwing his cloak. He was always going to be the hardest to convince, if only because he hated every word that ever left my mouth. I braced myself for the tongue lashing I was about to receive for such a stupid plan. I was open to ideas and I'd tell him so. If he could come up with something better, I'd be the first onboard.

Finally, he gave a deep sigh. "Maryanne's right. We have to split up. And Nottingham's the likeliest place to find Rob. We can meet at the stone cottage once you find Alan."

My shoulders sagged. We were screwed. Tuck hated my idea but couldn't come up with anything better, and worse still, didn't have the energy to tell me so.

No.

I wasn't thinking like that. We could do this. We would. The alternative was unthinkable.

"Good. Then get your things." I glanced at the place Rob had slept beside the fire last night. When I'd crept past his sleeping form this morning to go outside, I'd been so happy. Everything had been perfect. Now, just a few hours later, everything was ruined.

The Valentine's Day gift I'd given Rob—two pieces of soap brought with me from the twenty-first century—lay where he'd left it last night, waiting for him to pack it up this morning. "And if anyone can fit Rob's and Alan's things in their packs, take them, too." I picked up Rob's present and slid it into my pack, then opened the door and stepped outside, almost treading on a man coming into the hut.

I stopped dead, blinking hard.

What I was seeing wasn't real. Shaking my head, I took a step back.

That cloak, dark brown and lined with fur. The gait. And that smile.

It couldn't be.

"Rob?"

Two

I RUBBED my eyes because I had to be seeing
things, then met his gaze. It was Rob. Here. In
front of me. Standing on the rutted dirt cart path
that led to every house in the village.

"Did Alan come back yet?" He smiled down at
me as if he hadn't heard anyone screaming Alan's
name this past hour.

And, how was he here, anyway?

Tuck, Miller and John burst out the door,
silent, then all speaking at once. They hugged him,
and each other. And me. They whooped and
slapped each other's backs. All while Rob watched
with a slightly dazed expression on his face, which
was pretty much the way I felt, too. Villagers

smiled as they passed. Those who hadn't seen the soldiers this morning, had heard about them. Some had even put aside their work for a while to help hunt for Alan. We might be strangers here, but they knew who we were and what had happened.

I reached out to touch Rob's arm, just to make sure my eyes, and ears, weren't deceiving me.

"Maryanne. You look awfully pale." He put his hand over mine—I had wrapped my fingers tightly around his arm, half to hold myself up, half to prove to myself he really was here. "Do you think perhaps you should sit down?"

I shook my head, still trying to make sense of what was in front of my face. I'd seen Rob with an arrow in his back. I'd seen him thrown face-down and unmoving across the back of a horse. He'd been too injured to escape, and Gisborne's men had tied him so tight that he couldn't have anyway. "Are you okay?" I pulled from his grasp and walked behind him to check the arrow wound. "Do you need a healer?" There was no entry hole in his cloak, no blood, and from what I could tell, no wound.

Rob looked at me sideways, before glancing at the rest of his friends. "What's...going on?"

"We thought you were dead. I thought it was my fault for drinking too much whiskey and making us stay here last night." Miller grinned as the weight of all that guilt lifted from his shoulders.

A frown wrinkled Rob's forehead, his eyes still moving between each of us. "Why would you think that?"

"Lady Maryanne saw..." Miller stopped, his eyes widening with understanding. The same understanding that dawned on me at that same moment. Miller's face fell.

"Maryanne?" Rob tilted his head to one side, the frown still in place.

"The soldiers came. Gisborne came." I hadn't expected it to be this hard to tell him. Until a few moments ago, I hadn't expected to have to tell him.

Rob turned on the spot looking along the street. A boy ran past followed by a laughing group of kids, women cleaned clothes in buckets, or carried wood for their fires, and farther away, men worked in the fields. I knew what he was seeing. And what he was thinking. This was not a village recently ransacked by a group of Gisborne's soldiers.

"What did he want? Is everyone okay?" Rob's question was slow, like he didn't want to ask.

No one else understood. No one else had put all the pieces together. Except maybe Miller, and he wasn't talking. It was up to me to say it. "Alan's not."

"Alan's not what?" His frown grew deeper.

I swallowed, plucking up the courage to tell him the words I needed to say. He would blame me. I'd been there and done nothing. He was going to hate me.

His eyes widened and he looked at each of us, then poked his head through the door of the empty hut. "Alan's still not here?" he asked, his words slow as he turned back to me.

"We've been out searching for him, Rob." John's voice came from somewhere behind me. "Couldn't find a trace of him."

Rob took me by the shoulders, waiting until I looked at him. "Gisborne was here?"

I nodded.

"With soldiers? On horseback?"

I drew a breath and forced the words from my mouth. "Gisborne took Alan."

THREE

ROB shook his head as if he could repel my words.

"I thought he was you. It wasn't fully light, and I wasn't close enough to tell. I saw your cloak, and your hair." Alan's cloak, Alan's hair. "And it was exactly the way I'd seen it in my dream." I stopped because the words were coming so fast, no one would understand unless I took a deep breath and slowed down. "I yelled to you...to him, thinking he was you. He didn't turn." Because I'd been yelling his brother's name. "Then Gisborne..."

Rob closed his eyes for a moment like he could imagine exactly what I would say next. He straightened his back and met my eyes. "Gisborne...?"

"Shot an arrow into his back, tied him onto a horse and left." Might as well rip the Band-Aid off. There was no point in drawing this out. It just made it more horrific. "I'm sorry, Rob. I tried to get to him." To you. "But Gisborne stopped me with his archers." What a mess. We'd wasted so much time this morning. Especially me, feeling sorry for myself. "We didn't go after them because we couldn't find Alan. We thought he'd gone for a walk and gotten lost. We were just about to split up so we could search for you both."

Rob's shoulders dropped and he pulled me close. "It's okay. We'll sort this out."

He stroked the length of my back and my shoulders relaxed. He'd sort it. Of course, he would.

"Where have you been, Rob?" Tuck asked. "Didn't you hear us yelling for your brother? Maryanne screamed hard enough to split the forest when they took him."

I leaned back in his arms. Where *had* he been?

"I woke up and both Alan and Maryanne were gone." He shook his head. "I thought he'd convinced Maryanne to take him to the waterfall early. I went to find them." Alan had begged to go see the waterfall near here after hearing how much fun Rob had there last summer, and Rob agreed to take him. This morning, after we all woke up.

John looked along the cart path and out to the field. He licked one finger and put it in the air. "The river's upwind. And the waterfall's probably loud enough to cover any commotion we made. I didn't search that far away." John shook his head, an apology in his eyes as he looked at Rob.

"Neither did I," mumbled Tuck. "Should have, but I didn't think of it."

"I was hardly going to go off in the dark to a place I've never been." There was a snap in my voice as everything fell into place in my mind. This could have all been avoided if Rob had thought things through properly. He should never have gone to the waterfall to look for us. Then again, if Alan hadn't risen so early, or if I'd gotten to Alan before Gisborne got there, it would have worked out differently, too. So many things had fallen into place perfectly for this to happen.

Maybe we couldn't even put it down to bad luck. I'd told Rob about my dreams, even knowing I would die for it. I thought I was so smart when I escaped Gisborne and felt the magic shift because I'd done enough to keep us both safe. But maybe I'd just moved the problem to someone else. By telling Rob about my dreams, had I as good as signed Alan's death warrant?

I assumed Gisborne, in the dim light and a pain induced haze from the injuries we'd given him a few days ago, thought he was taking Rob, especially when he witnessed my reaction. But he could just as easily have targeted Alan when the opportunity presented itself. For months he'd been trying to hurt Rob by hurting us. This could be another step in that direction. The right one, from Gisborne's point of view. This would break Rob.

Rob looked down at me. "What was I supposed to do when I woke to find you both gone?"

"I don't know." Irritation filled my voice, fueled by my guilt for not preventing what I'd seen coming in my dreams. What good were dreams when I couldn't do anything about the things I saw? "That neither of us could sleep?" *Stop.* This wasn't Rob's fault.

He stiffened. "Maybe you should remember that when you call my name, I'll always turn around. If I don't..." He didn't need to finish his sentence. The blame was clear for everyone to see.

"Maryanne couldn't have stopped him." Tuck was the first to arrive as Gisborne rode off into the forest with Alan. He'd sprinted down from the village, watching it happen as he ran. "None of us could. We were too far away."

Tuck had never stood up for me before. Rob knew it, too. He looked at me and mumbled. "Sorry. I didn't mean that."

Tuck turned to me. "And Rob couldn't have known what would happen when he rose this morning."

Obviously. None of us could have known. I deserved the reprimand. "I'm sorry, too."

"Good." Tuck passed Rob's pack to him. He'd taken it as he left the hut. "Then, I suggest we follow Maryanne's plan and go get Alan back."

There were no horses in Huxley, so we followed Gisborne on foot. It was about the least practical thing we'd ever done. Especially when we needed to travel as quickly as possible.

"How close is the main trail from here?" Our pace was steady; single file along a trail with bracken and branches brushing against our faces, arms and legs. It was too narrow for horses, so we wouldn't run into soldiers, but it wasn't the fastest way to find Alan, either.

Rob shrugged. "A good hour's walk. Maybe longer."

"In which direction?"

Rob pointed off to the left at another thin trail. I started down it, waiting for the others to follow.

"Where are you going?" Rob asked, a sigh in his voice.

"To rob a carriage."

We reached the main trail just before midday, quietly splitting up and walking along either side. We'd have no warning today about who might be traveling through the forest in a carriage. We weren't acting on rumors. This carriage robbery would be different to any we'd done before and was going to happen on a moment's notice. It would only work if we ducked out of sight before the approaching coachman saw us.

The trail was deserted. Not a single carriage trundled toward us until mid-afternoon. Rob was growing impatient, ready to give up on this robbery plan. We were still walking toward Nottingham as we waited for the carriage, and making good time, too. But it was dangerous to travel on this trail—it was the one the soldiers used, and we didn't need them finding Robin Hood.

I was almost ready to give up, too, when we heard the rumble of carriage wheels approaching. We watched, hidden behind huge leafy trees at the edge of the trail, waiting for our opportunity. The carriage was small, pulled by just a single horse, but it would do.

At the last possible moment, Rob stepped onto the trail, leaving just enough time for the horse to slow. John and Miller stepped out behind him. And after them, me. This might be the most important robbery we'd ever committed. We needed them to think there were too many of us to fight.

"Move on!" called the coachman, shaking the reins in his hand.

Rob shook his hooded head. "Can't do that, sorry."

"I'll run you down."

I lifted the bow in my hand and aimed for the coachman at the same time Miller drew his sword.

"That would be unwise, sir. Not only do I have the men you see standing in front of you, but I have twice this many again, hidden in the trees, waiting to shoot you dead should you refuse to comply." Rob's arms rested casually at his sides. The commanding tone in his voice was the only weapon he needed.

The coachman glanced into the forest, his eyes darting from one tree to the next. He wiped his palms on his tunic. "We have no gold. Nothing of value."

"I'm not after your gold." Rob walked up to the horse and began pulling at the ties that hitched it to the carriage. Today, this horse was more valuable than anything else in the forest.

And for once, we were taking something for our own use. It didn't sit well with any of us, but no one wanted to leave Alan in Gisborne's hands a second longer than necessary.

"What are you doing?" The coachman moved to jump from the carriage, to stop Rob. From the trees, Tuck fired an arrow. It whistled past the man's leg and lodged with a thunk into the back of the seat he perched on.

"Sit. Down!" There would be no charm from Rob today. Today was about something entirely different. He had a brother to save.

The coachman sat, resting on the edge of the seat because Tuck's arrow was in the way. I wasn't sure he was going to remain compliant, and I fixed my arrow on him in case he stood up and whipped out his sword, which seemed like what he wanted to do.

"Rob!" Tuck hissed Rob's name from his hiding place among the trees.

The moment he spoke, I heard the reason. Horses. Coming this way.

"I hear it," Rob said evenly, not looking up and still working on the ties. The harness was stuck. His fingers moved around the knot, trying to pull it undone, but it wasn't budging.

"Rob." This time it was a command, rather than a hiss.

Rob shook his head. "Nearly there. Just a moment longer."

The horses rounded the bend in the trail, trotting in our direction. My heart sank. Soldiers. Their burgundy and gold cloaks spread over their horses' rumps, and chainmail glinting where the sun caught it.

It was more likely bad luck than bad management that they were on the trail right now. Although Gisborne probably expected us to follow, I doubted he expected us to use this trail for exactly the reason we were now facing. I also doubted he'd sent these soldiers back to look for us. They were probably heading somewhere else and we were unlucky enough to be in the wrong place at the wrong time. And now our bad luck had us staring down five soldiers on horseback.

When they saw the carriage stopped in the middle of the trail with the four of us crowded around, they kicked their horses in the ribs and galloped toward us.

I didn't know what to do. Did I raise my arrow from the coachman to shoot at the soldiers, and leave the coachman unguarded to do whatever he wanted to Rob? Or did I stay where I was until Rob had the horse free?

Miller clumsily sheathed his sword, pulling his bow from his back and stringing it. John still wasn't confident with his bow, had barely used it since Gisborne took two of his fingers, and with Rob busy, that left only three of us capable of taking out the soldiers from this distance.

Five soldiers heading our way—the beating of hooves on the ground growing louder by the second—a coachman and goodness knew how many inside the tiny carriage, surely no more than two, and hopefully they were unarmed.

We could do it.

An arrow whistled from the trees. Tuck must have decided he wasn't waiting for them to get any closer. It flew wide, and my decision was made. "John." I nodded toward the coachman, directing him to take watch.

John moved closer to the man, to where the staff in his hand was in range, and nodded his understanding. His eyes made a constant circuit; from Rob, to the coachman, to the soldiers.

I sighted the soldier on the second-fastest horse; Tuck was likely aiming for the fastest one. I let my arrow go. It hit the soldier in the arm, the force twisting him backward and off balance. He fell under the feet of the horse behind him. There was no time to celebrate. I pulled another arrow from my quiver.

"Nice shot." Miller aimed at one of the riders and missed. If only he spent as much time practicing with his bow as he did with his sword.

I glanced at Rob. His fingers were moving fast, still trying to free the horse.

He must have seen my movement and glanced my way. "Almost done."

I nodded. Even if he got that horse free right now, we had to stay and fight. If we ran, they'd give chase and we'd likely lose against their swords.

The soldiers that were left were spread wide across the trail. They leaned forward in their saddles and urged their horses forward with kicks and yelled commands.

I aimed for the middle rider just as the one to his left fell, hit by Tuck's arrow. They were getting close. Almost too close to use my bow. Time for one more shot. I took it. And missed.

"John!" I yelled. The closest soldier was almost near enough to hit John with his swinging sword.

We should have run the moment we saw them coming. An injury here would hinder us from getting to Alan. I didn't even want to think about the other option—the worse one.

John jumped between the carriage and the horse, ducking away from the soldier's sword. I let out a breath of relief that he was safe for now.

Until the soldier's eye shifted to his next target. Me.

Four

I FUMBLED with my arrow, my hand shaking as I attempted to nock it, knowing the soldier was bearing down on me. I couldn't get the arrow in place. There was no time. He was too close.

I glanced at him and he stared back, eyes fixed on the junction of my shoulder and my neck. The place his sword would slice into me if I didn't stop him first.

I had one option if I wanted to live, and it wasn't shooting my arrow.

Waiting until he was too close to change course, I lunged for the bracken at the side of the trail. His horse pounded past, hooves like thunder against the dirt. He cursed.

I jumped to my feet, bow in one hand, arrow in the other. He was not going to win. I would not let him hurt me or my friends. As he slowed then turned his horse, I nocked my arrow. He kicked his horse in the ribs, urging her forward. I drew the string back to my cheek. His day was about to get a whole lot worse. The horse began to gallop, and I took my shot.

My arrow slipped through the chainmail at his chest. He dropped his sword and fell forward, then toppled sideways on the ground. Dead. Or soon to be.

I twisted back to the carriage. John ran, staff clutched in one hand, to help Miller with the soldiers approaching him.

Sensing his chance, the coachman made his move. He kicked Rob in the face. His head rocked back like whiplash. I nocked another arrow and aimed for the coachman's chest. It found his heart and he was dead before he knew it was coming.

A soldier raced toward Miller and John, the metal of his blade shining. His sword came down at Miller's neck, but Miller blocked, and the soldier raced straight past. I turned and fired an arrow into his back, watching just long enough to see him begin to slide from his horse before twisting back and nocking another arrow.

One soldier left.

Adrenalin pumped through my veins. One more to kill and we were safe. But the soldier was already fleeing. I aimed my arrow anyway. His burgundy and gold cape reminded me of what was taken from us this morning, and of what Gisborne had done when he kidnapped me. I wanted someone to pay. It should have mattered that he was fleeing. It should have mattered that to stop him I had to shoot him in the back. But it didn't.

"Maryanne." Rob's voice broke into my thoughts.

"One more."

"Maryanne. Stop. He's leaving." Rob put a hand on my arm.

I shook him off, focused on the soldier's back. "Almost done."

"Maryanne. No. We're good. Look at me."

Something in his voice made me stop. He was right. We were safe. I blinked. The bloodlust that had blinded me a moment ago fell away. I dropped my arm and blew out a deep breath.

We were safe.

Rob's eye was already swelling where the coachman had kicked him, and blood dribbled from his nose. A smear where he'd wiped it with the back of his sleeve ran across his face. "We're good," he repeated.

I looked at the coachman behind Rob, hanging half off the front of the carriage with an arrow in his chest. Blood dripped from his body onto the leafy trail. I'd killed him. A civilian. Hadn't even thought twice. He probably had a family, children to feed. Now they'd have no one to look after them.

As if reading my thoughts, Rob put a hand on my back and turned me away from the dead man.

Bodies lay on the ground around us. Three of them. And two farther up the trail. It might not have been what we planned for, but it had worked out better than we could have imagined. There were five horses on the trail; four wandering around riderless, and the one Rob had finally unharnessed. And there were five of us to ride them. "We did it." I couldn't quite believe we'd come out on the right side of that battle.

He nodded.

The door of the carriage opened and a woman in her mid-twenties poked her head out. She wore a beautiful soft pink satin dress and had a fur mantle wrapped around her shoulders. Her face was stained with tears and she had a baby in one arm. In her spare hand, she held a long-bladed dagger. She climbed from the carriage and pointed the shaking weapon at Rob. "Let us leave. Or I'll kill you."

I had no doubt she wanted to. But all of us, including her, knew she had no chance.

"Get back in the carriage," Rob growled, without looking at her. This was so different from his usual charm and flattery. He must be truly stressed to speak to her that way.

She shook her head, the jewels in her hairclip flashing as they caught the sunlight. "No. I'll not sit in there and wait to die. I'd rather die fighting."

Rob stiffened and turned to face her.

I started to move between them. I didn't want him to do anything he'd regret because he was blinded by anger. She hadn't done a thing wrong. She just had the bad luck of being on the trail when we needed a horse.

But Rob caught himself. His voice was softer the next time he spoke. "Please go back inside. I promise I won't kill you."

She took a step toward him, her hand trembling so much, I thought she might drop the dagger. "You might as well! You're going to leave me here, in the middle of the forest with a tiny baby and no horse to pull the carriage."

Rob watched her a moment before glancing at the coachman. "And no one to take you any-where."

Her eyes followed Rob's gaze and she choked back a sob. Her shoulders sagged, and the way her legs wobbled, I thought she might faint.

I stepped toward the woman. "Get in the carriage. I promise you won't die." Not because of us, anyway.

Her eyes widened when she heard a female voice, but it seemed enough to make her do as I asked. Once she was inside, I said to Miller, "Go and round up the rest of the horses." Tuck had already grabbed the one that had rushed past the rest of us. He was patting her nose and talking gently to her behind us on the trail. And John was heading in the direction of another. Might as well round up the other two at the same time.

As he headed off after John, I looked at Rob. "You're angry at the wrong person." Gisborne should have been his target, not everyone else. We were all upset, but we couldn't do what we needed if we gave in to our anger. And this was one time we could not afford to let Gisborne win.

He sighed, his lips pursing.

"She's very brave," I added. Or terrified. Either way, she won my respect the moment she threatened Rob with her knife. There were plenty of women—and some men—in the carriages we stopped who cowered inside with silent tears running down their cheeks. "And she has a child with her."

"She does," he said, carefully. "But her coachman is dead, and we need her horse. I don't have time to take her where she's going, especially with a child."

"Then don't take her horse." We didn't need it. Not really.

He closed his eyes and rubbed his temples. "Five horses and five of us."

Yes, but we had been happy with the single horse we would have taken from this carriage until the soldiers presented another opportunity. One horse would have meant one, or maybe two of us could get to Nottingham faster. Four horses were even better. "I don't mind sharing." With him. Or any of the others, actually. Just so long as we didn't leave that woman and her baby stranded in the middle of the forest without means to care for herself.

He rubbed his temples again. "What if she doesn't know how to drive a carriage?"

"If you didn't know how to shoot an arrow, would you say *I won't attempt to rescue Alan because I can't defend myself?*" She was a woman stuck in the forest alone with her child who she wanted to protect more than anything in the world. She would find a way.

"That's completely different."

"Is it?"

He screwed up his face, struggling with indecision between doing the right thing or getting to his brother. "We'd be faster on five horses."

Undeniably. Although the carriage horse wouldn't be as fast as the soldier's horses—it wasn't built for speed. "But how's your conscience doing?"

He let out a deep breath that shook his shoulders, then guided the horse back to the carriage, shaking his head as he walked. "Did I ever tell you life was a lot easier before I met you, Maryanne?"

I smiled. "Maybe it was. But I'm sure it was never as much fun."

"Do you think he meant to take Alan? Or do you think he did the same as Maryanne and confused the two of you from behind?" River water lapped at Miller's boots as we waited for the horses to drink. Bright green moss and lichen covered the boulders on the opposite side of the river and grass grew right to the edge on this side.

"I think he thought Alan was Rob," Tuck said, hitching up his robe to keep it from getting wet as he led his horse down the riverbank.

I'd come to the same conclusion. If we were correct, it was terrifying. I couldn't even start to think what Gisborne might do to Alan in his anger once he realized he had the wrong brother. I kept my concerns to myself, but I doubted I was the only one thinking them.

"I think we need a proper plan before we do anything else." John led his horse up to a patch of grass. "Getting Alan back is going to be dangerous. We've been lucky so far, but going into Nottingham is a whole other level."

"We have a plan." Rob's back was to us as he rubbed the nose of the horse we were sharing. "Get in, get Alan, get out."

John shook his head. "It's not enough. Gisborne will be expecting us. At the very least, he's going to have Alan guarded night and day."

"John's right." We couldn't risk our capture or our lives trying to get Alan back from a hopeless situation. We needed a better plan. "If something goes wrong at Nottingham, we have to make sure all of us are safe."

"Unlike the last time we were there," mumbled Miller.

Rob's fingers curled in the mane of our horse and his body went rigid. He turned slowly to face us. "I got Maryanne out safely last time we were there. I can do the same for my brother." His reply was short and sharp.

I'd never seen Rob in such bad humor. I didn't expect his normal light-hearted joking at the moment, but I also didn't expect him to snap at anyone who spoke.

"Technically, you didn't get Maryanne out, she got you out." Miller's voice was light, but his back was to Rob, otherwise he'd have seen Rob wasn't in the mood for joking.

"Miller," I warned.

But it was too late. Rob growled in the back of his throat, threw down the horse's reins and stormed into the forest.

I turned to fix Miller with a glare, but he was watching Rob with his mouth open and a what-did-I-say-wrong stare. I'd talk to him later. I ran after Rob.

"Rob. Wait." He was just ahead of me. I kept catching glances of him through the trees, but the bracken was so thick, it was difficult to keep up.

When he finally stopped, we were far from the others. He kept his back to me. I rested a hand on his shoulder to let him know I was here for him. He'd been quiet on the ride, quieter than I'd ever known him to be. He was worried, I got that. I was worried too, and I'd happily share his burden.

He just needed to talk to me. "Miller was only kidding."

He stepped out of my grasp and turned to face me. "I know."

I sighed. He knew, but he didn't care. "He was trying to help. Trying to lighten the mood." I didn't want Rob to be angry at Miller. He hadn't done anything wrong, except offer that badly timed ribbing.

"I've known him a lot longer than you." Rob folded his arms over his chest.

I pursed my lips, hearing the unspoken, *so I know better than you what he was trying to do.* "Well, then I guess you'll know you hurt him by storming off?" I spoke softly. He might have wanted an argument, but I didn't.

He blew an angry breath out his nose, shaking his head like it didn't matter.

I pointed at him, hoping he'd see he wasn't alone in this. "Don't do that. Miller cares about you. If you're hurting, he is, too. We all are."

"Yeah, well, hurting isn't going to bring my brother back." Was there some sort of insinuation in those words? Because it sounded like he blamed me.

"I didn't say it would," I spoke evenly, but his bad mood and sharp comments were starting to get to me. "All we said was a good plan would be our best protection."

"Maybe I should sit out here in the forest and wait while you all do what I'm clearly incapable of."

"Rob," I whispered his name, stepping forward and placing a hand on his arm. "No one thinks you're incapable of anything. All of us know if we're ever in the same situation as Alan, it will be you leading the charge to free us." Some of us, like John and me, knew it from bitter experience.

He shook off my hand, staring at the place it had been. "Don't. I can't do this." He put his hands up in front of him. "Not today."

Why did it sound like that sentence was unfinished? Like he wanted to add, *maybe not ever*. Because that wasn't how it had seemed last night. Perhaps I was stressed and reading more into it. "Okay. If that's what you want. I'm still here for you as a friend, though."

"If that's what I want? What I want is for my brother to be here with me! If I hadn't been up so late last night with you, maybe I'd have woken as he left this morning and I could have stopped him." He glared at me. "And I certainly wouldn't have sat back and watched while Gisborne loaded him onto a horse and stole him away."

He couldn't have hurt me more if he'd reached out and backhanded me across the face. Those words were like a physical blow to my chest that radiated out across my entire body. They hurt because they were true.

I doubled over, hands resting on my knees. I couldn't breathe. Rob's accusation pushed all the air from my body. I was the only one there when Gisborne and his men arrived. I was closer to them than anyone else, probably the only person close enough to have made a difference. Instead, I let it happen.

All day, I'd been trying to ignore the nagging thought that I could have done more. Guess I wasn't the only one thinking that.

While I hunched there, trying to recover, Rob left.

Without a word and on silent feet.

I forced myself to stand and scraped a hand down my cheeks. He was right to be so dismissive. Here I was telling him to form a plan before we went to Gisborne, yet I hadn't bothered to do the same. I'd seen Gisborne take Rob—or Alan—so many times in my dreams, but never once had I come up with a way to stop him should it happen in real life. I thought I'd prevented it. But I hadn't thought beyond that. I was as useless as Rob thought.

I headed back to the river, pushing through the bushes and doing my best to look like Rob hadn't just shattered me into a million pieces. One glance from John and I knew I'd failed. "You're riding with me for the rest of the day, Maryanne," he called.

I glanced at the others. Just three horses. Rob was already gone. He'd left us behind.

"Don't worry." John beckoned me over, reading my mind as he often did when it came to Rob. "He'll meet us at Frog Rock. Just needs some space."

I smiled, or at least tried to. Rob wasn't the only one.

Dreams kept me from sleeping properly all night. Nightmares.

Not the premonitions that had plagued me until my escape from Gisborne. These were different. Disjointed and distant, they were more like memories of the dreams I'd once had, all of them jumbled up together. Gisborne telling the people of Nottingham they were safe from Robin Hood; Rob standing in Gisborne's place telling a gathered crowd that the poor needed to look after themselves; the crowd cheering and Rob smiling. At least, his mouth did. I could never quite see his eyes.

As I lay awake in the darkness waiting for the dreams to recede, I could see it all so clearly. If that were the price Gisborne demanded from Rob in order to return Alan to us, Rob would agree. Not because he thought his brother was more important than the poor he helped, but because he blamed himself for Alan's capture, and the only way to ease that guilt was to set Alan free by any means possible.

I wasn't having it. Rob was supposed to be out here in the forest, forcing the rich to question the laws they lived by, and using their gold to help the poor who struggled every day just to survive. Alan was supposed to be here with us.

I walked down to the river, squatting at the edge to splash some water on my face. I craved the icy coldness that would chase away the remnants of the dreams. I went swimming here once, when the weather was warmer. It was one of my favorite places, as much for its beauty as for the time I'd spent here.

The moon reflected off the water, lighting up something white at the river's edge. I picked my way over the large stones and crouched on the last one, reaching into the water to retrieve the item.

Soap.

Or to be more accurate, one of the pieces of soap I'd brought from the twenty-first century and given to Rob two nights ago as a gift. It was mangled, one side dented and out of shape, and water-logged. If I squeezed it, the entire piece would disintegrate. The second piece was bobbing at the far edge of the river. If I'd wondered whether Rob had meant what he said to me earlier, I had my answer. The gift I'd lovingly selected then carried around for weeks—the gift he'd seemed so excited to receive—tossed away, uncared-for. Ungrateful bastard. He could have given it to someone else rather than throwing it away.

What was that childhood saying? Finders, keepers. If he didn't want the soap, fine. But I wasn't going to leave it here to crumble. At least one of us wouldn't smell like we'd been rolling in manure.

"You're not coming." Rob wouldn't even look at me as he forbid me to travel into Nottingham Castle with him and Tuck. We'd ridden all day yesterday until we made camp farther south than I'd ever stayed before. It was close to Nottingham though, so it suited our purpose. There was an old stone cottage here—at least, there were four walls and a dirt floor. Ivy grew up the outside walls, and the slow creep of the forest blocked the door until Tuck and John cleared a path. The roof was long gone, but John was sure he could make something that would shelter us. Better still, there was a fireplace inside, with a huge hearth.

Out the front of the cottage was a grassy clearing with an outdoor firepit sitting unused in the center. A river bubbled past—just a few steps away and then a steep climb down to where the water ran, and there was a small waterfall upriver that brought the constant sound of rushing water.

We'd already decided we should go to the Nottingham dungeon to look for Alan. Now we were deciding who would do what, and I was determined I would have a part in their plan. I needed to ease my guilt just as much as Rob did.

"I've been in the castle more recently than the rest of you. I know my way around." Some places. But that was better than knowing nothing, which was how much they'd know if they didn't take me.

"She does have a point," said John.

"Can you use a sword yet?" Rob demanded.

He knew the answer. He was just being a prick. "No." Not enough to save myself, anyway.

"Then how do you plan to defend yourself if we're discovered?" Rob had a point, too, but I wasn't letting him win that easily.

"I'll have my dagger, and I'm not afraid to use it. I'll be fine." I also needed to be there to make sure Rob didn't do anything stupid. Like hand himself over to Gisborne the way I'd seen in my dreams.

"No." Rob checked his sword and bow for at least the hundredth time.

I pulled on my pack and touched the top of my boot where my dagger was hidden. "I'm going. You can either physically stop me. or you can get over yourself and admit I'm an asset to this plan. Either way, if we're doing this today, we need to leave now." I started down the forest trail, heading toward Nottingham. I wasn't exactly sure what I expected Rob to do now. I could equally imagine him putting me over his shoulder, dragging me deeper into the forest and leaving me tied to a tree in Miller's company, as much as I could imagine him agreeing I could go into Nottingham, so long as I did some thing he deemed paramount for my safety.

Rob marched past me, his long strides impossible to keep up with. "Keep your hood up," he said, leading the way into the city.

FIVE

THE dungeon beneath Nottingham Castle was the most depressing and revolting place I'd ever been. The smell of human waste filled my nostrils long before Tuck and Rob knocked out the two guards sitting at the door playing cards by torchlight.

It was dark, pitch black except for that one burning torch on the wall where the guards were stationed. And it was cold. Colder than the icy wind that sliced through my cloak on the cobbled street above.

We each pulled a candle from our bags, lighting them from the torch on the wall.

"Hurry," said Rob. "If those guards wake while we're down here..."

Neither Tuck nor I needed him to finish that sentence. We probably should have killed them, but we were hoping to get out of this with as little bloodshed as possible.

The castle belonged to the King, but in his absence the Sheriff was in charge and he ruled over his adopted home with an iron fist. He also allowed his most trusted advisor—Gisborne—free rein. Should either of them find us down here, it was likely a death sentence for us after the way we'd embarrassed them both at the tournament. We were just hoping to get in and out without disturbing anyone.

I didn't think too hard about what was squelching beneath my feet as I walked over the uneven stone floor and peered into cell—did they even call them that?—after cell. Rob did the same on the opposite wall, while Tuck started at the far end.

The place was huge, and it was difficult to know how many cells were occupied. Sometimes, as I held up my candle and looked through the bars, I saw no one. That didn't mean it was empty, just that it was impossible to see into the darkest corners at the back. Other times, people came forward, hands out and begging for food.

They were dirty and skinny, and their eyes were without hope. Tuck had suggested we bring bread, hoping one of them might be more inclined to talk, so I handed out small pieces to everyone I encountered.

"Alan?" I whispered.

The cell occupant grunted, and a hand shot between the bars on the door, reaching for my ankle.

I jumped backward into a puddle of something I didn't want to contemplate. Swallowing a squeal, I placed a chunk of bread into the waiting hand. "Do you know of a new prisoner named Alan?"

"No, milady." The hand shot out again.

I didn't have a lot of bread left and there looked to be so many more cells.

"Please, milady. I haven't eaten in a week."

My heart contracted. Alan might not have had food either. Would he understand what had happened, why he was being treated this way? I handed the prisoner another piece of bread. It was pointless to hope someone had done the same for Alan because no one in their right mind would come down here, but still, I wished someone was looking out for him.

As I moved to the next cell, the prisoner called, "Ain't had no new prisoners for near on two weeks, milady. And none by the name of Alan."

I moved back to his cell. I could see him now, sitting on the cold floor, leaning back against the stone wall, his cloak in tatters. "Are you sure?"

He nodded and pointed above his head.

I raised my candle to see lines dug into the wall. Fifty or more that probably felt like braille when there was no light in the cell.

"The ones with a cross are when they bring someone new in. I mark it when the guards do their morning rounds, so I can recall days."

"And the rest of them?" Although I was sure I knew.

"The time I've been here. Fifty-nine days. I expect I won't be here much longer. Everyone that came before me has long since gone. Unless you want to take me with you?"

A shocked yell came from the dungeon entrance, where the two soldiers lay on the ground, knocked out cold.

Rob was already running back the way we'd come in, calling to us over his shoulder. "Maryanne, Tuck! Let's go."

There was only one way in and out of the dungeon. Just the one door. If we could get back out and past the guard station, there were three possible exits; left, right or up the stairs. But being trapped down here gave us no options whatsoever.

My boots clomped on the slippery stone floor as I raced after Rob. My candle went out the moment I started running and all I could do was focus on the light from the torch at the door. Rob drew his sword, the metallic rasp biting into the stale air, and behind me, Tuck did the same. There were no more voices, no shouts for help. But there would be soldiers on the way. I was certain of it.

We skidded out the door to find one soldier standing over the two guards—Rob knocked him out with the heel of his sword—and six more blocking the corridor to our right.

The corridor was wide, rounding a corner to the left and stretching forever to the right; a stairwell was the only thing that broke it up.

"Escapees!" The soldier ran at us, his chainmail rattling. He was already puffing with the effort. "Shut the dungeon doors! Make sure no one else gets out!" He drew his sword, watching Rob. I guessed he wasn't expecting us to be armed, and the dim light probably didn't help. I doubted he even saw the sword before Rob shoved it through his stomach.

The following soldiers' steps faltered. Perhaps they were wondering how someone escaping from the dungeon had gotten hold of a weapon.

"Maryanne! Get behind me." Rob raised his sword stepping carefully toward the group blocking our way. Footfalls sounded on the stone floor behind them. Reinforcements were on their way. A lot of them.

This was exactly what Rob had worried about when telling me I couldn't come. I had to learn to use a sword. I didn't want to be left back at camp because I was a liability. I pulled my dagger from my boot. It was pitiful compared to the weapons we were facing.

Rob moved slowly to the right, waving his left arm behind him as he directed me to move with him. He swung at the soldier, the clash of their swords overly loud in the low-ceilinged corridor. Tuck was beside us on our left, trading blows with a different soldier. I backed up behind them both, against the stone wall.

Yelling sounded over the clash of swords and there was no mistaking the voice. Gisborne was on his way. He'd probably been waiting for us to do something exactly like this. We needed to get out of here before he arrived. If I could just get Rob away from this soldier, we could run.

I glanced down at the tiny dagger in my hand. Without letting myself think too hard, I drew my hand back. When the soldier raised his arm to bring his sword down on Rob, I threw as hard as I could. The dagger, to my surprise, buried in the soldier's side, below his ribs.

Rob spun to face me, his mouth open in surprise.

"Gisborne's coming," I said, ignoring his reaction. "We have to run."

Rob motioned me toward the stairs, the sound of many footfalls coming from along the corridor. "I'll help Tuck, then we'll follow."

The first of the next wave of soldiers ran toward us. If we didn't leave now, we never would.

"Rob..."

He shook his head, raising his sword as a soldier charged at him.

"Woodhurst!" Gisborne's voice echoed off the low ceilings, and he skidded around the far-off corner at full pace, sword drawn.

"Go, Maryanne," Rob yelled, between blows.

Gisborne waved a hand in Rob's direction and three more soldiers advanced on him.

"We'll follow in a moment or two." Another swing at the soldier facing him. I didn't know if he'd seen Gisborne yet.

Indecision made my feet leaden. Our plan was to run if we needed to. To get out of the castle and back to the forest, no matter what, and no matter if we had to leave someone behind. It was easy in theory. In practice, impossible.

"Go! Now!"

Another group of soldiers advanced on Rob and Tuck at Gisborne's command, and the odds of any of us getting out of here grew ever slimmer. If I had my bow, I'd have picked them off one by one. But none of us carried bows today. It was difficult enough getting through the inner castle gates; bows slung over our back would have made us even more noticeable.

Two soldiers were fighting Rob. I'd seen him beat two at once before. He could win. Except that he kept looking behind him to check on me. If I didn't do something, he'd end up dead for worrying about me.

Screw the plan. I wasn't leaving the castle without them. I'd find something to fight with and return. Even if it was just a set of knives from the kitchen. "I'll come back soon." I ran up the steps, stumbling on the tiny footholds.

"One's escaping!"

"Get him!" Gisborne's voice boomed.

There was a clash of swords and a grunt below me. The spiral staircase hid them all from view, and I didn't know if Rob and Tuck were still fighting, or if the soldiers had the upper hand. All I knew was there were footsteps on the steps behind me. I stumbled upward, my breath coming in uneven gasps. Each step was taller than I was used to, and narrower, too, and my thighs burned. I ignored the first landing and continued up, the footfalls getting closer by the second. I ran faster, stumbled more, and hoped

Rob and Tuck would survive until I got back to help them.

At the second landing, I ducked off the staircase and sprinted along the corridor. My own stomping feet and heavy breathing did nothing to disguise the footsteps still on the staircase behind me. Hiding was my only option.

I tried a door, using both hands to turn the heavy handle and slamming my shoulder against it to force it open. It didn't budge.

I cursed and sprinted for the next one. Using the same tactic, I launched myself at the door, begging it to move. It swung open and I stumbled through. Catching my footing, I slammed it shut and pulled down the lock. Drawing in a deep breath, I leaned my back against it.

I realized my mistake the moment I turned around.

Six

"MAUD Fitzwalter. Or whatever name it is you go by these days." The deep and melodical voice of Eliza Thatcher filled the small room. "How lovely to have you barge into my chamber, yet again."

I lifted my head to meet her eyes, my heart racing while I tried to control my ragged breathing. "Eliza." If she screamed, I was screwed. There were so many doors I could have chosen in this corridor, any other would have been better than this one. My smile was tight. "It's lovely to see you, too."

Her chamber looked much the same as it had the last time I was here. Dark, dingy, and cold. A narrow bed on one side, a desk and chair on the other—where she was currently seated—and shelf after shelf on the wall displaying glass jars of things I didn't want to contemplate. The difference was, today there were three wooden chests stacked beside her desk, filled with some of her many glass jars. Like she was packing. "Going somewhere?" I asked sweetly.

"Home. To Woodhurst Manor for a while. I want no part of what's happening here. I have other things to think about." Her stare went distant. I knew what it meant. There were only two people who were important to Eliza, and if she was leaving one it was because of the other.

"I'm pretty sure you just missed the full moon." Other than Edwinstowe, Woodhurst was the closest village to the Big Tree. And the Big Tree was the only place Eliza was able to see her sister, and only if the magic and a few other elements lined up properly. "Wait. Is that why you were in the forest when Gisborne captured me?" She'd helped me. Given me water, food, and some sort of cream that healed my wounds faster than I'd expected. I'd never questioned why she was there, had just assumed she was traveling with Gisborne.

"Full moon was last week, when Gisborne attacked you, you're correct. You're also correct that I didn't see her. But eventually Tabitha is going to bring someone to this time on a full moon. I intend to be there when she does. Not stuck in this dungeon of a chamber just because Gisborne demands it."

That was a change of heart. "I thought you wanted to be wherever Gisborne was."

She loosed a deep sigh, her words wistful. "Sometimes, I want the exact opposite." As if she hadn't shared something so personal, Eliza lifted her chin and looked down her nose, her voice turning cold once more. "Were you looking for me, or did you simply plan on turning my room upside-down again?"

I'd done that last time I was here. It wasn't entirely my fault. I was searching for the coin she'd stolen from me. "I was...looking for you." If I could keep her talking until the soldiers gave up searching this corridor and looked somewhere else, I might just have a chance of getting back to Rob and Tuck.

She stood from her chair and folded her arms over her chest. Eliza and her sister always looked stunning, and it wasn't just because of their clothing. It was in the way they carried themselves. Today, she wore an emerald dress with wide lace sleeves and a slim cut that showed off her tiny waist. Her black hair was pulled into a tight bun high on her head. The only thing that detracted from her beauty were the three lines that ran across her face—scars from scratches given to her by the real Maud Fitzwalter.

"And what is it you want from me this time?" Her tone said there was not a thing in the world she would willingly give. The closeness we'd shared high in a tree house in Sherwood Forest last week, was gone.

Two sets of footsteps raced past in the corridor outside. I tensed, waiting for Eliza to call out. When she didn't, I pretended like I hadn't heard them. I'd spoken with Eliza twice since returning to the twelfth century. There was something I should have told her both times. I hadn't kept it from her maliciously. I'd been too focused on staying alive to think about much else on both occasions, but she deserved to know and now seemed like a good time to tell her. "Would you like to talk to your sister again?" Talking about Tabitha was also the only thing that would hold Eliza's attention long enough to keep her from calling to the soldiers searching the corridor for me.

She blew a breath out of her nose and shook her head. She wasn't saying no. She thought I was playing with her. My own fault. I'd tempted her with her sister before without knowing if I could deliver on my promise. There was a chance I couldn't deliver this time, too. "If I could free Tabitha from the portal, what would you do for me?"

She shook her head again, a slow and mocking smile rising on her face. "Nothing. Because I don't believe you can do it."

Based on past behavior, I wouldn't believe me either. "You don't have to believe. You just have to be willing to keep your end of the bargain once Tabitha is free." *If* Tabitha was freed.

She pursed her lips, watching me carefully. It seemed like an age before she finally gave me an answer. "I'd leave. And never go near Gisborne again. Is that what you want to hear?"

I turned my lips down. Sounded perfect to me. But not for the reasons she imagined. I was not and would never be attracted to that man the way she thought I was. For Rob's sake, one day soon, I was going to make sure Gisborne died, and when he did, we didn't need the hassle of her hunting us down on some revenge mission. "Okay. Let's call it a deal."

Something sparked in her eyes. "You're going to get Tabitha out of the portal? Now?"

"Not now..." If everything went right, Tabitha would be free of the portal in two months. That was the timeline we'd agreed on. She expected me to return to the tree then, with Eliza.

Rage twisted Eliza's face. "You presume to trick me? In my own chamber?"

I thought she was going to pick up one of the many jars on the wall and throw it at me, so I put my hands out in front, hoping to calm her. "I can't contact her until the full moon. You know that. And we've already established that was a week ago."

Eliza glared.

I let out a dramatic sigh. "You know how it works as well as I do, Eliza." There was no way to speak with Tabitha in the middle of the lunar cycle.

Her shoulders dropped but the snarl remained on her lips. "Fine. Just don't expect me to trust you. If you want to walk out of my chamber today free of the guards that are currently running the halls in search of you..." Her snarl became a smirk. I guess it didn't take too much to realize if I was here, I was probably hiding. "...then I'm going to need some sort of guarantee that you'll do as you promise."

"I guarantee I will—"

She folded her arms and shook her head. "Don't be ridiculous. Your word means nothing." Her eyes went to Maud's engagement ring, still on my finger. I guess to Eliza, it represented something she desperately wanted. "Give me that. If you get my sister out of the portal this full moon or next, I'll return it to you."

I twisted the ring slowly off my finger. It had no sentimental value to me, but it had done its job. Wearing it had stopped Gisborne from killing me that day in the forest, because for that moment, he'd believed I was Maud. I'd intended to keep it safe on Maud's behalf, but I couldn't do that if I handed it to Eliza. Then again, there would be no chance to do anything if I didn't get out of the castle alive today, and maybe handing it over gave me a little more bargaining power. I took a deep breath already knowing what I was about to ask wouldn't go down well. "To keep my promise, I'm going to need your help getting out of the castle today." I gave the ring a final twist and held it between my fingers.

Eliza nodded, her expression resigned. "I guessed as much."

It wasn't only me who needed her help. I was about to play a huge bluff. "I need you to help Rob, too. He knows someone who might take Tabitha's place in the portal." I shrugged. "I just don't know who it is yet—he hasn't told me." I gave an internal shudder. None of that was true and I hated lying.

She tilted her head to one side, raised her eyebrows and waited.

I had no idea if she was listening, or just waiting for me to leave. I went with the listening option. "He's here. At the castle."

She closed her eyes and shook her head. "Are you saying Gisborne's greatest enemy is the key to me seeing my sister again? And that you need me to help free the man Gisborne has been trying to capture for months if you're to stand any chance of bringing Tabitha back?

I nodded. Put that way, I was confident I'd get what I asked for. Eliza wanted her sister back more than anything in the world. I'd told her I could get it for her. Rob, Tuck and I were home free.

"No."

My mouth dropped open. I didn't miss the little smirk of satisfaction that gave her. "What do you mean?"

"I mean no. Is there something about that word you don't understand?" Her chin rose with a mixture of serenity and fire.

"But..." I was gasping for words. Where had I gone wrong? "You don't want Tabitha back?"

Some of the serenity disappeared, and her eyes widened in panic for a second. "Of course, I do," she snapped. "But I don't believe you need *him* to help you."

Some of the tension left my body. She was bluffing. Like me. "And you're willing to take that chance? You'd allow yourself to get so close to happiness, just to let your loyalty to Gisborne snatch it from you? You give that man far too much. More than he ever gives you."

Her jaw stiffened and she stepped toward me. "What about you? Would you let your loyalty to a criminal stop you walking away from here today?"

We were millimeters apart. "I won't leave here without him, or Tuck. I'll go down fighting, because that's what I do for my friends. In the end, Eliza, I guess it will all come down to what you want to see the most. Do you want to watch us all die trying to get away from here today? Or do you want to watch your sister run into your arms in a couple of months when she is finally released from the portal?"

"Possibly released," she corrected, but there was indecision in her eyes.

"Help me, and I'll help you," I whispered.

Her stare was long and hard. Finally, she nodded.

SEVEN

"GOOD Lord!" John cupped his hands over his nose and mouth. "You all smell worse than the back end of a horse."

I glanced at my boots. They needed a good clean, not just the quick scrape I'd given them on the roots of a tree as we entered the forest. But it was nothing compared to Rob and Tuck.

By the time I'd convinced Eliza to help, Gisborne had captured Rob and Tuck, and thrown them in the dungeon. The side of Rob's face had swelled where Gisborne knocked him out with his boot to Rob's face. The guards had then dragged him, through the river of human waste and into a cell to await Gisborne's next orders.

Tuck, although not as dirty, had knelt on the floor of his cell to pray, and the bottom half of his robe had seen better days.

"Good to see you, too," mumbled Tuck, throwing his cloak on the dirt beside the fire without breaking his stride. He kicked off his boots and walked straight through our clearing. A moment later there was a grunt and a splash as Tuck dived into the river.

"I take it, it didn't go well?" John removed his hands from his face and took a deep gulp of air through his mouth.

Rob threw his own cloak in the dirt beside Tuck's, quickly followed by his tunic and undershirt. All done in stony silence with a stony face.

I turned my back as he pulled off his clothes, focusing on John and Miller. "He wasn't there."

John and Miller had spent the day making a roof for the stone cottage. They'd traded three of the horses for food, gold and thatch for the roof, straw for mattresses, pots, mugs and a couple of extra blankets. They'd finished the roof, and although it wasn't to a standard a thatcher would be happy with, it was better than camping out in the open while the weather was still cold. Rob thought it was a waste of time and money because we'd be leaving soon. I hoped he was right, but given how little information we'd discovered about

Alan so far, I got the feeling we might be here a while longer and was grateful for the boys' efforts. Might as well be comfortable.

"You mean you didn't find him?" Miller asked, his eyes bouncing between Rob and me.

Rob's sword landed on the dirt with a muffled thud. There was no point expecting him to offer anything to the conversation. He hadn't said a word to either of us since Eliza helped us escape the castle through an underground tunnel.

"I mean, he wasn't there. We searched the dungeon and I asked a prisoner. No one has been brought into the dungeon this past week."

"Shit," said John, under his breath.

I couldn't agree more.

"What do we do now?" Miller looked from Rob to John. One of Rob's boots hit the ground with a thud. I could hear his movements, but I refused to turn around to check his progress. Conversation between Rob and I had been strained since the day Gisborne took Alan.

"We go about our lives and pretend like I never had an older brother. Because it looks like my bastard of a younger brother has killed him." His other boot hit the ground and Rob padded away toward the river.

I turned and watched him go. His dirtied pants were slung low around his hips, the top half of his body was naked. In the middle of his back was the puckered scar that was the result of Gisborne's arrow all those years ago. The incident that began Rob's hatred for his brother. He disappeared down the bank of the river, his dirty clothing screwed up in his arms.

"Is that it?" Miller asked, following John inside.

I kicked off my boots, leaving them outside before rushing into the hut after them.

Miller dropped down to sit on a log they'd dragged inside and placed in front of the hearth as a seat. "Are we giving up?"

I shook my head. John did the same. "I don't know what we do next, Miller," I said, quietly. "But we don't give up. Not until we know for sure." His face was pale, his freckles stark against his skin today. I ruffled his hair. "There are plenty of places Gisborne could have hidden him, other than the dungeon." And there were. I just wasn't sure how likely it was that Gisborne had done such a thing. Nor was I sure whether he would have kept Alan alive, especially if he thought he had kidnapped Rob, only to find Alan instead.

Tuck strode into the stone cottage wearing just an undershirt that came down almost to his knees, his hairy, white legs sticking out the bottom. His newly washed robe was balled in one hand, dripping water onto the dirt floor. "I'm going to Woodhurst. To look for Alan."

"When?" John looked up from the fire he was using to warm his hands. He didn't seem particularly surprised. Certainly not as surprised as I was.

Tuck grunted as he hung his robe from a metal hook beside the hearth to dry, before sitting gingerly on the log beside Miller. He glanced at me crouched at the other end of the hearth, feeding logs onto the fire. "Maryanne's right. Alan could be anywhere. My guess is that he's somewhere in Nottingham, but I keep thinking, *what if he's not?* With Eliza going back that way soon, it just makes me wonder if we've come to the wrong place."

I'd passed on what Eliza told me as we walked back.

"I still know plenty of people back there," Tuck continued. "I can have a good look around without drawing too much attention. It feels like it'd be more helpful than anything I could do here. Plus, isn't it better that we split up, cover as much ground as possible at the same time?"

That was likely the best option. The faster we found him, the better it was for Alan. It was just unusual to hear Tuck so uncertain. It spoke volumes about the stakes of this whole situation. I nodded.

"The same goes for Nottingham, I guess." John ran a hand through his hair, making it stick out in every direction. "I'll go there tomorrow. Ask around. See if I can find anything."

Making a plan made me feel better. Being part of it made me feel better still. "I'll go, too. Maybe I can find Gisborne's servant, Xanthe, and get her to tell me something." Eliza had refused to answer any of my questions about Alan, and Xanthe was the only other person I knew inside the castle. She'd been good to me when I was staying there before the Sheriff's tournament, answering my questions and even loaning me her clothing so I could confront Eliza.

"I guess I'll keep an eye on Rob, then." Miller's shoulders slumped and his voice was glum.

There was a time, not so long ago, when Miller wanted to be with Rob every waking moment, to be exactly like him. It broke my heart that he was no longer excited to spend time with Rob. "It might be more fun than you think."

"You've seen him these last few days, Lady Maryanne. I know you don't really think that. Would you want to spend a whole day in his company?" Miller threw another log on the fire.

"Silly question, Miller." John grinned in my direction. "Maryanne and Rob have plenty to do in each other's company."

"Then you stay with him!" Miller turned pleading eyes on me. "I don't want him yelling at me."

The yelling was something none of us were used to. We excused it because of the stress Rob was under, but Miller was right, being around Rob was far from pleasant these days. I glared at John. "Rob and I...we aren't..." We hadn't ever really been anything other than friends. We kept heading toward something more, but it never went further than a kiss. I was surprised John hadn't noticed that Rob had barely spoken to me since the day Alan was taken.

He grinned, ignoring my words and my glare. "Today, perhaps. But tomorrow you'll both be wandering around with stupid smiles on your faces again." He had noticed then. He just didn't think it was permanent.

I wasn't so sure. Especially if Rob blamed me for not saving his brother. "Wait, is that why you're all in here huddled around the fire? Because none of you want to go out and check on him?"

Three sets of eyes looked at anything but me.

"He doesn't need to talk to any of us." Miller's voice wobbled with uncertainty.

"Don't you want to tell him what we're planning to do these next few days?" Now that I thought about it, there had been very little conversation between anyone around here these past couple of days. I was so wrapped up in myself I hadn't even noticed everyone else's relationship with Rob was equally strained.

"He'll come right in an hour or two. He doesn't need any of us sticking our noses where they aren't wanted." Tuck scowled as he wrapped John's cloak around his legs for extra warmth while his robe dried.

John shook his head. "You know that's not true. What he needs is to work some of his frustration off with his sword."

"He already tried that. Today at the castle. Didn't work." Tuck's eyes were on his feet.

"I meant with you," John said, his voice low.

Tuck shrugged and reached his hands out to warm them by the fire. "That's not what he needs."

John looked at me and let out a deep sigh. "Maryanne, if you wanted to talk to him..." John paused and lifted one shoulder. "If you did, you'd probably find him glaring at the water down beside the river."

Three sets of eyes focused on me. "What do you all expect me to do, exactly?" Chances were, my presence when he wanted time alone, would only make him angrier.

John shrugged. "Make him smile. Or make him yell. Anything's better than the silence we're getting from him at the moment."

I sighed and got to my feet. After the response I received the last time I talked to him, I wanted to do it about as much as anyone else, but someone had to try to pull Rob out of his funk.

As I stepped over the threshold to head down to the river, Tuck called, "Maybe ask him about Lizzie."

I spun slowly back to face them. "Lizzie?" That was a name I'd never heard mentioned before. A female name, at that. But it wasn't the fact it was a woman's name that had caused the little hairs to rise on the back of my neck. It was the way Tuck spoke it, a mixture of teasing somehow entwined with mockery.

John gave Tuck a shove and jumped up to stand between the two of us. His cheeks were suddenly red, and he drew in a long, loud breath, glaring at Tuck. "Don't," he spat through clenched teeth.

I wasn't sure if the word was for me or Tuck, but his reaction did nothing to fix the unease Tuck had made me feel. "John?" John rarely lost his temper, but in that single word he was as angry as I'd ever seen him.

He shook his head, his jaw set like he couldn't open it to speak.

Miller's eyes were wide, and he kept looking between John and me.

Finally, as my gaze moved from one to the next, John forced a few words out his mouth. "Go talk to Rob, Maryanne. But not about that."

"I know what you're doing," I said to Rob's back, trying not to slip on the dirt path as I crept down the riverbank toward him. Rob's washed clothing lay spread on the rocks. He sat in just his damp pants with his knees pulled up, arms resting on top and staring out across the water. He might be sitting in the sunshine, but the day had a bite that the sun did little to remove. He must be freezing.

Silence. It was mostly what we'd been getting from Rob since Gisborne took Alan. Now that I'd noticed he was this way with everyone, and with a few minutes to think about why, I was onto him.

I untied my cloak and placed it over his shoulders, then sat next to him. The river was wide here. And deep. It would be a perfect swimming hole in the summer.

"Pushing all of us away isn't going to make any of us give up on you. You know that, right?" Said the girl who'd once been an expert in doing exactly that. But it also meant I knew what it felt like to walk in his shoes. I knew what he might need from us to feel better. "We're not going to walk away from you. We're all staying right here. None of us are—"

"Then you're all stupid." Rob's voice was rough, and rusty from disuse.

"No. We're your friends. That's what friends do."

"Gisborne will kill you. One by one." His voice shook, but I couldn't tell if it was from anger or fear. Once Eliza agreed to help me get Rob and Tuck out of the castle, we'd had to wait until Gisborne left the dungeon to free them. Neither Rob or Tuck had said what had happened in that hour that Gisborne had spent with them down there, but the slow and sometimes labored movements of Tuck up in the stone cottage painted a pretty clear picture. The haunted look in Rob's eyes said that he'd been made to watch as Gisborne beat his friend. That coupled with Gisborne chopping off two of John's fingers a few months back just to get to Rob, and kidnapping both Miller and me, probably had him feeling pretty messed up.

Giving up wasn't the answer. "Only if we don't kill him first." Because with every day, and with every way Gisborne hurt us, my resolve grew stronger. He would die. And if it wasn't Rob who killed him, it would be me.

Rob let loose a deep sigh, dropping his head into his hands. "I can't keep doing this, Maryanne." His voice was small, and it seemed as if it took way too much energy to say those few words.

"Can't keep doing what?" I turned to look at him rather than the water ambling past.

Silence, again.

"You know, you let him win when you push us away." It was the same thing I used to do when I was screaming out for help after Josh's accident. In the days after, I'd desperately wanted to talk to someone who cared about me. When no one volunteered, I grew somber and morose, and pushed everyone away because it was easier than admitting they might not care for me as much as I hoped they did. Gisborne would laugh himself stupid if he knew he had Rob so petrified that he wanted us all to leave.

"If you and Eliza hadn't gotten us out of the dungeon today, Tuck would be dead by now." He met my eyes for a moment before dropping his head into his hands again. "I can't take the pressure. I can't sleep. Can't eat. I spend half my time thinking of new scenarios that Gisborne might force me to watch next time he gets hold of one of you." He lifted his head to stare across the river, silent for a long moment before continuing. "The other half is thinking of ways to set you all free from those scenarios. I have no room left in my mind to figure out what to do about Alan, yet he should be my priority. I can't keep you all safe. I can't make decisions about anything anymore." He turned my way. "I can't be what you all think I am, Maryanne. I especially can't be who you think I am."

His words were a plea. One that spoke directly to my heart.

I rested my hand on his. "Then don't." Whatever he thought we needed from him, we didn't. All we needed was for him to feel better again, for the worry to be gone. If it was the legend that was pressuring him, then screw the legend. Rob feeling like himself meant more to me than making sure he became Robin Hood. Once this was over, we'd find a way to bring hope back to the people of Sherwood Forest. But for now, it was the last thing Rob needed to think about.

His eyes were damp. "How...?"

"We can do all the things you don't feel up to doing. We want the same things you do, and we want them as much as you. You can trust us, Rob. We'll take care of everything. We'll get Alan back." After my brother's accident, I'd stayed in bed and hid myself from the world for weeks. For Rob, bed wasn't much of an option. But we could eliminate his stress in other ways. No matter what happened with Alan, I would make sure Rob got through this.

"Wait here." I jumped up, running into the stone cottage. Ignoring John and Miller's questioning looks, I grabbed the piece of soap I'd rescued at Frog Rock and ran back out to Rob, handing it to him.

His eyebrows rose as he took it, and for the first time in days there was something other than despair on his face. "Where did you get this?"

I shrugged, trying to seem nonchalant. "Found it. Seemed like it might have been going to waste."

"I was angry that night." He shook his head. "Sorry. I shouldn't have thrown it away." His eyes were glassy with unshed tears.

I lifted one shoulder. It suddenly didn't matter that he'd thrown it away. If he wanted to use it, it was all his.

He got to his feet and pulled me into a hug. "Thank you," he whispered. "For caring."

I put my arms around his waist and rested my head on his shoulder. Rob was breaking and it was everything Gisborne wanted. Seeing him like this felt like watching Gisborne win, and I'd never allow that to happen.

Miller handed me a mug of tea when I returned from an early morning wash in the river a week later, and John nodded to the biscuits he'd made for breakfast.

I raised my eyebrows at the special treatment. Breakfast was usually porridge or something equally simple.

"You'll need your sustenance so we can rescue Alan." John grinned.

"She's not doing any rescuing today." Rob walked back and forth across the narrow width of the stone cottage like a caged tiger, his feet light on the dirt floor.

"Relax, Rob." John handed him a warm biscuit. "I'm kidding, although we know there isn't much Maryanne can't do."

I already felt the pressure over today. I'd suggested talking to Xanthe a week ago, but we'd put it off until today in the hope that we'd get the information we needed without going inside the castle walls. The last time we entered the castle, it hadn't gone well. Going there today was a last and desperate resort. We had no other good leads. This was it. It was up to me to ask Xanthe the right questions and coax the answers from her, and not get caught while doing it. I hoped I was up to the task. "We'll be back by lunch." I glanced at Miller who was seated on the log in front of the fire, watching Rob out the corner of his eye. He wasn't the boy he'd been before Gisborne took him, but I was pleased to see him watching Rob. He used to do it all the time, and it was good to see him returning to a semblance of his old self. "Maybe you two might want to get out and do something while you wait for us to return?"

Miller's eyebrows rose slowly. "Like what, milady?"

I shook my head. "I don't know. Take him fishing or something. Otherwise it's going to feel like a very long morning." Especially since there was so much riding on this mission. We all wanted Xanthe to have the answers.

"I've got a better idea." Miller grinned, then clamped his mouth shut and refused to say anything more.

EIGHT

GETTING inside the inner castle gates was easier than expected. John paid a farmer who was bringing food to the kitchen to take us hidden in the back of his cart. The soldiers at the gates barely made him slow before waving him past They didn't even look under the canvas.

We scrambled out when he reached the kitchen and ran inside. We found an alcove just outside the kitchen entrance and tucked ourselves into it, watching while we caught our breath. The kitchen was a busy place early in the morning, with a steady stream of servants coming and going, but I didn't need to see her face to recognize Xanthe when she passed by our hiding place. She hurried into the kitchen, with an empty tray in her hands. She mumbled a quiet hello to another servant running in the opposite direction without breaking her stride.

A few moments later, she returned, her tray piled high with fruits and breads, plates and cutlery. We slipped into the hallway and followed her. We were working on the theory that so long as we walked purposefully, kept our eyes on the ground and looked like we knew where we were going, we wouldn't look out of place. It seemed to be working.

The moment Xanthe turned into a quiet corridor, we made our move. John grabbed her from behind, covering her mouth with his hand so she didn't scream. I scooped the tray out of her hands before she could drop it, then opened the nearest door for him to bundle her inside. With one hand balancing the tray, I pulled the door closed behind us.

The room was a guest chamber, similar to the one I'd stayed in when Gisborne brought me here, but this one hadn't been used in a long time. It was icy cold, the hearth boarded up. The bed was covered with drop cloths and the walls and floor were bare stone, with no tapestries covering them. Hopefully, the disuse of the room would work in our favor and no one would come in here.

Xanthe struggled against the hold John had on her. One hand remained over her mouth, the other wrapped over her chest, pinning her arms down. She was so little, and sometime over these past months, he'd bulked up, his shoulders and biceps bulging against the fabric of his tunic. She was no match for him.

"Xanthe, it's me," I said, putting the tray on the ground and moving closer to them both.

Her eyes widened when she heard my voice, and she stilled.

"John will take his hand from your mouth if you promise not to make any noise. Okay?"

She nodded, eyes still wide. She wasn't the only one worried. If she screamed now, John and I would have to run. From a room in the middle of the castle, there was little chance we'd get away. I just hoped she wouldn't scream.

John must have been thinking the same thing because he moved his hand slowly away from her face, ready, it seemed, to slap it back across if she made a noise. The moment she was free, she scrambled away from him. Away from the door, too.

I smiled, trying to calm her. "I'm sorry if we scared you, Xanthe. It wasn't our intention. We need to ask you a few questions. Then you'll be free to go."

She stared at me, wide-eyed.

"We'll make it worth your while." I held up a lump of gold that we'd gotten for selling the horses. It had been John's idea to bring it, and he was right. If Xanthe helped us, we should help her.

Her eyes grew even wider at the sight of the gold, and she nodded. "I'll try, milady. But I'll not do anything that will hurt anyone."

"And we don't want you to. We just need to know...has Gisborne brought a prisoner to the castle this past week?"

Xanthe stood in the corner wringing her hands. Her eyes went to the floor and her mouth clamped shut.

Perhaps we should start with something easier, something we already knew but which Xanthe might see as helping if she told us. She might relax more if we eased her into it. "Is Gisborne in Nottingham at the moment?"

She nodded, watching me a few seconds before answering. "Aye, milady. He arrived last week." She swallowed. "Has the witch with him, too, though I think she's leaving soon."

I wasn't entirely convinced of Eliza's magical powers, but I let it slide. "Do you know why he's here?"

"Are you going to kill him?" She shot the question back at me so fast, she took me off guard.

"No." Not yet, at least. And not inside the castle. "He took a friend of ours. Once we have him back, we'll leave."

Xanthe pursed her lips, like maybe she was trying to keep from speaking.

"His name is Alan. Have you seen him?" I felt like a child crossing my fingers and hoping I'd get the answer I desired.

Her face softened and she nodded. "Aye. I've seen him."

"Is he all right? Is he alive?" John asked the questions while my brain was still processing Xanthe's answer.

She nodded again. "He was hurt. But he's recovering." She glanced at me, her words pointed. "Gisborne's looking after him."

I bit back the urge to tell her the reason he was injured was because of the man she so desperately wanted to protect. "Where is he?" Because, if he was somewhere nearby, maybe we could get him out of here today.

Xanthe held up one hand. "I like you, Lady Maud, but if you don't let this anger with Gisborne go, you're going to end up dead." Her voice was as hard as nails. I'd never heard her use that tone before. She always seemed too frightened to say boo to a mouse. "Alan is guarded day and night. Inside and outside his chamber. Whatever you're planning, don't do it."

I swallowed. "I'm not planning anything."

She blew out a breathy laugh and shook her head. "I can see in your eyes how much you want Alan back. Gisborne knows it, too. That's why there are so many guards on his door. You must realize that?"

On some level, I knew. If Alan were still alive, he wouldn't be easy to get. That was a problem for another day. Today I was just glad to hear there was still hope.

"How many guards?" asked John.

She shrugged. "It varies. Ten. Sometimes more."

Ten guards. I had no idea how we'd get past that many. "And he's definitely all right? He's alive?"

She nodded. "Please believe me when I say Gisborne is looking after him. From what I understand, they're brothers. For the most part, Gisborne is treating him like one, too."

It was a start. Better than him being in the ground, that was for certain. But Gisborne's idea of how to treat a brother was very different from mine, and it didn't ease my fears the way Xanthe meant it to.

I fumbled in my purse and pulled out two lumps of gold, handing them to Xanthe. "Thank you. For helping me this time. And last time."

She stared at the gold as I dropped it into her hand, shaking her head. "I can't take this, it's too much."

It was a lot. Enough for her to get out of here. Enough to set herself up and get a place of her own so she didn't have to work for Gisborne. "You deserve it. For helping me so many times." I turned and started for the door.

"Lady Maud," she called, as I placed my hand on the handle. I looked back at her. "Alan asks for you sometimes. Calls you Maryanne, but I know he means you. He used to ask for your man, but Gisborne put a stop to that very fast." She balled her fist and swung her arm, leaving me in no doubt how Gisborne had stopped Alan using Rob's name. "Now he asks for you if he's had a bad day, or if he's feeling sad. He's a lovely soul and I try to make him feel better. I just wanted you to know that. I do try."

I knew there was a reason I trusted Xanthe. She was a lovely soul, too. "Would you tell him, if you can, that I haven't forgotten him? That *we* haven't forgotten him." There were so many other things I wanted Alan to know, like how we would come and get him, and how he needed to be brave, and how he should never mention Rob's name around Gisborne, but the reality was Xanthe probably wouldn't see him again anyway. With the gold in her hand, she'd be gone from the castle by lunch.

John and I walked silently through the busy streets of the Nottingham markets inside the outer walls of the castle. Peddlers called to us—and everyone around us—desperate to sell their cloth, or fish, or arrowheads or bread. Coin purses jingled, children ran between legs, people laughed. On another day, I might have enjoyed this marketplace. Today, I was only thinking about getting back to Rob and telling him what we knew.

The news Xanthe had given us was good. Better than good. Alan was alive. Getting him back would be difficult, but that wasn't a surprise. How to make it happen was more than I could consider right now. Especially while I was trying to ignore the images that kept throwing themselves at me of Gisborne's fist smashing into Alan's face, and Alan not knowing why. Perhaps he'd think it was because Gisborne thought he was stupid, and that thought shredded my insides.

John stopped to look at arrowheads, and I stopped at a stall selling knick-knacks beside him, to wait. We should be getting back to the forest, but telling Rob that Gisborne had Alan guarded by ten or more soldiers made both our feet slow.

He would be happy for about thirty seconds before switching to revenge mode.

The peddler at the stall I'd stopped at displayed an assortment of buttons, beads, string and old pieces of cloth. Although I ran my fingers over the coarse fabrics, I wasn't looking at any of it. I was inside my head, trying to formulate a plan to take to Rob.

"Good morning, milady. Can I interest you in some of our highest quality beads?" The peddler was a big man with a black beard and faint accent.

I shook my head, running my fingers over the top of a tray of buttons. Something shining among them caught my eye. I pushed the little wooden pieces of all shapes and colors aside, to look more closely. A ring. Silver, thin, and with a knotted design on the front. It looked a lot like the ring Rob had once worn on a chain around his neck. The one he'd used to pay the healer for my care when my arm was infected. His mother's engagement ring.

I picked it up, turning it over in search of something, anything, that would mark it as once belonging to Rob. The band was so thin, there was no room to engrave anything on it. Maybe I should buy it anyway and hope it was the one. "How much?" I held the ring up to the peddler.

He shook his head. "Ah, milady, you don't want that. Can I interest you in some beautiful buttons? These ones complement your eyes." He held up two gaudy yellow buttons.

I shook my head and turned the ring over in my fingers. The more I looked at it, the more certain I was that it had belonged to Rob. "No. I'd like this please. How much?" Affording it would be my next problem, since I had nothing but a few copper coins left after handing our gold over to Xanthe.

"That ring is cursed, milady. The woman who originally owned it saw two husbands buried. She died not long into her third marriage. Two of her children died..." He frowned. "Or maybe it was only one. And the other is..." He glanced at the castle and clamped his lips shut.

"The other is...?" I prompted. It sounded like Rob's family. His mother had married three times. Rob and Alan might both be thought dead.

"The other is a complete bastard, milady."

If he was talking about Gisborne, I agreed.

"And the healer who received this ring as payment for his services, gave it to his sweetheart and she died the next week. Death follows this ring. Like I said, you don't want it." He shook his head firmly.

Oh, but I did. It was Rob's ring, I was certain. "Please." I shrugged the hessian pack off my shoulder. Some of my possessions were still at our camp at the stone cottage, like the heavy dress from the Sheriff. But there were some things I couldn't bear to leave behind. Like the photo album Josh gave me when I left. And the two blocks of chocolate he'd included with the album. I glanced at the peddler who was still shaking his head. If he thought it was cursed, perhaps I'd pick up a bargain. "I don't have much, but maybe we could arrange a trade?"

He sighed. "Ten copper pieces."

I shook my head. "That's too much for a cursed ring."

He stared at me like he was calculating the most I would give him. "Fine, five copper pieces."

"Still too much." I pulled one of the king-sized blocks of chocolate from my pack, opened the packet and broke off a single piece. "How about a compromise." I handed him the chocolate. "Try it."

His eyes narrowed.

"If you like it, I'll give you five more pieces which you can either keep for yourself or sell. The nobles will pay more than a copper piece for a taste of the most delicious food in the world, I'm certain." They would, once they heard how good it tasted.

He held it up to the light, turned it in his fingers and curled up his lip. "Looks like something from the back end of a dog."

"Luckily, it doesn't taste that way." I smiled. "If you don't eat it fast, it'll melt over your fingers."

He looked at his fingers then wrinkled his nose when he saw I was correct. "This better not be a trick." He popped it in his mouth. His eyes rounded, then closed and he let out a deep sigh. "Oh my. That is the best thing I've ever tasted."

I tried not to smile. I felt much the same way about chocolate, which was why Josh had given me two huge blocks. "Do we have a deal?"

The man's nod was fast.

I slipped the ring on my finger, but it was too large, so I put it in the pouch I carried on my belt for safe keeping. I broke off the five promised pieces, just as a bell began to ring somewhere in the distance.

"Thank you, milady," said the peddler.

"All right?" asked John, coming up behind me as I slipped the rest of the chocolate block into my pack.

I had hoped to keep it longer before opening it, because once it was open, I knew I would eat it all. This was for a good cause though. I nodded at John just as the bell rang again, and the town crier climbed onto a small platform that backed onto the exterior of the inner castle wall. "Hear ye, hear ye, hear ye."

People stopped around him, but John and I put our heads down and pressed through the crowd. Getting stuck in a public gathering was the last thing we needed—it made leaving in a hurry almost impossible. Plus, we didn't want to risk anyone recognizing us.

"The roads of Sherwood Forest are safe again! Robin Hood is gone!" The crier paused to let the people around him respond with cheering and booing. I shook my head and pressed on. They could tell themselves whatever they wanted, if it made them feel safe. Didn't mean it was true. "The outlaw, Robin Hood, is no longer a threat to your safety, or the safety of your...goods." There was a small chuckle from the gathered audience. "Robin Hood has been captured!" A roar from the crowd and my heart dropped to my feet. Both John and I stopped, craning our necks to see over the crowd, to the man dressed in a red velvet jacket telling us they'd caught Rob.

I glanced at John. His lips were thin and tight. If they really had caught Rob this morning— which although possible, I doubted—we needed to know what they were planning to do with him. If they hadn't, we at least wanted an idea of what game Gisborne was playing.

The crier stretched his parchment out, reading the words. "There will be no punishment for Hood at this time." There was a beat of silence, then someone booed and the rest of the crowd followed. There were likely one or two people in the crowd who were afraid of what they'd lose should they meet Robin Hood on the forest trails, but not enough to cause a reaction like this. I was in no doubt that the soldiers standing around the market and up on the walls were the reason the peasants were reacting as if they were upset by this announcement.

The crier let them continue for a moment before his voice cut through their mock disgust. "Hood is the long-lost brother of the Earl of Woodhurst, Sir Guy of Gisborne, who is excited to see his only family again. The Sheriff has decided it is better to bring families together than to rip them apart." More lifeless booing from the crowd.

I glanced at John again. Something was off here. If they had Rob in their custody, they would never let him go free after everything he'd done, which meant the Sheriff and Gisborne were bluffing, begging the question; why?

"Show us!" yelled John, adjusting his hood so it covered more of his face. "If you have Hood, show us his face!"

I nudged him in the ribs with my elbow. We didn't need any sort of attention focused our way.

"You're in luck, sir," called the crier. "Sir Guy of Gisborne is pleased and proud to present his older brother to you all."

I stood on tiptoes, hoping to find both Rob's brothers standing side by side. It was the first time I'd ever willingly searched for Gisborne.

To our right, the crowd parted, revealing two servants, biceps bulging as they carried a litter between them. Slumped on it was a man in a cloak. His face was covered by his hood. He sat unmoving as Gisborne strolled casually alongside. Gisborne wore his chainmail and riding cloak, as if he had just come back from the forest His black hair was longer than I'd seen it, curls falling into his eyes. Or maybe I was just used to seeing it plastered to his head with sweat. Either way, his cold eyes sent chills down my spine, and all I could think about was the way he'd smirked as his fist slammed into my body again and again almost two weeks ago.

I took a step back, and John gave my shoulder a squeeze, a silent version of the question he so often asked; *all right?* I nodded. I was fine.

Gisborne had done worse to John and he wasn't cowering like a baby.

But that wasn't the only reason John asked his silent question. It was because of the cloak on the litter. Rob's cloak. Or Alan's. Brown and lined with fur. The same one they both wore.

Gisborne cleared his throat and climbed onto the platform beside the crier. He was smug as ever. One day someone would wipe that smirk right off his face. I hoped it would be me. Or at the very least, I hoped I was there when it happened. "Ladies and gentlemen of Nottingham, may I present to you, my brother Robin of Woodhurst." The man in the chair didn't move. At a nod from Gisborne, the crier marched over and whipped off the man's hood to a collective gasp from the crowd. I guessed they were gasping to see the face of the man that had terrorized the forest these past months. I gasped, too. Not because of the face under the hood, but because I'd seen a variation of this exact scene in my dreams. Usually I saw Rob up on that platform with Gisborne. Today, I was looking at the bruised and battered face of Rob's brother.

Alan.

John squeezed my shoulder again and gave a tight smile. Alan was alive. Hurt, but living. Just as Xanthe said.

His face was pale where it wasn't mottled with bruising, and the light in his eyes was gone. He moved rigidly on his seat, searching for comfort as if his face wasn't the only part of his body that was sore. My heart broke for him and I was glad Rob wasn't here to see this.

Gisborne's voice boomed out across the crowd. "My brother is ecstatic to be away from the hardships of the forest and is committed to keeping the families of Nottingham safe while stopping the violence within the forest. To that end, he's offered a remarkable bargain. He's commanded his followers stop stealing gold from the rich."

John blew a breath out his nose, something I understood as meaning *yeah, like that'll happen.*

Gisborne's eyes skimmed the crowd, stopping just over my shoulder. I turned to find four chain-mail clad soldiers striding toward the gathering. Their burgundy cloaks flared out behind as they walked, and the swords hanging from their waists glinted in the sunlight.

I turned back to face Gisborne and pulled my hood lower over my eyes. I didn't need anyone to recognize me, especially Gisborne's soldiers. Their boots clicked on the cobblestones as they drew closer, and I tensed, waiting for them to pass.

When they came to a stop, they were right beside us, one of them so close, his shoulder brushed mine.

Nine

I FOCUSED on Alan, pretending not to notice the chill of the soldier's chainmail as it rested against my arm. Two more soldiers stopped directly behind John and me, their breath warm on my neck. The last one stopped on John's left.

We had no weapons except a small dagger each, hidden in our boots. John never used a sword, and carrying his staff was impractical when we were trying not to draw attention. It was the same reason we didn't have our bows. Inside the castle while we were searching for Xanthe, a bow thrown over our backs would have given us away immediately.

John's hand was still on my shoulder. He gave it another squeeze, his chin high as he too, pretended to ignore the soldiers. The squeeze was for moral support. It also warned me to relax and act natural, that soldiers choosing to stand behind us was nothing more than a coincidence.

Gisborne cleared his throat, addressing the crowd again. "My brother wants word to spread that he has offered his own neck. Should anyone continue where he left off in Sherwood Forest, should anyone steal from carriages passing through the trails, my brother will hang. He will take the punishment for any robbery committed within the confines of Sherwood Forest."

I drew in a breath. I heard the threat in Gisborne's words.

Gisborne's eyes found mine for just a second. They moved away so quickly, that I might have imagined it if I didn't know the man in question.

He focused elsewhere and began speaking again. "Should any of his followers make threats against our family or attempt to abduct our personal servants..." He paused. This time, when his eyes landed on me, there was no imagining anything. He was watching me. I stared back. I didn't think he could see my eyes clearly beneath my hood, but I wouldn't duck my head and let him think I was scared, no matter how true it might be. "My brother will willingly go to the gallows for that, too. Spread the word."

Beside me, as Gisborne's eyes held me in place, John stiffened. He was probably calculating how fast he could get to the weapon in his boot. Not fast enough.

Gisborne stepped off the platform and nodded to his servants. They picked up the litter and the crowd parted, allowing them to move away. Their steps were a slow trudge through the inner gate and back toward the castle, with Gisborne walking beside them. John's hand remained on my shoulder as they left. I couldn't stop watching Alan. He'd pulled his hood up so I could no longer see his face. The rest of his body was hidden beneath his cloak and gave no clue to other injuries. All I knew for certain was that he was alive. Better than nothing, but I needed to know more. Not that I could do anything with the information if the soldiers surrounding us didn't allow us to leave.

The crowd dissipated, returning to their shopping or their stalls, the noise of their chatter filling the area again. John and I remained where we stood, flanked by Gisborne's men. I focused on my dagger. I wasn't going down without a fight. I would dive for it the moment we looked to be in trouble.

As soon as Gisborne disappeared around the corner, the soldiers moved away from us. One moment they were there, the next they were striding away, their shoes tapping against the cobbles.

The moment they were inside the inner wall, I let out my breath. Gisborne knew we were here. He'd made sure we heard every menacing word he said.

Without waiting a second longer, John put a hand on my back and wordlessly guided me from the city.

"A threat." Miller paced up and down the length of the little clearing outside the stone cottage, his hands flexing and then balling into fists over and again. "All because we stopped a carriage this morning?"

Miller, to his credit, had gotten Rob to do something he hadn't done in months. The two had stopped a carriage together and by Miller's account, Rob had even enjoyed it. It was impossible Gisborne's announcement had come because of the carriage robbery—there hadn't been enough time.

John ran his hand through his hair, the light wind making long strands dance around his eyes. "Not because of you. There's no way he would have learned of this morning's activity so fast.

Gisborne knew Maryanne and I were there, though. Xanthe must have told him. Why else would he provide such a public scene?"

I threw my cloak on the ground and sat on it, letting the afternoon sun warm the chill that settled in my bones the moment Gisborne met my eyes. "He knew, all right. He looked straight at me as he threatened us with going near Xanthe or Eliza again." Bastard. "If only I'd had my bow with me." I was all talk. There had not only been no room to raise my bow in that crowded marketplace, but with two soldiers beside me, doing so would have been a death wish. I was just so sick of Gisborne getting the better of us again and again.

"If you'd been caught with a bow in the castle, you'd both be dead by now." Miller continued to pace as he spoke, flattening the long grass with every step.

I wasn't quite willing to let go of my bravado. "Yes. But, so would he." I was a good shot. I would have hit him.

John and Miller gave a quiet chuckle. Tuck, who'd arrived back from Woodhurst a few minutes before John and I returned from Nottingham, stared quietly at his feet, while Rob leaned a shoulder against a tree, his eyes fixed on the cold embers of the old outdoor firepit at the center of the clearing.

"How was he?" It was the first words Rob had spoken since our return—the first words I'd heard from him all week—and it was a question I'd asked myself over and over while we walked back from Nottingham.

I still felt guilty. There had been no possibility we could rescue Alan *and* get away alive, but the fact remained that I was free and Alan wasn't. It made me feel bad. "He was upright." That was probably the most positive thing I could say. "Xanthe told us he's getting better each day, and I believe she's telling the truth."

"Yes, but how did he seem?" Rob's shoulders were stiff, and he wouldn't meet anyone's eyes. His nostrils flared as he spoke.

I sighed. Truthfully, Alan hadn't looked great. I'd hoped to keep that from Rob—he didn't need the added stress—but I should have known he'd push hard for details. "Hurt. His face was pale and bruised. He was slumped in the chair and it looked like it hurt to move."

Rob made a pained sound in the back of his throat.

"But considering he had an arrow through his back just over a week ago, he's probably doing all right." He'd even raised a hand to wave. "Xanthe said Gisborne was looking after him, Rob. If that wasn't true, I don't believe Alan would have been sitting up."

Rob's eyes remained down, his hair falling forward and hiding the emotions I knew would be on his face; anger, guilt, horror. That was okay. He could hide as long as he liked. I'd told him we had this, and we did. Now we knew where Alan was, we could work on a plan to get him back.

"We'll go to the castle tonight. Break him out." Rob's voice was flat. Almost as if he didn't expect to succeed. Which, of course, he wouldn't. Not without a well thought out plan.

"No." I shook my head. "Xanthe said he has guards on his door constantly. Lots of guards."

Rob shrugged, his chin finally rising. "I'll kill them."

I threw a pleading glance at John. He was there this morning. He knew as well as I that this was not the way to get Alan back.

"We can't get in there like that. There has to be a better way." He shook his head and folded himself down to sit on the grass next to me.

"Yeah?" Rob gave a caustic laugh. "And how would we do that? Perhaps by marching up to Gisborne and asking for Alan back? I'm sure that would work just as well."

All of us watched him carefully. All of us remained silent. It wouldn't matter what anyone said now, Rob wasn't going to like it.

Tuck let out a deep sigh and ran both hands down his face. Not even he was willing to pull Rob back into line. We all felt Rob's pain, and Rob was the only one who didn't realize it. Tuck's voice was as gentle as I'd ever heard it. "It's a trap. You know it is. Gisborne held Alan out like bait in front of Maryanne and John this morning. He's expecting you to come for Alan tonight. Which is exactly why you're not going."

Rob sneered at Tuck. He sauntered over to his friend, folded his arms over his chest, tilted his head and looked down his nose. "Try to stop me."

"Oh, I will." Tuck copied his stance. I'd seen the two of them behave like this before. In a moment, one would draw his sword and the other would follow. I'd hated it then, and I despised it even more now. Rob was in such a dark place that I wasn't sure he'd know when to stop.

But Tuck was right. Going to Nottingham tonight to break Alan out of wherever Gisborne held him was as good as walking up to Gisborne and saying *hang me now*.

Gisborne held all the power and he knew it. We needed leverage. Something we could use against

Gisborne the same way he was using Alan against us.

"Eliza Thatcher!" I jumped to my feet.

Rob and Tuck, each of them with a hand on the hilt of their swords, turned to me, mouths open and staring like I might be mad. They might be right.

"She's our leverage." It was so perfect, I didn't know why I hadn't thought of it sooner.

"Our what?" For once, Tuck didn't glare like I couldn't possibly know what I was talking about. Maybe because we both wanted to offer Rob an alternative solution than the one he was a breath away from enacting.

"Our way of making Gisborne return Alan unharmed."

John turned his head to look at me. "You know I believe in you, Maryanne, but why would Eliza make Gisborne do that? And how would we make her?"

For the first time in a week, I was tingly with hope. I looked at each of the faces staring at me. All of them wanted the same impossible thing, and maybe this was our way of getting it. "Gisborne said if we stole any more gold, Alan would hang. What if we stop a carriage, not for gold, but for the person inside?" They continued to stare blankly at me. "Eliza is going to Woodhurst any day now. She told me so, and I saw her packing for the trip. If we were to interrupt her travel and have her stay with us here at the stone cottage for a night or two, perhaps Gisborne could be persuaded to make a swap. Eliza for Alan."

Rob shook his head. "No. Gisborne said he'd hang Alan if we stopped any more carriages." He released his grip on the hilt of his sword and folded his arms over his chest. At least his fight with Tuck was momentarily forgotten.

"He said if we stole any more gold. We'll leave all her gold and...whatever else she travels with. We'll just take her." It was working to the very limit of Gisborne's command. I just hoped Eliza's life meant enough to him to secure us some bargaining power.

"It might work," said Tuck. He dragged a log out from under some bracken, depositing it in front of the firepit beside John and sitting down. Our patch of sun was growing smaller by the minute, but there was still enough room for both of them to bask in the last rays before it disappeared behind the trees. "But it's a risk..."

It was. Gisborne cared for Eliza. He'd chosen her again and again. Even after he thought Maud had returned and had promised he'd get rid of Eliza, she was still with him. No matter how much he seemed to want Maud back, he wanted Eliza just as much. Maybe more. "Eliza might be the only thing in the entire world that Gisborne loves more than himself."

John nodded. "You might be right." He turned to Rob. "Surely it's worth a shot."

"It's better than any other plan we've come up with," Miller added. I threw him a grateful smile. It was a big deal for Miller to back someone other than Rob.

I drew a deep breath. "If we get this wrong, we're essentially killing Alan." The question was, would the risk be worth it?

Rob shook his head, his voice quiet. "How would we do it?"

"That's what we need to figure out," I said.

Five days later, Miller came running back to the stone cottage out of breath. "Today! Eliza's leaving Nottingham today!"

I tied off the lashing I was finishing for the cage at the back of the cottage where we planned to keep her and walked outside. My heart was racing. This was it. The day we might finally get some leverage on Gisborne.

Miller had watched the stables at Nottingham Castle every day this week. The moment he saw anyone touch Gisborne's carriage he was to get back to the cottage as fast as he could. Which seemed to be what he'd done.

Rob strode up from the river. He ducked into the cottage, grabbed his sword and strapped it around his waist. John, who'd been checking his bow outside, threw it over his shoulder and picked up his staff. By the time I had a quiver strapped to my back, Tuck and Rob were already waiting, and John and Miller were walking out of the clearing.

We'd discussed how this would go again and again these past few days—it wasn't like we had much else to do. Our plan was simple and probably easier than stopping carriages for gold. The stakes were so much higher, though. If we didn't manage to get Eliza, Alan would die because we'd gone against Gisborne's rules. Plus, the main trail this close to Nottingham was busy. It would be a miracle if we weren't interrupted by another carriage or passing soldiers.

Because of that, we'd carefully considered the place to stop them. Rob, Tuck, John and I had walked up and down the main trail for hours over the past few days, searching for the place that gave us the best chance of success. The spot we finally decided on was at the bottom of a small rise. The carriage would be on a roll down the hill, so if they saw us, turning would be almost impossible. In the other direction, the trail was straight. If anyone came around that far-off corner, we'd have plenty of time to slip into the undergrowth and run.

I relaxed my hand from around my bow, shaking out the cramp my nerves had given me, then re-gripped it. I would stay at the edge of the trail where I was currently hidden. My job was to shoot anyone that got in the way of us taking Eliza captive. I'd done this at carriage robberies in the past, but every other time, I'd had Tuck to back me up. Today, when the boys stepped out on the trail, Tuck was going with them. He thought I had enough skill with a bow to manage the task on my own, and if hand-to-hand fighting happened, he could swing a sword far better than I could. It was a compliment from Tuck. Only the second one he'd ever offered me.

A little farther up the trail, hidden in the undergrowth, Tuck stiffened. I heard it, too, the bumping rumble of a carriage on the trail. Five sets of shoulders tensed, looking to the top of the hill, searching for that little white carriage with the *G* painted on the door.

The carriage that rolled over the hill and began its descent was not white. Nor was it little. It was large and ornate, painted black with swirls of gold around the windows and door.

"Wrong carriage," Rob turned from farther up the trail and whispered loudly. "Relax and let it pass."

I'd seen this carriage before and wracked my memory to place it. I moved through the undergrowth to where the rest of them were standing. "Is that...Bridgette Sutherland's carriage?"

Rob nodded and I caught a hidden smile from John and Miller. I'd embarrassed myself the day I'd last seen this carriage by firing a warning shot when there was no one coming. All because I was jealous. Not today.

"Let's stop it."

Rob spun around to look at me. "Are you out of your mind? You know what Gisborne said."

I did. But I had an idea. A better idea than the one we were currently pursuing. "Not for the gold. For Bridgette."

"Eliza means more to Gisborne. We stick with the plan." Rob turned to watch the carriage's progress.

"Yes, but Bridgette Sutherland's very rich husband means more to the Sheriff. If the Sheriff refuses to barter with us to get Bridgette back, he'll make an enemy of her husband. Not to mention the gold he'll no longer receive because her husband will stop backing his projects. Call it added protection. We take them both." I wasn't entirely sure who was calling the shots in Nottingham. Gisborne seemed to have a level of autonomy, but he'd still bowed to the Sheriff the day of the tournament. Surely, we were better off using everything we could to plead our case for Alan.

"For leverage over Gisborne *and* the Sheriff," said Miller, nodding. "I like it."

Rob shook his head. "We don't need it. Eliza will give us all the power we require. Stopping a second carriage is dangerous. So is changing the plan at the last minute. You've said so yourself in the past. You're the one who's always insisted we have clear and well thought out plans before we do anything."

It might be dangerous, but I was certain I was right. The more we could hold over Gisborne and the Sheriff, the more likely we'd be to get Alan back. I wasn't going to sit around and miss a chance like this, no matter how much Rob hated the idea.

Not even if I had to do it alone.

I pulled up my hood and stepped onto the trail, my bow raised.

TEN

"MARYANNE! Get back here." Rob spoke through gritted teeth, but I refused to listen. He wasn't the only one who could make decisions around here.

"Join me. Or don't. But I'm bringing Bridgette Sutherland home with us tonight." I looked at the carriage as I spoke to him, putting up a hand to stop the horses.

The coachman slowed. Tension pulled at his shoulders and jaw. "The Earl of Woodhurst said to remind any bandits we might meet that he will kill your leader should you take our gold."

"Oh, I don't want your gold," I said.

The coachman's eyes widened for a second, then he laughed and flicked the reins. "You're a girl? I'll not stop for you."

"That would be unwise." John stepped onto the trail behind me. I could have hugged him. "She's a woman used to getting what she asks for." The end of his staff hit the leafy dirt with a muffled thud.

The coachman looked from John to me and back again as if trying to decide whether we were a threat. His carriage moved slowly toward us, but when Rob and Miller stepped onto the trail, he pulled his horses to a stop. "What is it you want, then, if not gold?"

"I want you to open the carriage door." Actually, I had hoped Lady Sutherland might open it of her own accord, but so far, no luck.

The coachman shook his head, a hand going to the sword at his waist. An arrow flew from the trees, landing beside his left knee. I'd wondered if Tuck had stayed hidden because he didn't agree with me. Now I realized he was taking on the role I would have when we stopped Eliza's coach.

"I wouldn't do that if I were you," said Rob. "If you value your life, you'll do as the lady asks."

The coachman swallowed, looking up the trail in front of him. I guess he saw nothing helpful because he finally jumped to the ground. He knocked on the door, then opened it.

"Tell Lady Sutherland to step outside," I called.

He did, holding up a hand to assist her from the carriage.

Last time I'd seen Lady Bridgette Sutherland, I was overcome with petty jealousy. I'd thought she was the most beautiful woman I'd ever seen, and had disliked the way Rob told her so. Today, I still thought she was beautiful, though, this time I saw her without the filter of jealousy, and she wasn't quite as stunning as I'd first imagined. Her dress was orange, with white lace overlaying the sleeves. A very wide matching hat sat upon her head and a large emerald adorned her neck. We were going to have to find her new clothing; she was wearing the equivalent of a fluorescent safety vest and she'd be easy to spot when the Sheriff sent his men searching for her. "Good afternoon, Lady Sutherland." I inclined my head. "I'm Maryanne. I believe you've met my friend Rob before." I pointed to Rob behind me. "The two of us were hoping you'd join us for dinner."

Lady Sutherland smiled at Rob, then shook her head. "I'm sorry, but I have a prior engagement. I must decline." She turned and lifted her skirts to climb back into the carriage. Tuck let another arrow fly, this one landing in the middle of the open door to the left of her head. She let out a squeal and her coachman pushed her behind him. Before the man could draw his sword, Rob and John were on him, each taking an arm and holding him back. We would not kill or injure anyone. We didn't want to give Gisborne any reason to hurt Alan.

I stepped around the boys and held out my hand. "I'm sorry. But you don't have a choice." I gave a pointed glance at the coachman, now struggling in Rob's headlock.

Lady Sutherland looked from Rob to me. Her shoulders dropped. "I just need my purse."

I shook my head. It was better that she leave whatever gold or jewels she had in the carriage so Gisborne couldn't accuse us of stealing them. "Actually, could you please remove that emerald from your neck."

With a sigh, she did as asked and passed the necklace to me. I reached into the carriage and placed it carefully on the seat, then took her arm and guided her away. At the edge of the trail, I turned back to her coachman. "If you want to see Lady Sutherland alive again, you need to do three things for me."

The coachman struggled in Rob's grasp again, finally nodding when he realized he couldn't get free.

I held up my hand, counting on my fingers, thumb first. "First, tell the Sheriff of Nottingham that Lady Sutherland will remain unharmed so long as our friend currently in Gisborne's custody is not hurt." I counted off the next finger. "Second, tell him she'll be returned at the time our friend is returned to us." I held up a third finger. "Finally, remind him we kept to Gisborne's rules today. We stole no gold or jewels." I narrowed my eyes. "And if you so much as think about stealing any of Lady Sutherland's fortune which is still inside her carriage, you're a dead man."

Rob gave the coachman's neck another squeeze and he let out a groan. "Are we clear?"

The coachman nodded.

With that, I used Lady Sutherland's elbow to lead her off the trail and through the bracken.

Bridgette Sutherland sat quietly on the leafy floor of the forest, her hands and feet tied and a gag in her mouth, while we took Eliza from her carriage. In contrast to Lady Bridgette, Eliza kicked and screamed, scratched and yelled. Rob was in no mood for it, gagging her as well before lifting her over his shoulder to haul her away.

I took the ties from Lady Bridgette's feet and offered her a smile. "It's all right. We won't hurt you. And if you're quiet, I can remove that gag."

She nodded, and I did as promised.

She straightened her back, her chin lifting at the same time. "Tonight, maybe. What about after that?"

Lady Bridgette would have to share the cell we'd built for Eliza. It would be cramped, but we couldn't risk either of them escaping. "You won't die, if that's what you're worried about. We don't intend to hurt you."

"I'm not worried about dying," she said quietly.

Lady Bridgette walked slowly toward the stone cottage, both because of her uncomfortable-look-ing boots and her wide dress and hat that caught on every possible snag slowing her down on the narrow trails. Miller and I took her the long way; we couldn't risk her bringing someone here if she escaped. It was safer for everyone.

"Are you going to leave these on me all day?" She held up her wrists, still tied together. They were another reason she moved so slowly; she couldn't raise her hands for balance on the uneven trail.

"I'm sorry." To my utter surprise, I already had a great deal of respect for the lady. She hadn't shed a single tear since we took her. She'd dealt with it all with grace, a straight back and a high chin. The complete opposite of Eliza.

One side of her mouth kicked up. "You think tied hands will stop me from running? These boots and this dress are doing perfectly well in that department all on their own."

I glanced at Miller. He raised one shoulder and I wasn't sure if he thought she wouldn't try to escape if we removed the ties, or if he was leaving all decisions surrounding her care to me, since I'd taken her without discussing it with them first. Likely both.

I wasn't sorry about my last-minute decision to kidnap her. It was the right thing to do. "Give me your wrists." I untied one of them. Then I wrapped the rope from her unbound wrist around my own, so we were tied together. "Better?"

She shrugged and followed me through the forest, our pace the slightest bit faster.

By the time we arrived at the stone cottage, the others had made themselves comfortable. The fire inside roared, and John had set up a spit to roast a venison shank. "Where did we get that?" I asked.

John glanced at Rob and that was as far as the conversation went. Perhaps that's what Rob was doing while I finished the cell this morning.

Rob couldn't have answered, even if he'd wanted to, anyway. He was battling to keep a screaming Eliza in the cage of sticks at the back of the single room cottage. Eliza kept throwing herself at the wooden bars, making the whole thing wobble.

I indicated for Lady Bridgette to sit on the log in front of the fireplace and she dropped down on it with a heavy sigh. Leaning forward, she unlaced her boots, one-handed. I watched her awkward movements for a moment before giving in. "I'll untie us. But if you run, all of us will come after you. Like you said, you can't hide in that bright dress or run in those uncomfortable shoes, and we'll all be faster than you. Okay?" I really hoped she understood because we'd do everything in our power to keep her here.

She nodded, not that we could have heard her speak above Eliza's screams, anyway. Once the rope was off, she rubbed her wrist, then pulled off her boots, followed by her stockings. Her toes and heels were blistered and bloody, and she gave another deep sigh as she released her feet. She hadn't made a sound of complaint as we walked.

After John offered to tie himself to Eliza so she could come out of the cage for dinner, she finally stopped screaming.

The boys were in good spirits as we ate. Miller and John cracked jokes and even Rob smiled like he hadn't since before Alan was taken in Huxley.

Tonight, we all had hope. We'd been running low on it until now.

The girls picked at their food and watched us as they listened to our talk. Once John offered them both more comfortable clothing—which Bridgette accepted and Eliza refused, preferring to remain in her pale yellow gown—then wrapped their legs in our spare blankets, they relaxed. We didn't want them to feel like prisoners, even though that was exactly what they were.

In a lull between stories, Rob said, "Maryanne, can I talk to you for a moment?"

It was the first time he'd initiated conversation in a week—with me or anyone else. I nodded, too surprised to speak.

He got to his feet and I followed, knowing every set of eyes were on us.

He walked across the grassy clearing and disappeared down the riverbank to sit cross-legged on a flat rock at the river's edge. I watched from above for a moment before following and sitting beside him. The night was dark—the thin sliver of the moon hid behind a bank of clouds—and cold, especially after the fire-warmed cottage. I was glad to be sleeping in there tonight and not out in the open.

Rob's smile was fleeting. "I just wanted to thank you. Taking Bridgette was a good idea. I should have backed you as soon as you suggested it."

I watched his face trying to gauge his mood, but he guarded his feelings closely and I was left with no idea. "You're welcome." I sounded so formal. When had this happened to us?

"You're trying to help Alan. I should trust your judgment." He sounded formal, too. Like we were talking to each other for the first time.

"We'll get him back, Rob." It was what we were all working toward.

He turned his head away, looking out at the bubbling river in front of us, leaving me to see only his profile in the dim light. His jaw worked. I would have given anything to hear his thoughts. He ran both hands through his hair, which was loose tonight. I always thought it suited him best this way. "Everything was perfect right before it happened. Now nothing is."

I touched the back of his arm with my fingertips, waiting for him to flinch away, the way he'd had so often lately. He didn't. "Nothing is perfect right now. But it will be again soon."

"You don't know that." His voice was so soft it was almost lost in the rushing of the water.

"No one does. Not for sure. But once Alan's back, we can make things as perfect as they were before." Some things, at least.

He looked at me, shaking his head. "And us, Maryanne? How do you propose to make us perfect again?"

I stared at him, my mouth falling open. He was the one who'd put the distance between us these past few weeks. I thought anything *us* was off the table at the moment, and it shocked me to have him mention it. The way I felt about him hadn't changed. I'd go back to Valentine's Day in Huxley in a heartbeat. I'd relive the whole night without changing a thing. It was Rob who had issues to work through. "Time? I can wait as long as you need." And I would.

He shook his head, a snarl growing in his voice. "Ignoring it won't make it go away."

His words were barbed, and I didn't know why. "I don't understand."

He looked across the water again before speaking so softly I had to lean in to hear him. "I know you know about her. I heard Tuck tell you last week."

I released a slow breath.

Lizzie. The name Tuck had thrown at me and I'd refused to contemplate since. For weeks Rob had pretended he was going home to his girlfriend every time he left us. He'd finally confessed that it was Alan he was living with, and even though there was no girlfriend that time, I wasn't willing to jump back into that trap. And with the mood Rob had been in lately, I hadn't wanted to bring her up, either. But now, it seemed like I had to hear about her. I sighed. "Fine. Tell me about her."

His voice was almost too soft to hear. "If you cared about me at all, you'd have asked about her sooner."

Something flared inside my chest. I was partially aware that the person speaking wasn't the Rob I knew, that he was hurting over Alan and wanted someone to make him feel better. It should have been me, but I couldn't go there. I couldn't be okay that there was a *Lizzie* who clearly meant a lot to him, especially after he'd already hurt me by letting me think he had a girlfriend once before.

I tried to keep my voice even as I replied. "No, actually. It's because I care about me that I didn't ask after her. Because my feelings for you mean I can't keep following you down these paths you want to lead me. I died inside when you lied about having another girlfriend. Now another name gets thrown around, and John acts like saying it is the biggest transgression in the world. I have eyes, Rob. I know where asking after her leads and I can't deal. Not at the moment, not right now. I don't want to go there."

I climbed to my feet and glared down at him, my hands balled into fists. There were so many other things I wanted to say, but when he refused to look at me, I started back up the riverbank toward the stone cottage. Halfway up, I stopped. Screw it. I had more to say. I turned to find him watching me, mouth slightly open. I pointed a finger at him because, although I could keep a lid on the screaming I felt like doing, I was upset and I wanted him to know it. "But you should have told me. You shouldn't expect me to ask about something I know nothing of. You want life to be perfect again? Well, it will never happen when you refuse to speak to anyone." I stared at him a second longer, then turned on my heel and walked away.

Just as I reached the top of the riverbank—a few steps away from the door of the cottage—his voice floated toward me, so soft I wasn't sure if he expected me to hear. "You're wrong. My life can't be perfect unless you're beside me. And that's never going to happen."

I pushed the door open, slinking back into the stone cottage and sinking down in front of the fire to stare at the flames. I felt every set of eyes on me, but their conversation didn't miss a beat.

Rob remained outside, and I wasn't surprised. Ever since I'd first met him, he'd always needed time to recenter himself after a disagreement. Time to think. Time alone. But the enjoyable part of the evening was over for me. He'd stolen that when he picked a fight.

I probably should have let him tell me about her. It might have been good for us both. But everything I'd said was true. I couldn't keep dealing with all these hidden parts of Rob's life like they didn't affect me at all. If he cared about me, he'd understand that.

Suddenly the cottage felt small and stuffy, and the hidden glances my way felt intrusive. I got up and walked outside, this time the chilly air hitting my face was pleasant. The one horse we hadn't yet sold whinnied softly from the back of the cottage when she heard my movements.

As I'd expected, Rob was gone from the riverbank, so I returned to the place we'd sat together and dropped my head into my hands. Once, I'd wondered if I was his Marian. I'd even come back to this time thinking I must be. But with each new argument and the distance it wedged between us, that hope died. My connection with Rob was dying, too. I wasn't her, but just by being here, I was part of Robin Hood's legend. Maybe it was time to make my own place in it and leave Marian's place for the person who would one day forge that connection with Rob. The idea hurt so much, I thought I might break in two. But it was the right decision. There was no point trying to hold onto something that was no longer there.

"Need to talk?" John's boots crunched on the dirt and loose stones as he trotted down the riverbank. He settled onto the rock beside me without waiting for my answer.

I shook my head, then spoke anyway. "Did you hear us?" I'd tried to keep my voice down, but the stone cottage was so close, and privacy was a luxury in the forest.

John gave a small shrug. He might as well have said the whole forest heard. "Talking sometimes helps."

I blew a laugh out my nose. "Sorry, but I'm not in the mood to hear all the reasons why I should give Rob a break at the moment." I knew every single one of them, and every one was valid. I hated that thinking about *her*, about Lizzie, cut me to the bone. Because, in the grand scheme of things, it was nothing. I was being pathetic. I hated that, too. It was the reason I needed to step away from whatever I'd once had with Rob. I couldn't help anyone when I felt this way.

"Maybe you don't want to hear this, but you need to keep trying with him. You're making a difference that none of the rest of us can."

Nice of him to say, but not true. "I'm his punching bag, you mean."

"He's angry. But not at you. Maybe try seeing it from his view. In the last few months, Gisborne's taken me, Miller, you and now Alan. He's hurt us all. And it's all been to get to Rob. Now Rob's trying to push us all away, so none of us get hurt again." John rubbed the back of his neck. "Please don't give up on him. He needs you."

"Well, he's got an odd way of showing it."

He tried to smile. "Please. I'll talk to him. Tell him to be nicer."

Whether he needed me or not, that wasn't the reason for our latest disagreement. "Who's Lizzie?"

There was a long breath of silence. "You two haven't talked about her?"

Maybe he really hadn't heard us. I shook my head.

John drew in a deep breath. "Tuck had no right mentioning her. He should have left that to Rob."

"Yeah, well, he doesn't seem so eager to talk about her, either. I'm assuming she's his girl-friend?" I didn't even need to ask because, what other option was there?

John nodded, his lips pressed together like he wanted nothing to come from them, yet the words found their way out anyway. "Lizzie was Rob's first girlfriend. It's not yet a year since they broke up."

"His choice or hers?" I wasn't sure I even wanted to know.

"Hers."

Hearing that told me more than I needed to know about the situation. John had once warned me not to hurt Rob, now it made sense. "Is that why you told me to be careful with him?"

"It took Rob a long time to get over her. I didn't want him to go through that again so soon." He shrugged. "But Lizzie and Rob were nothing like you and him. They were never right together."

That admission made me feel better than it should have. "He couldn't see it?"

John gave a bitter laugh. "Oh, he sees it now."

He was over her, and they were no longer together. I didn't understand all the drama. "Then, what's the problem?"

A movement behind made me turn, and I found Rob behind us, cloak wrapped tightly around his body. "The problem is..." He shrugged. "I'm still engaged to marry her."

ELEVEN

I STOOD and turned slowly to face him. "You're what?" Surely, I hadn't heard him correctly. Because if he were engaged to someone else, he'd never have acted like he wasn't.

"Engaged." This time as he spoke, Rob looked at his feet.

I folded my arms over my chest. "And yet you kissed me. Twice?" One of those times I could forgive. He thought I was going home, and we'd never see each other again. It was still a dick move, but I got it. The second time he had no such excuse and had kissed me anyway, knowing he had no right. Worse still, that kiss at the Valentine's party in Huxley had meant so much.

It felt like it was the start of something real between the two of us.

John stretched his arms up toward the dark sky and gave a loud and very fake yawn. "It's getting late. Must be my bedtime." He stood and walked up to the stone cottage without another word to either of us. Great. Now Rob and I were making others feel uncomfortable.

"That's it," said Rob. "Hate me."

I marched up the bank to where he stood looking down at me and pushed his shoulders. Hard. He took a step back to steady himself. "No. You don't get to do that. Don't expect me to tiptoe around you like we've been doing for a fortnight. Not over this. This, we talk about. This, you own." I pushed him again, just to make sure he understood.

"Don't push me," he said quietly.

"Or what? You'll storm away into the forest the way you always do without talking about the real issues?" Just because I was mad, and embarrassed not to have seen this coming, I pushed him again.

He caught my wrists in his hands, holding them tight enough that I couldn't push him again, but gentle enough that he didn't hurt. His fingers felt like silk on my skin, his touch set my pulse racing.

I jerked my arms away, disgusted with myself. This was my problem around Rob. One touch, one look, one word, and my knees turned to jelly. My brain, too. He was engaged to someone else. Whatever tactics he'd used in the past to get me on his side, weren't going to work today. I couldn't let him. But I couldn't think of anything else to say, either, and I stood there, staring at him and hoping he couldn't hear the rapid beating of my heart.

"I should have told you about her. I shouldn't have expected you to ask. And I shouldn't keep running into the forest to hide from difficult conversations. I'm sorry." There was some of the old Rob in his tone, the Rob that cared, and it did exactly what he probably expected; turned my insides to mush.

I straightened my spine. He'd lied. It would take more than a few pretty words to earn my forgiveness this time. "Whatever." I jerked my arms from his grip, turned and stalked toward the cottage.

"Maryanne, wait." He ran to stand between me and the door. "Please can we talk?" He gestured to a log Tuck had moved beside the outdoor firepit. Right outside the cottage.

"I hardly think everyone wants to hear us argue while they try to sleep."

Rob lowered his voice. "I don't intend to yell." One side of his lips kicked up. "Or say anything that will make you want to yell, either."

I closed my eyes. A day ago, hell, an hour ago, I'd have given anything to see that tentative smile on Rob's face. Now, I hated it. I hated it because of what it did to me, and what it meant I'd say. I wanted to be strong, to walk away, to not listen to whatever spin he was about to feed me. But that smile made it impossible. I already knew how the next few minutes would go. No matter how much I wanted to walk away and leave him stewing out here while I went to bed, I wasn't going to. That smile made certain I'd hear him out. What it didn't guarantee was my reaction at the end. This was his only chance. If I didn't like what he told me, the two of us were done.

I opened my eyes to find him watching me, eyebrows raised hopefully. I pushed past him and sat on the log with my arms folded over my chest. No sense making this easy on him.

Rob sat at the other end. The distance between us wasn't great, maybe a meter, but it was the farthest apart we'd ever sat when it was just the two of us, and it hurt. I picked up a stick, only burnt at one end, and threw it onto the cold coals hoping Rob couldn't see any of what I was feeling on my face.

He waited until I was still again before he began talking. "I met Lizzie when I was fifteen."

Almost four years ago. That was some serious history and it just served to remind me that Rob and I had so little.

"We were friends for a long time before it grew into something more. I thought I was in love with her."

"Thought?" *Oh my God! Shut up!* So much for not showing him how I felt.

He shrugged. "You know my history. There wasn't much love in my upbringing. But I thought that was what the two of us shared."

If he'd wanted to use those pretty words he was so fond of, right then would have been the perfect opportunity to express how knowing me had changed all that. But he didn't.

"Lizzie always knew what she wanted. She never hid it from me. I was just good at blocking it out. Or storming away when she said something I didn't want to hear." He gave a faint smile.

"Some things never change," I said quietly.

He met my eyes, the intensity in them something I hadn't seen since the first time we met. "I never wanted to hurt again the way I did with her. Storming away has always been easier than sticking around to have my heart torn out."

"So, instead you tore out mine."

He pressed his lips together and looked at the grass beneath his feet. That was a low blow, especially when he was trying to explain. I should feel bad about it, but I didn't.

"I thought Lizzie and I had a lot in common. She wanted a home, a place she felt safe and loved." He didn't need to add the words, *like me*, we were both thinking it. "But to her, a home was four walls and a roof. I thought she'd change her mind. Or maybe I thought she'd want to be with me enough that she wouldn't care where we lived. Because, there was no way I was living in a village or town."

He said it like he was worried Gisborne might raid that imaginary town, and he might have been. But it wasn't the only reason. Rob thrived in the forest. He lived to see the stars at night, or to hear the river babbling as he woke. He'd have gone crazy living inside a house in a village. I didn't know how he managed it when he was looking after Alan. At least here, at the stone cottage, he was in the middle of the forest.

"Like I said, I thought I was in love with her. I thought she was in love with me. She wanted to be married so I got down on one knee and proposed."

I couldn't look at him because I didn't know what he might see on my face. Obviously, his story was leading to this point, but it still felt like a dagger to my heart to hear it. "What did John think about that?" I got the feeling John wasn't fond of Lizzie. I wondered if he'd told Rob at the time or left him to make his own mistakes.

"John was in a difficult position. Back then, Josephine was married to Lizzie's brother, her children are Lizzie's nephews, so he kept his thoughts to himself. But Tuck wasn't happy with my decision, and he told me so in no uncertain terms."

Good to hear that Tuck hated all Rob's female friends equally. It wasn't just me. "Josephine? John's sister?"

He nodded.

"Wait. The first day we went to Clipstone, after the soldiers attacked, was Lizzie's brother in one of the graves?" We'd stood at the edge of the forest and watched John hand out the gold that day that seemed so long ago. Rob had wanted to stay anonymous.

He nodded. "I was hiding from Lizzie. Couldn't even go down and offer my condolences."

"Because she hurt you?" At least, that's what John had said.

"Because of that. And because I was just starting to wonder if maybe, she hadn't hurt me at all."

I frowned as I watched him because that made no sense, but he gave me no time to speak.

"When I proposed to Lizzie eight months ago, I meant it. I'd have done everything to keep her safe for the rest of my life. I'd have provided for her. I hoped to have a family with her. After she said yes, I spent time considering our living arrangements and decided to compromise. I would go to live at Clipstone with her. It was close to Tuck, John and Miller, so I'd still be able to see them. But when I got to Clipstone to tell her, I found her with someone else."

I raised my eyebrows, silently nodding. That was low. No wonder Rob was hurt. Especially since this was all so recent. It had happened just two months before we first met.

"In bed with him," he clarified. His voice shook, the anger from that day still bubbling somewhere near the surface.

"Rob, I'm sorry." No matter how upset I was, that was still a horrible thing to walk in on. I wouldn't have wished it on anyone.

He shrugged like it was no big deal.

I knew better. "What did you do?"

"Nothing. Never went near her again. I focused on my desire to kill my little brother and tried not to think of her. Closest I've been to Clipstone was that day with you, where I wanted to go down that hill and hug Jo for her loss, but I was terrified of coming face to face with Lizzie and what's-his-face." He met my eyes, shaking his head. "Don't look at me like that. I don't need your sympathy. I'm not that broken." He paused, then added quietly, "Not anymore. Not since you arrived."

I ignored that last comment. We weren't there yet and I wasn't ready to discuss us. And he'd seemed pretty damn broken these past couple of weeks. "You should have told me." It wasn't as bad as it sounded. For all intents and purposes, the engagement was off.

"I should have. But life when you're around is...hectic."

I allowed my lips to twitch. Hectic was an understatement. "Feeling's mutual, buddy."

"It was wrong of me, and I apologize."

I shook my head. He'd made a big deal where there was none. "It wasn't wrong if the engagement is off."

He licked his lips. "Yes, well."

"It's not off?" How could that be? He'd admitted they hadn't talked or even seen each other in months.

"Neither of us actually called it off. Jo says she still wears the little silver ring I had made for her. She also says that things between Lizzie and what's-his-face aren't so good anymore. Plus, Lizzie..." He screwed up his face like he didn't want to say the words. "She's somewhat...territorial."

"Meaning...?" I could put it together, but I wanted to hear it from him.

"That night in Huxley, I hadn't planned to kiss you. I'd actually wanted to leave it a few days longer, to make sure we were both ready. But you looked beautiful, and I planned to go to Clipstone the next day to get my ring back from Lizzie and end our engagement. I didn't think she'd have a problem with it because she hadn't tried to see me in six months. I didn't know she was unhappy with what's-his-face. It was stupid of me, and I'm sorry."

"Because you never made it to Clipstone?" Alan had been kidnapped the following morning. There hadn't exactly been time for anything but rescuing him. And until we got him back, we were staying in the south of the forest, far from Clipstone and Lizzie.

"Jo brought a message with her that night in Huxley. She told me as she left. She said Lizzie wanted me to know she was ready to marry me."

I snorted. As if that was going to happen. Not after the way she'd treated him.

The ghost of a smile came to Rob's lips. "I reacted the same way. Until she gave me the rest of the message." He ran a hand down his face.

"Which was...?"

"That she's pregnant. And since she's publicly engaged to me, she's my responsibility and I need to do something about it."

"But...everyone will know it's not yours if you haven't been near her in eight months." I couldn't see how that was even a threat.

"People will see what they want to see. She's engaged to me, therefore the baby must be mine. And even if it's not, she wears my ring, so I'm responsible for her. Jo thinks she's only doing it now because she heard about you. She didn't want me when she could have had me, but now she has competition, she's marking her territory. And there's not a damn thing I can do about it, except marry her the way I promised I would." He gave me a caustic smile. "See what I mean when I say my life won't ever be perfect again? It could have been, I think, with you challenging me every step of the way, making me laugh, making me mad, and maybe loving me, too. Instead now I'll have to spend it trapped inside a house away from the forest with a lying tart for a wife."

I raised my eyebrows even though Rob had every right to speak that way about her. "I'm sorry."

He shook his head. "This is all my own stupid fault. I hope you will decide not to hate me. But I understand if you do."

If only he knew. My heart, although no longer pounding the way it had after he touched me, had settled into a beat that was both faster and louder than when he wasn't around. Hating him wasn't an option. I imagined it to be something that would take years of practice, and I'd have to want it very much. Which I didn't. I leaned over and put a hand on his. "I don't hate you, Rob. I don't think I ever could. We can fix this. I don't know how at the moment. I don't even think we can afford to spend time thinking about how until we've got Alan back. But if you really don't want to marry Lizzie, we'll find a way out of it. Her baby should not be your burden." We'd have to sort this out before it became obvious Lizzie was pregnant, but I hoped we had a few weeks before that happened.

He turned his hand over and closed his fingers around mine. "John told me I should tell you. Told me so right after Huxley. Said if anyone could make me feel better about it, it would be you."

John put too much faith in the way I dealt with Rob. "Was he right?"

Rob squeezed my hand. "He was. I'm glad it's no longer a secret standing between us."

TWELVE

THE next morning Rob, Tuck and I rose early and walked to Nottingham. The others stayed back to look after our prisoners, and so they could come and rescue us should something go wrong. I hoped we'd be fine. I'd dreamed of Alan last night. He'd been playing a throwing game in the cobbled courtyard of Nottingham Castle with a group of children. They were laughing and cheering, the way he had been the day I'd first met him.

"What if Bridgette is lying?" I asked, leaves crunching beneath my feet as light slowly brightened the forest.

"Then we're in trouble," said Tuck. The fact he was here, even knowing that, told me Tuck thought we had no other option but to trust her.

We needed to make certain the Sheriff, and Gisborne for that matter, understood our terms including when and how we'd return our prisoners. Although we gave both coachmen messages for the Sheriff, there was no guarantee they relayed them correctly. The Sheriff needed to understand we were serious. We'd return our prisoners in exchange for Alan.

Telling him in person was the best way to achieve that.

We'd considered so many ways to make that happen, until Bridgette offered a solution. She said he was known to take a walk around the castle grounds early in the morning, often dragging Gisborne with him. They always walked through a small wooded area inside the castle walls, before heading to the stables and going out for a ride.

"She wants to go back home," said Rob. "She can't if we're in the dungeon because she's set us up. I think we can trust her." Rob seemed happier this morning, actually contributing to the conversation as we walked, rather than staring morosely at the trail ahead. It was amazing what hope could do. Not to mention unburdening oneself.

Although I'd told him I'd help fix his Lizzie problem, I was still mad at him. Lizzie was obviously a piece of work, but he should have told me what she was doing to him. I'd spent a sleepless night thinking about it from all angles and driving myself crazy. This morning I'd decided not to think about it at all. At least for a while. Right now, we had bigger worries.

"I hope so," said Tuck.

So did I.

Rob held a branch back off the trail so I could pass. "There's no way we can be ambushed because she can't get a message to the Sheriff's guards. We'll go in carefully. Check everything out. If anything feels off, we turn around and return to the forest. If it's all as Lady Bridgette said, we continue as planned."

The wooded area at the castle sat between the inner and outer walls on a gently sloping hill. The little grove was thick with trees almost as tall as those in Sherwood, and an under canopy so dense, very little light entered. Trails heading in every direction crisscrossed the grove; most were overgrown and rarely used, but there were also a number of wider and well-traveled trails. It was on one of these that Bridgette said we'd find the Sheriff.

My heart almost beat out of my chest. The guards at the gate barely gave us a second glance as we entered, our weapons hidden in what we hoped looked like piles of cloth carried across our arms. It was market day, and we blended right in with everyone else streaming through the gates hoping to sell their wares.

Heading to the grove, all three of us took separate hiding places as far from those main trails as we could. Bridgette said two of the Sheriff's guards would walk the trails before he entered, checking it was safe. Once they were gone, we'd be free to speak with the Sheriff uninterrupted.

The guards passed closer to me than I would have liked, chatting to each other about a pretty servant girl and taking no notice of anything around them. Once they were gone—according to Bridgette, back to guard the entrance to the grove—Rob and Tuck moved closer, and we waited.

We heard the Sheriff before we saw him, the timbre of his voice carrying through the trees. I didn't know what he was saying; my heart was beating too loud in my ears to hear. He was easy to spot, his burgundy jacket trimmed with gold edging doing nothing to hide him among the greenery of the trees. Gisborne, walking beside him, was also easy to see, his burgundy cloak around his shoulders.

As they drew closer, Rob stepped out in front of them. He bowed respectfully. His hood covered his head, and with the long shadows of early morning, I doubted the Sheriff or Gisborne could see his face. "Good morning, Sheriff. May I have a word?"

The Sheriff continued walking as if he hadn't heard Rob, making to step around him. He seemed relaxed, except for the one hand hovering above the handle of his sword.

Rob planted his feet, refusing to back away. "My name is Robin Hood."

The Sheriff wrapped his hand around his sword hilt, though he didn't draw it. He stopped walking, and his voice was careful when he answered. "We have Robin Hood in our custody."

I flexed my hand on my bow, waiting for my cue.

"I believe you're mistaken, my lord." Rob pulled back his hood.

In the same moment, Gisborne drew his sword and Tuck and I stepped onto the path, our bows nocked and aimed at the chests of the Sheriff and Gisborne, ready to fire.

"I suggest you remain quiet, my lord, and listen carefully. We will shoot should you yell. Are we clear?" Rob's hands were out in front of him, empty of weapons, and he spoke fast and urgently.

The Sheriff glanced at Rob's waist. He knew as well as I did that there was a sword beneath his cloak, which he could draw and use before the Sheriff's guards could arrive.

"No!" Gisborne moved half a step forward.

"Stand down, Gisborne." The Sheriff looked down his nose at Rob, then nodded, agreeing to his terms. "Let the man talk."

"Good decision." Rob looked him over. "You have something I very much want back. And I have two somethings you will want returned. I'd like to arrange an exchange."

"I presume you're speaking of Lady Bridgette Sutherland." The Sheriff's voice was cold and hard, and he glared at Rob like he was something smeared over the bottom of his shoe.

Gisborne leaned toward him and mumbled. "They also have Eliza Thatcher, my lord."

I hid my smile. Both coachmen had returned safely to Nottingham, then. And done exactly as we asked.

The Sheriff paused a moment, calculations running behind his eyes. "You can keep them. They are of no benefit to me."

My heartrate ramped up and my hand grew slick around my bow. We'd misjudged everything by presuming the Sheriff would negotiate on the women's behalf. If he refused, we had no way of bargaining for Alan.

"But—" Gisborne's cheeks and neck turned bright red. He clamped his mouth shut and swallowed like he was trying to stop himself saying more.

Rob kept his cool. When he spoke, there was no trace of the panic I was feeling. "I have it on good authority, my lord, that Lord Carston Sutherland is a very generous benefactor to the city of Nottingham. I'm also led to believe he cares deeply for his young wife. I believe his generosity will dry up should he not get his wife back unharmed." That was the theory I'd worked on when we took Bridgette. It was something she'd confirmed over dinner last night.

The Sheriff paled. His mouth opened and closed, no words escaping his lips. Bullseye.

"We will return both prisoners the moment you release Alan of Woodhurst from your custody."

The Sheriff glared at Rob, his lips pressed tightly together.

For once, we had all the power. For once, we could make demands.

"I'm nothing if not fair," said Rob. "Two prisoners for your one. That's all I ask. Agree, and both women will be back in Nottingham before lunch. Disagree, and..." We had no plans to hurt

Eliza or Bridgette, but it would do us no good for the Sheriff to know that.

"I don't make deals with outlaws." The Sheriff spat the words, his lips drooping in disgust.

My heart fell. This wasn't the answer he was supposed to give. This was where he was supposed to be so grateful to get the women back that he jumped into action right away in preparation for their return.

Rob didn't seem quite so shocked by the Sheriff's response. He shrugged and started to turn away, speaking at the same time. "That is, of course, your choice. But do make sure you know what you plan to tell Lord Sutherland when he discovers you chose not to save his wife's life."

The Sheriff's lips pressed together so tightly, they turned white. "Three days."

Rob swiveled on his heel to face the Sheriff. "I beg your pardon, my lord?"

"Three days. We'll make the swap in three days."

Rob swallowed. We didn't want to wait. We wanted to make the exchange today. His shoulders tensed as if he could feel the deal slipping away. "And why would I agree to that?"

Why, indeed? A delay would surely give the Sheriff the opportunity to set a trap for us. We had to refuse.

A slow smile spread across the Sheriff's face. "What choice do you have? I will not hand over Alan of Woodhurst until sundown in three days. You, of course, are welcome to hand your prisoners back prior to that time." His smile grew wider.

We would not be giving our prisoners back early. We'd give them back only once we saw he intended to return Alan to us. He was right. We had no choice but to agree.

Rob must have come to the same conclusion. "Very well." The tension humming through his body said he wasn't happy about this development. "But if you're deciding the time, we'll decide the place."

The Sheriff's lip curled. "And I'd agree to that because...?"

Rob lifted one shoulder. "Same reason. Because you have no choice. I'm not coming back to Nottingham to walk into a trap you've had three days to set. We'll met you at the village of Bestwood in Sherwood Forest at sundown on the third day from now. And don't even think about trying to trap us there. It's surrounded by forest, and we'll be watching the village until we get Alan back."

There was a beat of silence before the Sheriff said, "Can you guarantee the women are unharmed?" His hand still hovered near his sword.

"Can you guarantee my brother is unharmed?" Rob shot back, his voice growing more accusatory as his hold on his emotions slipped.

"Rob," I cautioned. This wasn't the time for blame or anger.

Gisborne's head swiveled my way, as if he'd only just noticed anyone else was here. "Maud?"

I pulled back my hood. "Good morning, Gisborne. My lord." I nodded to them both, hoping the movement might placate them if Rob's tone had riled them.

"Do we have a deal?" Rob asked, moving ever so slightly to place himself between Gisborne and me.

The Sheriff pursed his lips before finally nodding. "Sundown in three days at Bestwood. Your two prisoners for our one."

Rob bowed his head just as Gisborne took a step forward, eyes soft and focusing on me. He should have learned by now. I wasn't her. I didn't even act like her. And I certainly didn't want to be anywhere near him.

"Don't take another step," Rob snarled, his eyes remaining on the Sheriff and a protective arm gesturing me to move behind him. "You did more than enough damage the last time you were near her." I'd never heard Rob's voice so filled with hatred and anger. Gisborne must have heard it to, because he shuffled back.

The Sheriff's sword screamed as he dragged it from its scabbard. He brought his arm up, ready to swing at Rob.

I loosed my arrow. It whistled through the air and buried in the Sheriff's arm. He dropped his sword with a clatter and let out a scream.

Crap! This was *not* how this was supposed to go. But I'd had no other choice. He was going to hurt Rob. I nocked another arrow and pointed it at Gisborne. Tuck's arrow was also on him.

"Gisborne. Kill them!" The Sheriff spoke through his teeth, his hand gripping his arm where the arrow protruded.

Gisborne raised his sword. Rob had yet to draw his own weapon. Gisborne could kill him before he had the chance.

"My lord," I called, gripping my bow tight, hoping to pull Gisborne's attention from Rob.

Gisborne's eyes darted to me, searching, as always, for the girl who looked so much like me.

It was about time he realized Maud wasn't coming back, and I wasn't anything like her. "Drop your sword. Or I will shoot you."

"Gisborne!" The Sheriff growled at Gisborne's shift in focus.

Gisborne looked between the three of us, then let his sword fall to the ground with a muttered curse.

Rob, Tuck and I sprinted from the grove, and once we were out of the castle grounds, we ran until we couldn't breathe.

I took Eliza to the river to bathe after we returned from Nottingham. To a place upstream from our camp, past the waterfall and surrounded by willows. It was more private than the nearby swimming hole we could see from the door of the cottage. She'd been tied to John all morning and complained that she needed to wash. It seemed like a fair request. Miller was listening from back at the stone cottage in case I needed help.

I sat on a rock watching Eliza pick her way with bare feet over boulders and down to the river. She still wore her city clothes, a pale-yellow gown that was now covered in sap from the walls of the cage she'd thrown herself against again and again yesterday. She'd declined our repeated offers of a tunic, pants and boots—which Tuck had gotten from a nearby village—refusing to wear them. I couldn't tell if it was because they were men's clothes or because they came from the poor.

"You know he'll be searching for me, don't you?" Eliza hadn't yet reached the water but glanced back over her shoulder at me.

"Gisborne? He wasn't hunting for you when we saw him this morning." But he *had* known about her. And I imagined she was right; if he wasn't personally searching for her, he would have his soldiers out looking.

She flinched. "Because he didn't know where to look. He would have had people follow you back here. They'll be here any moment to rescue me."

We'd worried about that. Had walked in purposeful circles because of it. No one had followed us from Nottingham. If they found us, it would be through sheer luck. But with the luck we'd had lately, it wouldn't surprise me to have a soldier stumble across our campsite when he was lost in the forest.

"Have you kept your end of our bargain?" She crouched beside the water, pulling up her skirts so they didn't get wet, and dropping her voice so anyone else who might be lurking in the trees— which was no one—didn't hear.

Meaning, did I know if her sister was getting out of the portal. "Not sure if you've noticed, Eliza, but I have a few things going on in my life at the moment." I hadn't even had time to think about the deal I'd made with Eliza since leaving her chamber that day.

"Is that a yes or a no?" She turned to look at me.

"I'm working on it." Or, I would be, in a day or two. Once everything settled down. "Are you really trying to bathe while fully dressed and without getting your dress wet?"

She folded her sleeves up her arms, then dipped her hands in the river and splashed water on her face.

I didn't hear her answer as I stood and stumbled down the riverbank to where she crouched at the river's edge, unable to take my eyes from her arms. "What happened?" Both arms were a mass of bruises in varying colors, especially above her elbows. Black, purple, yellow and everything in between. I'd seen bruises like that before. On me.

Eliza dragged her sleeves down, not bothering to dry herself. "Nothing." She stood and folded her arms.

I took her wrist in my hand, turning it over. On the inside of her forearm were four purple circles, where someone had held her so tight, they'd left marks. "Did Gisborne do this?"

She pulled from my grasp. "What if he did? I must have deserved it."

I shook my head, my eyes on her arms that were now hidden behind the material of her dress. "There is not a thing you could have done to deserve that." And it hadn't been just one beating. Some of the bruises on her arms were old, some newer. "Does he do it often?"

She shrugged. "Often enough."

"Is that why you helped me after Gisborne hurt me?" She was the last person I expected to see that day. Definitely the last person I expected to nurse my injuries.

She shrugged. "When he's hurting someone else, he's not hurting me."

I moved toward her, needing to see it again in case my eyes had deceived me. "Is it just your arms?"

She jumped away and shook her head, winding her arms tightly and protectively around her body.

"Are you in pain?" It now made more sense why she'd screamed when Rob threw her over his shoulder yesterday. And perhaps why she hadn't wanted to change clothes—in case we saw what he'd done to her.

She shrugged. "I'm used to it. When I anger him, he hits anywhere but the face. Everything else can be hidden." Her voice was bitter, and it was the first time I'd heard her speak of Gisborne with anything but love or reverence. "Gisborne doesn't love you," she said, making an abrupt change of subject.

No. He loved a girl who looked exactly like me, who he'd hurt so badly she had no intention of returning to him. "He doesn't love you, either. If he did, he wouldn't treat you that way." I wasn't trying to be mean. I wanted Eliza to see the truth. To maybe search for other options, especially if I failed to get her sister out of the portal.

She shook her head, her lips curling in disgust. "You think I don't know that? You think I don't remember how he treated you before you left. How he used to look at you? How he looks at you now you're back, even though you've been nothing but cruel to him? I'll take it, because I love him. And because I don't have a whole lot of other options, in case you haven't noticed."

"I'm sure there's someone out there better for you than Gisborne." He might have prestige and power, but what was the point when he hurt her that way?

"Not all of us have a forest full of boys waiting to drop everything to do our bidding. Not all of us have men going gooey-eyed at us wherever we go."

There wasn't a forest full of boys. There wasn't even one boy. "Not everyone's life is the way it looks from the outside. Sometimes, what people let you see is totally different from their reality."

She shook her head, her face twisting in anger. "Screw this. I'm done. You are nothing more than a whore. And you'll never get Gisborne back, no matter how hard you try to make me leave him." She turned on her heel and ran. Up the riverbank and into the forest, her bare feet slapping against the dirt.

Damn. I stumbled up the bank behind her. "Miller!" She was fast. Gone through the undergrowth, sticks breaking as she ran.

Ahead there was a thud and a squeal. Miller came walking toward me, carrying Eliza over his shoulder. I couldn't think of a better time for him to emulate Rob, but I also hoped he wasn't hurting Eliza. I must remember to tell her I was Maryanne—that the ring she took from me wasn't mine, but Maud's. Like everyone else, she'd seen it on my finger and assumed.

I went back down to the riverbank to get my cloak. By the time I returned to the clearing, Miller was stalking around the edge with measured steps, boots thumping against the ground. John, Tuck and Rob had gone hunting and I thought it was Miller's choice to stay behind. "Miller, if you wanted to go with them, you should have said. I'd have been fine here on my own."

"I know that," he snapped.

"Then...what's wrong?" Something, clearly. But I had no inkling what that might be.

He hadn't bothered to lock either of the girls in the cage, instead tying one hand of each of them to a stake he'd hammered into the ground in the middle of the grassy clearing. They could sit and work on undoing the ties, but neither of them were. I wasn't sure if he didn't think they'd run, or if he was certain he could catch them should they attempt to get away. I kept them in the corner of my vision as I watched Miller pace, in case they decided to make a break.

Miller picked up a rock off the ground and threw it so hard at a tree that part of the rock broke off. "She broke up with me."

I wracked my memory for any mention of a girlfriend and came up blank. "You have a girlfriend?"

"Had."

How on earth had he had time, with everything else going on? "What happened?" I had so many more questions that needed answers. Who is she? Where did they meet? Was she the girl from the party at Huxley? Was she good to him? How had I become so wrapped up in my own problems that I'd completely missed something so huge in Miller's life?

"Went to visit her this morning. While you were at Nottingham. She told me it was over, that she'd met someone else."

"Oh, Miller." It seemed none of us had much luck in the love department. I reached out a hand to place it on his shoulder. He ducked away.

"I loved her!"

"What was her name?"

"Alice." He stopped pacing and leaned back against a tree. Then he slid down it until he was sitting on the ground, his knees up to his chin.

I didn't recall him ever mentioning that name. "Where did you meet her?" There was just so much I didn't know.

He gave me a look that was all wide eyes and raised brows, and when he spoke, it was like he thought I should have known. "Huxley."

Maybe I should have. He'd drunk a lot of whiskey that night, and now I thought about it, it wasn't like him. More likely, he'd been trying to impress her. "How did you see her this morning?" We were too far from Huxley for a day trip, let alone a morning visit.

"She came south just after us. She's staying with her sister in Arnold." He put his head in his hands. "I loved her so much, Maryanne."

It was on the tip of my tongue to tell him two weeks wasn't long enough to fall in love with anyone, but it had taken less than a month for me to know I felt something for Rob, so who was I to judge?

I did, however, have something that might help.

I went into the cottage and pulled the open block of chocolate from my pack, then I walked back out and sat next to him, resting the chocolate on my knee. The girls watched openly.

"What's that?" Miller asked.

"Well, in my time, it's...it's...a remedy for a breakup." I broke off a square. "It's called chocolate."

He narrowed his eyes. "What do I do with it?"

"Eat it." I smiled, my mouth salivating from the sweet smell. I could easily sit here and scarf the entire block. And even though I had more in my pack, I wouldn't. This was the only chocolate I'd see for the rest of my life. I planned to make it last. Plus, it made me feel closer to Josh because he'd given it to me.

"How would eating something that looks so revolting take away the agony of what happened?" He looked at it as if it were something he wanted to wipe from the bottom of his boot.

I shrugged. "Maybe it won't take it away. But it'll make you feel better for a moment or two. Trust me." I glanced at Eliza and Bridgette, both watching us. They could use some, too. I broke a piece off for each of them.

With another dubious look, Miller edged it into his mouth. He blinked a couple of times, then grinned, his eyes widening. "It's good."

Bridgette sighed in agreement and Eliza closed her eyes as she swallowed.

I couldn't wait any longer. I put a piece into my mouth and let the creamy texture melt over my tongue and slide down my throat, silently thanking Josh for the gift. "You know, Miller. It might work out. Alice might decide it's not working with her new man and come running back to you."

"Doubt it," he said, glumly.

I passed him and the girls another square of chocolate. "I once thought someone I loved was with someone else. Turned out, he wasn't. The day I found that out was one of the happiest of my life." Until it wasn't.

He looked at me sideways. "If you're trying to give me hope, you're failing. You're talking about Rob and all you two ever do these days is argue. Love sucks. I'm never falling in love again."

Thirteen

By the time I sorted Miller out with another two pieces of chocolate, it was too late to take Bridgette to the river to wash. Not that she seemed bothered. If I didn't know better, I'd think she was enjoying her time with us. Nothing seemed to phase her, and she was always cheerful.

"I've got a joke." Miller put his last piece of chocolate into his mouth. He was clearly feeling better—or perhaps he was simply trying to distract himself into feeling better.

"Go on, then," smiled Bridgette.

Miller cleared his throat. "What do you call someone with no body and no nose?"

I shrugged when he looked at me, unsure if telling jokes was a good idea. I'd heard some of the crass jokes the boys told, and I doubted Bridgette or Eliza would appreciate any of them.

"I don't know," said Bridgette, still smiling.

Miller looked at Eliza, but she looked away, refusing to be drawn into the conversation. He shrugged and said, "Nobody knows."

I smiled. That was probably the tamest joke in Miller's repertoire, and perfect for our guests.

Bridgette doubled over with loud, bubbling laughter.

Eliza sat in stony silence and Miller narrowed his eyes. He got up and walked over to her, crouching in front of her. "I have another joke. Want to hear it?"

Eliza rolled her eyes.

"Miller. Just..." I shook my head. Eliza probably didn't feel like laughing with the people holding her captive.

His eyes remained on her. "Did you know I was named after King Richard?"

There was a long silence where Eliza's jaw jutted. Miller remained crouched in front of her, unmoving. Finally, she blew out a deep breath and met Miller's eyes, her voice overflowing with contempt. "Your name's not even Richard."

Miller lifted his eyebrows. "I know. Like I said, I was named *after* King Richard."

Laughter bubbled out of Bridgette. Eliza stared at Miller for the longest time. Then her lips twitched, and she looked away.

"Ah, she does smile." Miller met my eyes with a grin.

He and Bridgette took Eliza's reaction as permission, the two of them banding together to do all they could to force a laugh from her. They tried every joke they knew; dirty, clean, silly. With each joke, Eliza's lips twitched a little more, and her shoulders lost a little more tension.

But it wasn't until the two of them impersonated the Sheriff and Gisborne that they got an actual smile from her. Bridgette cheered like she'd won the lottery and Miller threw his arms in the air. "I knew you had a smile in you," he said.

Once Eliza had smiled once, there was no going back. She giggled along with the rest of us at the jokes on offer.

When the laughter died down, she taught us a game that was similar to tic-tac-toe. Her and Miller turned out to be very competitive, yelling and laughing when they won. And sometimes if they lost.

The following morning, I took Bridgette to bathe in the river. I didn't have to watch her the way I'd watched Eliza. She'd made no move to run and, after the games yesterday, had even helped John with dinner. She'd asked everyone to stop calling her Lady Bridgette, or Lady Sutherland, so we were now on a first name basis with her.

At the river, she pulled off her borrowed tunic and pants, and dived straight in, not caring about the cold. And even though the weather was warming up, I wasn't sure it was warm enough to dive into the river yet.

She washed quietly and dried herself on the bank while I sat in the sun with my back turned. The sound of a child crying reached us on the breeze. I got to my feet trying to work out which direction it was coming from as she walked up the bank to stand beside me. We weren't close to any villages. There shouldn't be anyone out here.

"Should we go and check it out?" Bridgette whispered, her long black hair dripping down her back.

I nodded, hoping it wasn't a trap, and let her lead the way. We walked farther from our camp to find not one crying child, but two, standing by the bank of the river. The older of the two was probably around seven and had her arms around her little brother. Their clothes were torn, faces dirty. The girl carried a little sword strapped around her waist, which she moved to pull out the moment she saw us.

I put my hands in the air and crouched on the mulch-covered ground in front of them. "Are you lost?"

The older child waved her sword in my direction but remained silent.

"Where's your ma?" It was dangerous out here in the forest. Worse for children.

The girl stared up at me with huge, tear-filled eyes. Her shoulders drooped, and her little brother answered. "Our pa died." Big tears sat on his lashes.

Bridgette crouched in front of him. "Oh, my dear. I'm so sorry." She pulled the younger child to her chest and he relaxed into her. "What are your names?"

"Mary," said the girl. "And Simon."

"Did your pa die recently?" It would explain why they were out here alone and so upset.

Mary nodded. "The soldiers killed him. A few weeks ago. There's no food in our village. Ma told us to go out and find something for us and the babies to eat. We're not to come back until we do." Tears threatened to spill down her cheeks, but she held them back, her chin wobbling with the effort.

I held out my arms to her and, having decided we weren't a threat, she ran into them, dropping her sword in the dirt.

"How long have you been out here?" Bridgette asked.

"All night. We found some spring berries and were going to take them home. But Simon was so hungry—"

"So were you," Simon interrupted.

She shrugged. "We were both so hungry, we ate them." Tears filled her eyes again. "We should have taken them back. For the babies."

I shook my head. "It's important for you to eat, too." There was only one solution here. "Tell you what. Why don't the two of you head back to your village. I'll get some food and bring it to you."

Mary shook her head, adamantly. "No! Ma said we wasn't to come home without any food."

Their ma must be desperate to send such young children out alone and refuse to let them come back unless they found something to eat. I ran a hand down my face, thinking. "Okay. How about you wait for me down there." I nodded at the river. There was a willow tree they could wait under and stay hidden until I returned. "I'll be back in an hour or two and I'll bring some food that you can take back to your ma. Okay?"

The two children nodded, their faces solemn as we led them down to the tree. I strung my bow and checked I had enough arrows in my quiver.

Bridgette grabbed my arm. "What are you doing? You can't hunt in the King's forest!"

I shook her off. I didn't need a scalding from a rich woman. "What do you think you've been eating these last few days? I don't know how things work where you come from, but here in the forest, meat doesn't turn up already cooked. We have to kill it first. If we don't, we starve."

"But, it's the King's." She didn't sound quite so confident this time.

"And his laws are unfair. Plus, he entrusted the Sheriff—the most unjust man in Nottingham—to take over in his absence, and the Sheriff used the *King's* soldiers to kill the children's father." And they probably stomped all over their crops at the same time. "I'd say he owes these children some food. Come on. I'll take you back to the cottage."

Bridgette pulled her shoulders back. "I...I want to come with you."

I stared at her. "You want to come hunting?" I couldn't believe a noble woman would choose to break the law.

"Please," she added quietly.

I sighed and nodded, and started down the trail, Bridgette following closely behind.

It took a couple of hours to get the children two rabbits. Rob would have been faster, probably knew exactly where the rabbits liked to hang out; he'd had more practice at it than me. I was just pleased I could take something back to them. I made a mental note to find out where they were from and go to their village with some gold once we had Alan back. Anything to make their lives easier.

The children were where we left them, and their faces lit up when I handed them a rabbit each.

"Ma will be so happy," Mary whispered. "Thank you."

"We'll walk you home, if you like?" I offered.

Mary shook her head. "You've done enough, taken enough time from your day." She touched her hip. "I've got my sword. We'll be fine." She gave each of us a hug, pushed Simon in front of her and headed down the narrow trail.

We watched as they walked away. Their steps were light, and they talked quietly to each other. No tears now. It filled my heart. And Bridgette's, if the smile on her face was anything to go by.

As if they had been waiting for them, two soldiers suddenly stepped out of the dense forest and onto the trail in front of the children.

"What have we here?" The taller of the two asked.

I started down the trail after them. I'd been here before. I'd seen soldiers stop a child on the trail, I knew exactly how this would end.

"Is that the King's game in your hands?" one of the soldiers asked.

Mary drew herself up. "Please, my lord. It's just two rabbits. My baby brothers are starving and will die if we don't bring them some food."

Bridgette rushed past me, raising her hood and marching straight up to the tall soldier. "What's going on?"

"Are these your children, ma'am?" he asked.

"No. But they are friends of ours."

"Well, they're each about to lose a hand." The children gasped. Bridgette may have, too. I wondered if she'd ever seen the forest justice system up this close. "For stealing."

"They're starving. Can't you show them leniency?" Bridgette pleaded. She glanced at me, her face grim.

I was going to have to own up to killing the rabbits if I wanted to save the children's hands.

"The law is the law," the soldier said.

I stepped toward the soldier. "They didn't—"

"Maryanne. Quiet!" Bridgette demanded, raising a finger in my direction.

"But——" I needed to help the children, and the only way to do that was to admit to my part in this.

"One more time," she said to the soldiers, drawing herself up. "Are you going to show them leniency and let them go home to feed their family?" Her voice had grown as hard as steel, and I wondered where this version of the noblewoman who'd spent two nights with us had come from. We definitely had never seen this side of her.

He raised his chin. "I most certainly am not. We have laws to uphold."

"And you're willing to trade your life over two little rabbits?"

What was she doing? We had no weapons. My bow lay resting against the tree where we'd said goodbye to the children, and even if I had it in my hand, it was no good up close. I did have the dagger I kept in my boot, but it was no match for the sword hanging from the belt of each soldier.

The tall soldier laughed. "Our lives? What exactly should I be worried about? The children attacking me?" He eyed Mary's little sword and laughed again. "Or two women?"

Neither, was my bet. I could yell for Rob, but where there were two soldiers, there were likely more, and I couldn't risk them finding our camp. Or finding Eliza.

For that matter, what the hell was Bridgette doing? These soldiers could rescue her. Bring her home to her rich husband and beautiful clothing. Why wasn't she asking them to do exactly that?

Bridgette twisted and lunged for Mary's sword, pulling it from her belt. In one movement she turned back to the soldier and stabbed the sword, which was much thinner than the one Rob used, into his gut. Her hood flew off as she drew it out and whipped around to face the other soldier. Clumsily, he drew his weapon, holding it defensively in front of himself. "You're Lady Sutherland. I'd recognize that dark hair anywhere. We're looking for you. You don't need to fight us."

She swung her sword at him, and he moved fast, blocking her. "If you're going to cut off the hands of starving children, I'm afraid I do need to fight you."

She swung again. He blocked and brought his sword down in an arc toward her. She turned, twisting away so it missed, then she blocked his next blow. I'd never seen anyone fight like her. She was light on her feet, like a dancer. Ducking, weaving, twisting and turning. Rather than brute strength, speed was her weapon. As the soldier raised his sword to bring it toward her again, she ducked beneath it and buried hers in his stomach, pulling it free when he crumpled to the ground.

She rested her hands on her knees, puffing, and looked up at the children. "You're safe now. Or as safe as it ever is within the forest. I think there will be more of them around, so stay off the trails. And maybe hide the rabbits."

The children nodded, eyes wide.

Bridgette wiped the blood off the sword with a leaf and handed it back to Mary.

"I hope I can fight like you one day," the little girl said. "I've never seen a girl fight before."

Bridgette smiled. "Practice every day and you'll be able to. Now, go."

They hurried away, ducking off the trail, their rabbits hidden under their shirts. Once they were gone Bridgette's shoulder's sagged. She stared at the bodies of the men at her feet. "I've never killed anyone before." Her voice was quiet, and her body trembled.

I put an arm around her shoulders. There was nothing I could say to make her feel better. Killing didn't get any easier to deal with. In my experience, it seemed people just became better at hiding their horror. "You know they could have saved you." She'd had a ticket out of here and had let it go.

Bridgette looked slowly up at me and shook her head. "No. They could have dragged me back to a place where I might as well be kept in a cage. Out here, I feel free. I'm not ready to go back yet."

Oh, the irony in that statement. "But you're a prisoner."

She shrugged. "Apart from the way you all watch me to make sure I don't run, you don't treat me like a prisoner. You talk to me, you let me do what I want to do. Cook, or swim." She gave me a wry glance. "Or fight. You treat me like I'm one of you."

I smiled. I thought I could understand where she was coming from. "It is freeing, being out here in the forest, isn't it?"

She spread her hands wide, lifted her head to the sky and turned in a circle, laughing, if slightly hysterically. She would come right soon. Once the adrenalin wore off. "So much."

"Where did you learn to fight like that?" I wished I had half the skill with a sword as her. And the courage.

"My husband likes me to be happy. I guess he knows on some level that I'm really not. He paid for a tutor, after I spent six months begging him to allow it."

I didn't know anything about Lord Sutherland, other than he was old and filthy rich. "Does he like the fact that you can use a sword better than most men?" I couldn't imagine he did, given he'd had to *allow* her to learn in the first place.

She gave a coy little shrug of her shoulder. "I may have led him to believe I don't have all the skills you just saw. I don't want him to decide he's spent enough on my lessons and stop them. I love it so much. It's the highlight of my day." She watched me sideways. "I saw you shoot the arrow to save your man at the Sheriff's tournament."

Everyone had seen me shoot that arrow. Some liked what I'd done, some hated it. As a noble, Bridgette would usually have been firmly on the side of the haters. After her display with a sword, I wasn't sure where she stood.

"I know you're not Maud." She spoke quietly, like she was sharing a secret. "We were friends, Maud and I, before she...died, or whatever happened to her. I knew her well enough to be certain there's no way she would ever have picked up a bow, let alone taken the time to learn to shoot one." She pressed her lips together, as if debating whether to speak what was on her mind before spitting the words out in a rush. "And even if she had, she would never in a million years have pointed it at Gisborne, no matter how badly he hurt her."

She was probably right about the last part. It was the first part that bothered me. It didn't hurt to have people think I was Maud. Being her opened doors that might otherwise remain bolted firmly shut. "People change."

"Perhaps. No matter how many times he hurt her, she still had love in her eyes when she looked at him. That day at the tournament, you looked at him like you hated him."

"I did hate him." *Do* hate him. "He's not the...person I thought he was." It was a weak comeback. I should have been able to do better, but she'd taken me by surprise. The last thing I needed was her going back to Nottingham and screaming from the rooftops that I was an imposter. That would just give the Sheriff more reason to want me locked up.

Her stare told me to quit it. That I wasn't fooling her. "She'd never have slept out here, night after night, on a straw mattress on the ground, in the cold, with no one to bring her food, no nice clothing. Plus, your friends call you Maryanne."

"I think you underestimate Maud Fitzwalter. She's a resourceful lady. She'd do whatever she needed, to survive." Like living on the streets for two years, eight hundred years in the future, for example.

"I'm not trying to scare you. If you want to talk, I'm available. It's not like there's a lot of other women out here for you to bond with. I like you. Even if you're not Maud, we should be friends. I see her spirit in you."

Tuck, John and Eliza were the only ones at the cottage when we returned. They were quietly playing Eliza's version of tic-tac-toe. John knew the moment we stepped into the clearing that something had happened and made us share. He and Tuck listened with their brows drawn together.

When we finished, John said, "I know better than not to believe something you tell us, Maryanne. But Lady Bridgette using a sword?" He shook his head. "I don't think so. The nobles don't let their women learn that sort of thing."

"I can show you." Bridgette's chin jutted, but her words were soft.

John shook his head. "I don't own a sword. Tuck's the only one currently here who has one, and you can't show us much on your own."

"Well..." She stretched out the word. "I might have one hidden in the dress I was wearing when you took me." She looked at her feet.

I stared at her with my mouth open. We'd never searched Eliza or Bridgette for weapons. We'd certainly never checked Bridgette's pile of clothing after she removed it. None of us thought either of them were a risk in that department.

"Go on, then." Tuck got to his feet. "Show us what you've got."

Bridgette jumped up and ran into the cottage where she'd left her dress folded neatly on the ground in the back corner.

"Who's showing us what they've got?" Rob strolled into our clearing with Miller close behind.

"Maryanne and Bridgette have been killing soldiers. Bridgette's about to show us how," said John.

Rob lifted an eyebrow.

"With her sword," added Tuck, his tone dry.

Miller's eyes rounded when Bridgette returned with her sword, a little larger than the one she'd used today, but not so big as what the boys used. He took a step toward her, his eyes on her weapon. "Whoa. You have a sword? Can you use it?"

Rob's smile was confused. "You mean you've actually killed soldiers today?"

I nodded, and let Bridgette tell the story.

Rob's face grew more and more serious, the longer Bridgette talked. When she was finished, he pointed his finger at me. "You are not to leave the clearing unless one of us is with you." He glanced at Bridgette and Eliza. "None of you women are to leave the clearing."

"Don't be ridiculous." I didn't need to be wrapped in cotton wool or treated like a prisoner.

We'd come away alive today. That was all that mattered. "It wasn't even that dangerous." Understatement. But he wasn't ever going to tell me what I could or couldn't do.

"To be fair, you were considering handing yourself over to the soldiers," said Tuck.

I glared at him. Bridgette left that part out when she told Rob. I wasn't sure if she'd just forgotten to mention it, or if she knew how Rob might react, but I'd been grateful. Should have known Tuck would do what he could to drop me in it.

"You were what?"

I shrugged. "You wouldn't have done anything different."

"I would have! Because I wouldn't have walked into a fight unarmed. You're reckless, Maryanne. It will get you killed."

I already knew how close we'd come to dying today, I didn't need to be reminded. But I also didn't need him telling me I was stupid or reckless. I hadn't run into that fight the way I'd done once before. I'd gone to help children who needed us, and he would have done the same if he'd been there. "Yeah, well, I guess I learned from the best."

I turned away. My buzz from the fight as dead as the soldiers Bridgette killed. I'd sit down by the water to calm down. Then maybe later, I'd try to have a proper conversation with Rob about this.

"I mean it, Maryanne. You're not to leave the clearing unless someone else is with you."

I whirled on him. "And I'm not your property to command." Bridgette had been amazing today. I'd come back to the cottage on a high because of what she'd done. I wanted to learn to fight that way. But Rob had just pointed out that I couldn't do even a fraction of the things Bridgette could. The reason he treated me like I couldn't look after myself was because, hand-to-hand, I couldn't. Miller gave me occasional lessons, but I never took them seriously. His sword was too heavy for me, and I'd never been interested in that sort of fighting because surely, against any man with his strength and reach, I'd lose.

Except Bridgette hadn't. She hadn't even used her own sword to win. It felt as if Rob was rubbing my uselessness in my face.

"I never said you were my property. But I will demand you stay in this clearing with one of us until things die down with the Sheriff and we have Alan back."

The correct response would have been to agree I was wrong and start taking proper sword lessons. But the anger on Rob's face made my hackles rise and lit a fire inside my chest. I folded my arms and raised my chin. He wasn't stopping me from doing things just because he could. "Make me."

My words ignited the same reaction in him. His lips tightened at the edges and he pulled himself up tall. "Oh, I will. Just try me."

Stop! Stop! Stop! My brain yelled at me to let it go. I couldn't. I was past the place of making rational decisions, driven by anger instead. "So, you're going to make me a prisoner in this clearing just because I've done something you don't like?"

His eyes narrowed. "I don't know. Maybe you could just keep doing your own thing, making your own decisions and not telling anyone important information because you think you know best. Would that work better for you?"

That was a pretty accurate assessment of the way I'd been acting. But it wasn't totally my fault. True, I'd taken Bridgette on a whim, but in most situations, I talked things through with him—when he was available. But he'd been MIA ever since Gisborne took Alan. I glared. "You're not making me a prisoner."

"And you're not going anywhere."

That sounded like a challenge. I met his eyes. "Yes. I am." I stormed past him out onto the trail that led from our camp.

"Maryanne! Come back here!"

I shook my head. I was over his chest beating.

"Last chance. I mean it." He spoke through his teeth.

I ignored him and continued walking, pushing past the branches hanging over the trail.

I didn't even hear his footsteps, but he did exactly as I'd told him he would. He raced after me, swept me up over his shoulder and marched back to the campsite.

Fourteen

I KICKED and yelled. I hit his back, and when that didn't work, I tried to scratch him, too. But weeks in the forest had left me with next to no nails, so that didn't hurt him either. Without a word, he deposited me inside Eliza and Bridgette's cage and backed out while I aimed a kick at his shins. He wound the tie around the door, locking me in without looking at me, and said, "I'll be back once you cool off." Spinning on his heel, he stalked toward the door. Over the threshold, everyone else stood watching, their mouths hanging open.

I was angry and humiliated. And I wasn't finished with him yet. "That's right. Run away into the forest like you always do!"

Almost out the door, his step faltered. Then he continued walking like I hadn't spoken.

I turned away from the horrified looks, moving to the back of the cell to lean against the stone wall and wallow in my humiliation.

How had I let my anger get the better of me? I'd just had a very public screaming match with someone I had no right to be yelling at.

On second thought, why was I so surprised? This was me. It was what I did. Especially around Rob, just usually not *at* Rob. The first few times I'd been able to use my bow again had only happened because I'd let my emotions take over. The same thing had happened here today.

"You were pretty hard on him." Bridgette walked inside and sat, resting her back against the wooden bars of the cage. She stared straight out the cottage door.

Great. Now someone else wanted to have a go. "He was hard on me."

"He was." She twisted toward me, a huge grin on her face. "But you were fierce. I wish I could be like that. Stand up to people that way." Her voice dropped to a whisper. "But I also wish I had someone who cared for me enough to do what Rob just did."

"Newsflash. He didn't drag me in here because he cares. He did it because he likes to make all the decisions for everyone, and he hates it when I question him. And he likes to beat his chest like an ape." I was wild about the way he'd treated me. This wasn't the way men treated women in my time. I'd never been on the receiving end of such behavior, and it was worse because it came from someone I cared about.

"You don't believe that," she said, her voice soft.

I didn't know what I believed. I was so damn angry I could hit something, but every time I thought about our argument, my cheeks burned over the way I'd acted. And then I realized I was locked in a cage and I wanted to hit Rob for putting me here. I let out a harsh laugh. "If he did this because he cares, he has a strange way of showing it."

She sighed. "You'd only need to ask that boy to jump, and he'd say *how high?*"

She looked so different from the fine woman I'd first met when we robbed her carriage months ago, whose clothes and hair were elaborate and never out of place. Her tunic was stained with something dark—grass, or more likely, blood—and her shirt was rolled up at the sleeves. There was a leaf in her hair, and her cheeks had a glow that hadn't been there a few days ago. But she didn't know what she was talking about. "He's engaged to someone else."

She lifted one shoulder. "Entrapped, more like it. But I believe you will think of a way to fix that. Or a way to live with it."

"They told you?" Because everyone had sat on that information rather than sharing it with me.

"I asked. I was trying to understand what was going on with the two of you."

"Nothing. And there never will be. Especially when he locks me in a cage because he doesn't like what I say."

"I'd have locked you in a cage for baiting me that way, too."

"You think I should apologize to him." It wasn't a question. And I wasn't sure I'd listen to her answer.

"I think you two need to have a proper conversation for once. Tell him how you feel."

I wasn't telling him that. I still owned a single shred of dignity.

"I've spent a lot of time watching since I've been here, and you're the only one who can get Rob to do anything once his mind is made up. Hell, you told him not to storm off, and there he is, sitting at the top of the riverbank." I followed her gaze. Rob was sitting alone, staring out across the water. "Why do you think that is?"

The obvious answer was because he felt something for me. I shook my head. "He locked me in a cage."

Bridgette got to her feet. "You're not locked in. He only pretended to wrap the ties around the door. You can get out any time you see fit."

I didn't leave the cage immediately after Bridgette walked away. I watched Rob's back through the not-locked door. He sat with his knees pulled up, barely moving. Could Bridgette be right? Rob hadn't stormed off into the forest because I'd told him not to? John kept telling me I could talk Rob into anything. It wasn't entirely true, but he did listen when I spoke. A lot. I was also done with fighting with him. So much had changed since we first met, now we had to find a way to work our relationship—whatever it was— around those changes.

I stood and brushed off my pants, then pushed on the cage door. Like Bridgette said, it wasn't tied shut. Something I'd have known if I'd bothered to look properly. I walked quietly past the empty outdoor firepit where no coals glowed, but where everyone else sat talking and pointedly ignoring me as I passed.

I stood behind Rob a moment, growing my courage. Then I stepped up beside him and looked down.

"I'm sorry," I said. "For all..." I waved my hand in the direction of the cottage. "...that."

He looked up at me. "I'm sorry for all of that, too. I shouldn't have——"

I shook my head. "Don't dissect it."

He nodded. Maybe neither of us wanted to relive our behavior.

"Truce?"

He nodded again and shuffled over so I could sit. I imagined everyone was straining their necks to watch us. Best we didn't give them any more entertainment for the evening. "I only want you to be safe, Maryanne."

Of course, I knew that was all he'd wanted when he told me not to leave camp on my own. I just hadn't liked the way he said it. "And I want you to stop worrying about me." I had a plan about how I'd look after myself going forward. But first I was taking Bridgette's advice and talking. Properly. "Is that the only thing you want?"

He blew out a humorless laugh. "You know it's not. I want you, too. But since that's never going to happen, I'd settle for having what we had before you went home. You know, if we're making wishes here." His lips quirked up on one side.

I stared at his hand sitting in his lap. Then drew a deep breath and took it in mine. "I want the same thing. I want to never fight with you.

And..." I took another long breath. "I want you to get me a sword. I want Bridgette and Miller...or you...to start teaching me. And I want to learn properly."

"Done." He opened his mouth to speak further but no words came out, and he finally shook his head.

"What is it?"

"Don't leave. Don't go back home. I know I've been a complete bastard lately, today especially, but please, just...don't."

I tilted my head to one side. "I know you think the sun revolves around you, Rob, but a few arguments aren't going to push me over the edge. I'm here. And I'm here for good. You are all my family now, like it or not."

He nodded, his shoulders dropping in relief. Then he looked at me and lifted his eyebrows. "The sun revolves around me?" His grin was tentative. "That's an interesting notion. One I could see great benefits from."

I tried not to smile, but against my will, a grin stretched across my lips.

"Like never having to sit in the dark with a beautiful lady, unable to see her face."

I shook my head. "Don't think one compliment will fix everything that's wrong between us." Try as I might to stop it, I was still smiling, so he probably wasn't going to believe anything I said.

"What about two compliments? You, Maryanne Warren, are by far the bravest and most selfless person I've ever met."

I shook my head again. "Still, no." Although I'd take this over the last few weeks any day.

Rob licked his lips. "I'm sorry, Maryanne. For how I've behaved these past weeks. I didn't want to blame myself for Gisborne taking Alan, so I somehow made myself believe that it would never have happened if I hadn't been so focused on us. Plus, I've been livid with myself for letting everything with Lizzie get so out of control. Somehow, I took it all out on you."

I got it. I'd been an expert in finding ways to blame myself for Josh's accident and everything that happened after it, and then passing that blame onto others. Now I was annoyed at myself for not having kept my frustration in check.

"The reality is, we wouldn't be getting Alan back without you. I'd never have considered taking Eliza prisoner, and I didn't think taking Bridgette was a good idea either. But it was. I'm so grateful. I just hope that one day you'll stop hating me."

I sighed. This journey back in time had turned out so different from what I'd imagined. Worse in many ways. "I came back here thinking there was a place for me in your legend. Turns out, I was

right. It just wasn't the place I thought. I'm here
for a reason, Rob. And it's not to be the woman
hanging off your arm, like I expected. I am here
to help you be the best person you can be." I had
skills that could help him be an amazing Robin
Hood if he chose to once we had Alan back, and I
was proud of that. I was prouder still to find I was
braver than I'd ever imagined I could be. Needs
must, I supposed, but I had no qualms with
fighting to the death if it meant ridding Rob of
Gisborne for good. Especially if it gave Rob more
time to live as Robin Hood. "I don't hate you.
Never did. Never will."

A slow smile lit Rob's face. "You seem very
sure of that. You do realize I'm a complete
bastard, right?"

"I think I'm starting to." I smiled.

"Good. Best you understand that right from
the start." He leaned back on his elbows, more relaxed than I'd seen him in a long time. "Hanging
off my arm, huh? This sounds like a piece of the
legend you've neglected to tell me. Sounds like a
part I need to know. Especially if it involves you."

The timbre of his voice lit flames in my stomach, as it always did. I tried to ignore them. I
wasn't explaining the role of Marian in Robin
Hood's legend to Robin Hood. He could find out
about her all on his own, when he met her. I tilted

my head like I was trying to remember. "You know, I think the legend said something about how absolutely infuriating Robin Hood could be and how I would likely climb up your arm on the way to wrapping my hands around your throat." Okay, so I wasn't good at making things up on the spot, but he'd get the picture.

He laughed. "I do not believe that for a moment. But you're welcome to climb over me any way you like."

Now, *that* was an invitation. I pressed my lips together, trying not to smile. "Like I said, infuriating."

The three days with Eliza and Bridgette went faster than I imagined they would. Eliza remained surly—to everyone but John and Miller, who spent hours quietly playing her game with her—while Bridgette slotted into our group as if she'd always been here. Whenever she found me idle, she pressed her sword into my hand and made me swing it, or she made me practice moving around the clearing fast on my toes, or any of a hundred other things that she said would help me in a fight. I was going to miss her when she left.

"Do you want to change back into your dress? Do you want me to help you?" I asked Bridgette when we were almost ready to head to Bestwood to meet the Sheriff.

"I think I'll go as I am," she said, quietly.

"You're not worried what everyone will think, seeing you wearing pants and a tunic like a man?" Like me, she found it easier to get around in the forest without the hinderance of a dress.

Her face creased into a wide smile. "With any luck I'll give Carston heart failure and I'll be free to come and live out here with all of you." She pulled me into a hug. "Thank you," she whispered. "For kidnapping me. It's been the best few days of my life."

"Come back anytime. We've enjoyed having you here." I squeezed her tight, wishing I could ask her to stay. She clearly didn't love her city life as much as she enjoyed living with us in the forest. I couldn't though. She was the key to getting Alan back, and no matter how much I enjoyed her company, I couldn't leave Alan with Gisborne a moment longer. "Keep up those sword lessons. You never know when they might come in handy."

We started the trek to Bestwood long before dusk, all of us quiet as we walked. I didn't trust the Sheriff. I hoped this handover would go as we planned, but I doubted that would be the case.

The intense dreams I'd had about the future had stopped after I escaped Gisborne. I still dreamed, but they didn't feel as real, or as urgent. I'd spent hours since we made the deal with the Sheriff trying to recall those dreams, trying to find something that would give us an advantage tonight. Problem was, I'd never dreamed of Bridgette or Eliza, so no matter how hard I tried, I didn't remember anything that would help.

Rob fell into step beside me. "Feel like company?" The afternoon was warm, and he'd pushed his sleeves up to his elbows. His bow was slung over his back and his sword rested at his waist.

I moved over on the trail. It was narrow, but we could walk side-by-side at a push. "Are you worried about how today is going to go?"

"Terrified. Neither the Sheriff or Gisborne are trustworthy." He shrugged. "But this was our plan. Apart from the three day wait, we're exactly where we hoped to be. We have no choice but to see it through. We just have to be prepared for anything since we have no idea what we're walking into." He'd been better since our fight. Better actually, since he told me about Lizzie. It made me wonder if the guilt he'd felt over her had been a major part of the reason he'd been so withdrawn.

"There's always a choice." I said the words by reflex.

He shook his head. "Not this time. Not if we want Alan returned."

I sighed, because he was right. We'd felt so smart to put ourselves in this position. but it was our only chance. Neither of us were stupid enough to think Alan would be alive by sunrise tomorrow if anything went wrong at sundown tonight. Neither of us wanted to be responsible for his death. "Will you be happy with what you've done in your life if this is a trap and the Sheriff kills you?"

Rob gave me a sidelong glance as he held a branch out of my way. "That's very deep."

I shrugged. I'd come back to his time to make him a legend, and I was certain I'd done enough for him to be remembered as a hero. But with more time, there was so much more we could achieve. So, my answer to my own question, was no, I wasn't happy with what I'd done in my life so far.

I wondered about Rob, though, and what he would have been doing if he'd never met me. According to the legends of my time, he'd have been a criminal by now, preying on rich and poor alike, their gold going straight into his own pocket. Instead, he'd been handpicked for a job he hadn't known he wanted. Had I forced him into this lifestyle? Was he satisfied with the people we'd helped? Did he wish he'd never become this version of Robin Hood? "I just mean, is there anything you wish you'd done? Or wish you'd done differently?"

"Sure." He shrugged. "I have a few regrets. Doesn't everyone?"

"I guess so."

We fell back into silence as ahead of us John gave Eliza's arm a friendly nudge and she let out a quiet burst of laughter. Farther up the trail, Tuck, Bridgette and Miller walked quietly in single file.

"Four." Rob held up his fingers. "That's how many things I wish I'd done differently in my life." Rob began counting on his fingers. "I regret not moving the deer you shot the first day we met."

I frowned. That wasn't something I expected to find on his list of things he wished he could change. "Why?"

"Because if the soldier hadn't seen it, you wouldn't have had to shoot an arrow at my chest that day in Nottingham."

"I never wanted to shoot at you, but I'm not sorry it happened. I learned a few things about myself that day." And learned to like what I saw.

He held up his next finger. "I regret not killing Bridgette's coachman the first day we stopped her carriage."

"Because then he'd never have been able to tell everyone you were Robin Hood?"

He nodded. "And because everything that happened after that led to you leaving me." He marked off another finger. "I regret not killing Gisborne after he took you hostage."

It was easy to know why he regretted that one. "Because Alan would still be with us if Gisborne were dead. I thought that would have been first on your list."

He lifted his eyebrows. "I was listing chronologically. Because of Alan, yes. And also because it killed me to see you so wounded that day. And I did nothing about it."

He had done something. He'd made sure I could get away from there. "And the fourth one?" There hadn't been anything really big that happened since Alan was taken, so I had no idea what it might be.

He was silent for so long I twisted to face him as I walked. "The fourth one isn't chronological. But I do regret it every day."

"Okay?" I lifted one shoulder. He could list them in any order he liked.

"I wish...I'd greeted you the way I wanted to when you returned to this time. For those few minutes, I thought you were Maryanne, and everything was like it used to be. Then I saw that ring on your finger and everything changed." He shrugged. "Anyway, I regret it."

My cheeks heated. I knew exactly what he'd wanted to do that night. He'd told me. But it wasn't what I said. "You wish you'd greeted me with a smile and a hug?"

His lips twitched, and he shook his head. "No. That was how I actually greeted you. It had something to do with a tree."

Another flash of heat went to my cheeks and I looked at my feet, pretending to check for roots I might trip on as we walked. If the others hadn't been so close by that night, I wouldn't have complained about being greeted the way he'd wanted to, either. "I don't recall."

He shuffled closer, until he was almost touching me. Our pace slowed to a crawl and my heart rate ramped up. "Yes. You do." He spoke in my ear and it took every piece of resolve I had inside me not to shiver.

I totally did, but still I shook my head. "Sorry. No clue."

He licked his lips. I saw the movement out of the corner of my eye. "I wanted to...ravish you against a tree."

I drew in a deep breath to hear him say it. At some point, we'd stopped walking. His lips were so close, if I turned slightly, I could kiss him. I wanted to. I always wanted to with Rob. I forced myself to lean away, then met his eyes. "Why didn't you?" Not what I was planning to say. There was no point encouraging him, not with Lizzie still in the picture.

"Didn't know how you felt. About me."

I didn't believe him. "I've felt the same way about you since almost the moment we met." I hated how my voice came out all breathy when Rob was this close.

"Ah." He nodded. "Good thing I didn't do anything then. I was such a prick when we first met that I'm sure you wanted to put a knife through my back."

He had been. But he'd also been kind and generous and caring. "I guess nothing much has changed."

He laughed and started to walk again, the spell broken. "You know, there's a tree over there that's perfect for ravishing." He nodded somewhere off the trail. There were probably a hundred trees in the near vicinity that could be used for that purpose.

I lifted my eyebrows. "Have you fixed things with Lizzie?" He hadn't. We were at the opposite end of the forest from her. As much as I wanted to kiss him, it wasn't an option while he remained engaged. I wouldn't let him hurt me again. I didn't even know why we were talking about it.

He shook his head. "But I will. I'll end things with her once and for all. I'll tell her to leave me alone."

"She won't." Lizzie wasn't after Rob. She was either after someone to marry, or she wanted gold. One of those things was much easier to give her than the other. I fiddled with the pouch strapped to my waist. It was the place I kept everything important that I owned, which consisted of a single lump of gold and the hairclip Rob gave me on my birthday. If I could have fit my photo album in there, I would have.

I held the hairclip out to him. It was the most beautiful and expensive gift anyone had ever given me. "Give her this, if you can bear to be parted from it. If she takes it, make her return your ring. And tell her that will be the last time you see her. Tell her, if she takes it, she agrees that the two of you will never marry."

Rob's eyes were on the clip. He shook his head. "That was a gift for your birthday. I can't take it from you to fix my problems."

His problems were my problems, and I was okay with that. "Do you want to be married to her for the rest of your life?"

He shook his head, his jaw stiffening. Living anywhere but the forest would kill him, and never seeing him again might just kill me. But I wasn't doing this for me. I was doing it to help him, no matter what happened between us after.

I pressed it into his hand. "Take it, Rob. If it works, great. If not..." I shrugged. There would be another option to stop him marrying Lizzie, we'd make sure of it. "If it makes it any easier..." I put my hand in my pouch again, searching for the other item I kept in there. The one that didn't belong to me. "I got this back for you." I held up his mother's wedding band. The ring he'd traded to save my life after the wound Gisborne gave me became infected. The cursed piece of jewelry I'd bought for five pieces of chocolate.

His eyes rounded and he took the ring between his fingers. He held it up toward the sky for a better look. "Where did you find this? How did you...?"

I shrugged. "Long story. It's hers, though. Right?"

He nodded, still looking at the ring. "Is there anything you can't do?" he breathed.

So many things.

Like press my lips to his. "You're welcome."

FIFTEEN

THE Sheriff's soldiers—around thirty of them—stood in a single line looking toward the forest. There were about the width of a football field away from where we hid among the trees, their backs to the village. We used these few minutes before announcing our arrival to the Sheriff to catch our breath. And to check for obvious traps before stepping out and letting them know we were here.

Each soldier held a bow in one hand, an arrow in the other, and carried a quiver on their back. The Sheriff was here, too, and my shoulders drooped in relief. There was a part of me that expected he wouldn't turn up.

"I don't see Alan," said Rob, craning his neck to look through the trees.

I didn't see him either. "He must be here. Why else would there be so many soldiers?"

"Miller, Tuck, Maryanne. Ready your bows. John, keep hold of the girls, and all of you stay hidden for now. I'm going to step out of the forest for a better look."

Miller, Tuck and I spread out along the edge of the forest. I nocked my bow, keeping one eye on Rob, the other on the unmoving soldiers across the field.

Rob's bow remained slung over his shoulder. He had nothing in his hands. Practically unarmed, there should be no reason for the Sheriff to renege on this deal.

The moment Rob moved out of the forest, the Sheriff's voiced drifted across the field. "Robin of Woodhurst. Where are your prisoners?"

Rob nodded over his shoulder. "They're safe. Where is my brother?"

There was movement in the line of soldiers and Gisborne pushed his way through, smirking across at Rob.

"I mean my older brother." Rob's voice held a scowl.

"Show me your prisoners first." The Sheriff stepped up beside Gisborne.

Rob turned and nodded to John, who walked out of the forest, one hand around Eliza's wrist, one hand around Bridgette's.

"Show me Alan," Rob called.

The Sheriff's reply was loud and clear. He rested his hands over his ample belly. "I'm disinclined to trust a thief such as yourself. I don't believe you intend to return the women to us, despite what you say."

Panic rose in my gut. I'd expected something from the Sheriff, but I wished he'd proved me wrong.

Rob spread his hands wide. "I have no reason to lie. Return Alan of Woodhurst, and you can have both these women." With his body angled away from me, all I could see was the tension in his jaw, the only sign he shared the panic rising in my own gut.

"On the contrary. I'd say you have plenty of reasons to lie. Here's how today is going to work."

Rob's hands balled into fists, and I watched helplessly as our plan drifted beyond our reach.

The Sheriff's voice boomed over to us. "We need a display of goodwill before we release your brother, therefore, you will release Lady Bridgette Sutherland to us now. Should you do that with no loss of life to my soldiers, no injury, no weapons drawn, then we will return to this same place tomorrow and swap Alan of Woodhurst for Eliza Thatcher."

Without turning, Rob said quietly, "John. Take the ladies back into the forest. Take them in deeper than the edge. Miller will come to you once we've made an agreement here." He lifted his voice and spoke across the field as John and the girls sank back into the forest. "That's not what we agreed upon."

"Perhaps." The Sheriff's shoulders rose and fell as he spoke. "But after taking time to reconsider your offer, it is now the only agreement I'm willing to make. Refuse, and your brother will die at sunrise tomorrow."

Rob's fists clenched and unclenched at his sides, and I thought he might refuse. He couldn't. Alan would die if he did. With the Sheriff's deal, we still had hope. I could change his mind. At least, that's what John and Bridgette thought. Now seemed like as good a time as any to test that theory.

"Rob." I moved along the forest edge until I stood behind him, then called in a low voice. "Rob. Can you hear me?"

He gave a single nod.

"Offer Eliza instead. She's far less valuable to the Sheriff."

Rob gave no indication he'd heard me, but after a beat of silence, he called, "This isn't the deal we made. We will swap Eliza Thatcher now as a gesture of good faith. You'll get Bridgette Sutherland back when my brother is returned."

The Sheriff stared across the gulf between us. Finally, he licked his lips. "No deal. Bridgette Sutherland today. Eliza Thatcher tomorrow."

I shook my head. We couldn't agree to this. Eliza meant nothing to the Sheriff. He'd never honor a deal like this.

Rob might as well have read my mind. "No. We all know which of the two prisoners is more important to you. If we give you Bridgette, you won't return with Alan tomorrow. Eliza is the only prisoner I'll offer first."

The Sheriff's hands over his gut flexed. "You have no choice but to trust me."

Rob took a step back toward the forest. "Oh, I have plenty of choice." He turned, his movements slow, like he was walking away but waiting for the Sheriff's next move.

"Wait!" The Sheriff ran a hand down his face. "You have my word."

"You word means nothing!" Rob's voice echoed around the field.

The Sheriff dragged his other hand down his face. "I have been promised...I mean...the city of

Nottingham has been promised a substantial sum of gold should I manage to have both women returned unharmed. But Lady Sutherland must be returned first."

Bridgette extracted herself from John's grip by giving a hard, sharp tug on her arm. She ran to stand next to me and looked out across the field. "Carston's here." She licked her lips and directed her next words at Rob. "Ask the Sheriff who promised him the gold."

Rob did, and the Sheriff shot the answer straight back. "Lord Carston Sutherland."

I looked at Bridgette, trying to gauge her reaction. "Do you think this is true? Can we trust your husband?"

She nodded, her eyes on the Sheriff.

"But..." Anxiety made my heart race. We had to make this decision fast, and it had to be the right one. "I thought you were unhappy with your life with him."

She lifted her shoulder. "I am. But that doesn't make him untrustworthy. He's a good person. Old and boring, but good." Her eyes drifted to him, standing alone out the back of the soldiers. "My unhappiness is not because of him. It's because I can't stand the shallowness of the city. And because I'd rather be outdoors than in. Carston might never have met Eliza, but he'll hate the idea of either of us being out here against our will, and he'll want to make sure the Sheriff does everything he can to have us both returned."

Rob spoke without turning. "So, we trust him?"

Bridgette nodded. "He's an honorable man, Rob. With Carston involved in this deal, you can be sure you'll get your brother back." Her shoulders fell and I squeezed her hand.

"Maryanne?" Rob still didn't turn. I guess he didn't want the Sheriff to know about this conversation.

I trusted Bridgette. If she thought this wasn't a trap, then I believed her. "I think we do it."

"He's lied to us once. Alan isn't even here. What's to stop him lying again tomorrow?" Rob whispered back.

Nothing. But if Alan wasn't here tomorrow, we wouldn't hand Eliza over. Doing this today, wouldn't waste all our bargaining power. And if the Sheriff didn't show up tomorrow, we'd go directly to Gisborne. He wanted Eliza back. I believed he'd do anything to make that happen.

Rob blew out a deep breath and his shoulders slumped. He called across the field to the Sheriff. "You have a deal. We will return Bridgette tonight as a show of good will, and tomorrow we'll swap Eliza for Alan."

I hugged Bridgette tight. "Like I said, you can come and visit us anytime. You know that, right?"

"I look forward to taking you up on that offer." She lifted her chin, both of us knowing that would never happen. Chances were, we'd never see each other again. "Stay safe."

From the edge of the forest, I watched Lady Bridgette Sutherland walk with purposeful steps across the field toward the village of Bestwood. As she drew closer, a group of ten guards rushed to greet her, forming a human shield around her body and walking her into the village where they loaded her into a carriage, and bundled her away.

Rob backed into the forest and let out a sigh. His face was a mixture of anger, disbelief and sorrow.

"Well, that's the first part done. By tomorrow night, Alan should be back with us," said Tuck, coming to stand beside him.

"Think positively, Tuck," said John. "There's no should about it."

Mid-afternoon the next day, Tuck called me over to where he sat, alone in the shade at the edge of the clearing. "You had another dream last night, didn't you?" He paused a moment before adding, "I was awake when you cried out. I heard you trying to calm your breathing."

I'd dreamed Gisborne was leaning over me last night, fist drawn back to hit me. A memory. Not a premonition. "It's fine, Tuck. We'll be fine." I said it as much for my own benefit as his. I wasn't sure I believed myself. Bridgette had been so certain, but I had trouble trusting the Sheriff.

"I doubt that. This is the Sheriff we're talking about, and we've bested him one too many times to hope this will go the way we want it to."

My insides turned cold. I needed reassurance that we were all going to walk away tonight, including Alan. "Wait. Even you think this is a trap?"

He gave a non-committal shrug.

"Then why aren't you telling us not to go?" Tuck was usually the first to say if he didn't agree with something. He hadn't said a single bad thing about going today. In fact, it had been a long time since Tuck had said a bad thing about anything.

"Do you have a better idea? The Sheriff has him locked up too well at the castle. Going there would certainly end in all our deaths. At least there are no walls around Bestwood and there's a chance we can run if it all goes wrong." Tuck focused on his sword for a moment before looking up and switching subjects. "I want to apologize. In case tonight is a trap and I don't get another chance."

I stood up to walk away. He wasn't doing this. We weren't saying goodbyes today. "You know, I'd rather wait. Get that apology, whatever it might be for, once we're all back here safely later tonight." This was the sort of attitude that would get people killed, and I wanted no part of it.

"I always believed you were her," he said to my back. "No matter how many times you said you weren't, or Rob said it, or even hearing Miller or John call you Maryanne. I always thought you were Maud."

I turned slowly back to face him. "And you don't now?"

"You look so alike." He continued as if I hadn't spoken. "You talk a little differently than her, but the resemblance..." He shrugged. "You've heard it a million times, how much you look like her."

I had. It was old news.

"I thought you were her, pretending to be someone else...pretending to be you. Until I saw you pale and shaking when you thought it was Rob that Gisborne had captured rather than Alan. Then I knew you weren't Maud Fitzwalter. She was a noble. She'd never have fallen for him, not in a million years. But you had. I could see it in your reaction. I've been horrible to you because of it, despite seeing how good you are for Rob. He changes when you're around. For the better. You make him happy. I'm sorry. You didn't deserve it."

Okay. Now he'd mentioned Maud, I was listening, and my interest was piqued. "Do you hate her because of the bribe she once saw you take from Rob's uncle?"

His head reared up and he looked at me with round eyes. "You know? You *are* her?" He shook his head and got to his feet, holding his hands out in front of him. "I knew I was right. I knew—"

"Relax, Tuck. I'm not her. But I have met her, and I would have told you so had there been any time for campfire stories since I came back." I felt as if I'd been constantly running for my life since I returned to the twelfth century. "She told me not to trust you. She said she once watched you take a bribe."

Tuck's lips were set in a thin, straight line. "Have you told Rob?"

"No." I didn't know the details. Only that it had something to do with Rob's uncle. It must be something big, though, since Maud didn't trust Tuck. And since Tuck didn't want to tell Rob. Another secret that could drive a wedge between friends if he kept it that way. "But perhaps it's time you did."

"He would hate me forever," he said quietly.

I hoped not. Tuck had saved Rob's life when his family had tried to kill him, and numerous times since. Rob loved him like a brother. "He might be mad. But I can't ever imagine him treating you with the contempt he gives Gisborne."

"I can." Tuck didn't even pause to let my words sink in before throwing his reply back at me.

"Well, I'm not going to tell him, Tuck. As you're so fond of saying, it's not my story to tell." I took a couple of steps back toward the middle of the clearing. "But given what we're doing tonight and how you expect it to go, maybe it's time you did."

Rob returned to the clearing soon after. He'd left before daylight this morning on the one horse we'd kept since heading down this way with nothing but a mumbled *I'll be back by dusk*. From my seat on the log in the center of the clearing, I kept one eye on Tuck, wondering if he'd tell Rob his secret. Wondering exactly what his secret was.

Tuck remained sitting in that same place at the edge of the clearing, cleaning his already shining sword until it was almost time to leave for Bestwood. Then he stood up and called Rob over. Even as I watched out the corner of my eye, and John watched openly, I still didn't think Tuck would tell Rob whatever secret he'd kept for so many years.

I stilled myself and listened as hard as I could, but this wasn't a conversation Tuck wanted us to hear. He beckoned to Rob and they went down beside the river for privacy.

Miller, John and Eliza looked at me, all wearing similar brow-raised expressions. "What?" I asked.

"You were talking all hush-hush to Tuck earlier, and now he's taking Rob away for a private chat." Miller narrowed his eyes. "What's going on?"

I glanced in their direction but could tell nothing from their stances. "I don't know. Tuck said—"

"You did what?" Rob's hands went to his hips, his voice louder than the burbling water.

Tuck's answer was inaudible.

"Forgive you? No. Can you forgive this?" Before any of us could move to stop him, Rob drew his hand back and punched Tuck in the face.

I jumped to my feet. This wasn't how these two fought. They used weapons and talked about how much they wanted to hurt each other, but never actually did it. "You need to stop this," I demanded of John.

But John was already running in their direction. Miller and I were only steps behind. Even
Eliza, unrestrained today, followed to find out
what was going on.

John pushed his way between the two of them.
Blood streamed from Tuck's nose and dribbled
down his chin. Rob rubbed his knuckles, his face
hard as if he wanted to take another crack at
Tuck.

"Rob." John placed a hand on each of their
chests to stop them. "Whatever is going on,
now's not the time. We have bigger things to deal
with."

Rob's lip curled into a snarl as he looked
around John at Tuck. "No. I'd say this is right up
there with one of the biggest things that has ever
happened in my life. Get out of my way, John. I'm
going to kill him."

John moved a half step closer to Rob, his hand
still on Rob's chest, asking Rob to stop. His voice
was calm, as always. Quiet, even. I didn't know
how he did it. My heart was racing, and I imagined my voice would waver if I tried to talk.

Rob's glare was hard. His fists were tight balls
and his jaw was rigid, and it looked like he really
did want to kill Tuck. No wonder Tuck hadn't
wanted to share his secret. I'd encouraged him to
do it. I'd caused this. I needed to attempt to fix

it. "He's your friend, Rob. You're not going to kill him."

Rob gave a hard laugh. "I used to think so, too. Only, real friends don't try to have so-called-friends killed."

Tuck's lips were pressed so firmly together they almost disappeared.

"Don't be daft, Rob. Tuck has never tried to kill you." John gave a tense laugh. I thought of the fight I'd seen between the two of them after Gisborne found out Rob was still alive. John must have remembered it too, because he added, "Not for real, anyway."

"Why don't you ask him, if you're so sure." Rob's body was coiled tight, like he was about to spring. When he did, we all needed to watch out.

John, keeping his eyes on Rob, said, "Okay, then. Tuck, have you ever tried to kill Rob? For real?"

"Yes." Tuck's reply was so quiet it was almost a whisper.

All of us turned to stare at Tuck. That was not the admission any of us expected. Rob took the opportunity to pounce, lunging at Tuck with a closed fist while John wasn't watching. He struck Tuck high on the cheek before John grabbed him from behind and wrapped his arms around Rob's chest.

John dragged him away from Tuck. "There must be some sort of misunderstanding."

"There's not," spat Rob. "Right, Tuck?"

Tuck swallowed deeply and shook his head. Already, the skin around one eye was turning purple, and there was a red mark on his cheek from Rob's latest punch.

"Well, tell them." Rob struggled against John's hold. "They won't believe it if they hear it from me." Something in Rob's voice made me think he wouldn't have believed it either, had he not heard the words from Tuck's own mouth.

"The previous Earl of Woodhurst, Rob's uncle——" because we all knew how much Rob hated to call that man his father, "—paid me to drag Rob's body out into the forest on the night Gisborne tried to kill him."

Well, that wasn't so bad. If Tuck hadn't been with Rob, he wouldn't have survived his injuries.

"He was in pain, bleeding, and slightly delirious. There was a healer in Woodhurst who could have helped him, had I chosen to go against Jerimiah that night. I didn't. For years, Jerimiah had paid my mother. The gold started coming after Edward died. I guess Jerimiah felt bad for organizing the fight that killed my brother." He shrugged. "Jerimiah paid us well and our family was far from poor, but as the years went on, his money came with...expectations."

"Expectations?" asked Miller.

"He expected Ma to do things for him. Things he didn't want to do himself. Little things usually, that were of no consequence. And when I was home, as I was that day, he expected the same obedience from me. What he was asking that day didn't bother me. That's what I told myself. Rob killed my brother, what did it matter if he died? So, I dragged Rob far into the forest. I left him bleeding on the cold ground beneath the Big Tree and returned to Woodhurst to collect my pay." He looked at me. "Or bribe. However you choose to look at it." Or however Maud chose to look at it.

Miller shook his head. "But...you saved him. That's what you told us. You nursed him back to health." He shook his head again. "You're lying. You have to be."

I didn't want to believe it either. Tuck might not be my favorite of these boys, but I knew I could count on him to have my back when it mattered, because Rob trusted him. It ripped me apart to think everything between the two of them was built on a lie. It tore me up even further to know it was true. But it was. I'd seen it once, in a dream years before I'd known any of these people. I'd remembered that dream the day Rob told me his family had tried to kill him. My dream had matched Rob's version until the very end. In my dream, I'd been Rob. And I'd been terrified of the person trying to save me, because somehow, I knew he had hurt me. Before I even came here, before I knew these people, I'd known what Tuck did to Rob.

Tuck sighed, his entire body sagging. "I'm not lying. I chose gold over the life of a child. I've hated myself every moment since."

"So, you didn't nurse him back to health?" It was the first John had said since calming Rob down, and he seemed to be having as hard a job reconciling this as the rest of us. Rob, however, had gone limp in his arms, the fight leaving his body.

"I climbed into bed that night, the gold under my pillow, expecting to dream of all the things I might spend it on. But there was nothing I wanted. Nothing I could use to tempt myself into feeling better. Except the life of the child I'd just condemned. So, I got up, took three gold pieces from the purse and left the rest with Ma, bought some salves from the healer—who wasn't happy to be woken in the middle of the night—then went back to the forest to find Rob. I didn't know if he'd still be alive. I'd left him alone out there for hours. He was." Tuck shrugged. "You know the rest."

"He could have died because of you?" Miller shook his head.

"He nearly did." Tuck let out a deep sigh. "Nothing's changed. You're all still as important to me as you've always thought you were. I never saw Jerimiah again. He kept paying Ma until he died. Gisborne stopped those payments the moment he took Jerimiah's place."

I was stunned. How stupid was I for suggesting Tuck own up? Rob was always going to be pissed at this story. Had I known what he'd done, I'd never have suggested it. Or at least not suggested it today. The timing was so wrong. Especially when we all needed our minds clear when we went to deliver Eliza to the Sheriff. "He might have died, Miller. But he didn't. Because of Tuck."

Miller's lips curled in disgust; a look I'd never seen him wear before. "Tuck left him out here where anything could have happened. I thought you were a good person, Tuck! I thought you loved us all. It's been nothing but a lie. You only help us because you feel guilty!" He turned and ran back up to the cottage.

I watched him go, not even surprised. Miller's bond with Rob had always been strong. Of course he would take something like this harder than anyone else.

"I'm sorry, Rob." Tuck's voice broke and his head drooped in defeat.

Rob shook his head. John had released his grip, but waited, tensed, should he lunge again. Rob stood lifelessly, though. He wouldn't try to hurt Tuck again, even if John hadn't been poised to stop him. "I'm sorry, too," he whispered and turned on his heel, walking away from the clearing.

John motioned with his head for me to follow. "I'll sort things here," he whispered, as I walked past. "You get Rob back to us so we can go get his brother as planned."

I nodded and started after Rob at a trot.

I found him sitting with his back against the same willow Mary and Simon hid beneath while I hunted for them. Leaves were beginning to unfurl on the tree, giving its branches a tint of green. The river babbled past almost close enough to touch.

Rob's head was in his hands. "Don't say it," he said, as I approached. "Don't tell me it doesn't matter because I didn't die, because it does!"

"I'm not going to tell you how to feel." I sat against the tree beside Rob. Getting him focused on his brother again was something I didn't know how to approach. He was hurting. What he really needed was time to digest what he'd just learned. Time we didn't have.

"He should have told me sooner."

I nodded, but Rob's head was still in his hands and he couldn't see me. "He should have." The result would have been the same, but it wouldn't have felt like so many years of lying had finally caught up with them.

"I hate him," Rob spat, pulling his head from his hands and turning to me.

"You don't. He's been good to you. You'll see it—"

"Not Tuck. My uncle."

Ah. He had good reason. "Does it help to hear that I hate him, too? And I never had the displeasure of meeting him." Rob's lips turned up faintly at the ends. It had been helpful, then. "Would it help to know that Jerimiah is the entire reason I got to come back in time and meet you?"

Interest lit Rob's eyes and I jumped on it. Anything to get him to release his anger with Tuck so we could focus on helping Alan. "My father—"

"Another person I have trouble liking." He glanced at me, checking he hadn't overstepped a line. He hadn't. I'd once felt the same way about Dad, but not anymore. "Because of the things he's done to you." Like sending me back in time without my consent, or barely talking to me for years.

"He's made some bad decisions, but where they involved me, I believe he thought he was helping." Right or wrong, I'd come to understand my father had only ever had my best interests at heart. But that wasn't what I wanted to speak of. "My dad knew your father—your real father." I paused, allowing that little nugget of information and all that it entailed, to sink in.

Rob frowned. "He time travelled, too? To my father's time?"

I nodded. "Dad was with your father the night they were set upon by your uncle. They were outnumbered and taken by surprise, and Avery fought that night so Dad could go free. Back to the safety of his own time." I recalled the way Dad stared out the window as he told me this story. Avery Woodhurst had meant a lot to him. "He felt terrible guilt over leaving Avery behind, and when he discovered in the history books that Avery had a son, he spent years researching your life. He sent me back to this time because he was certain you were going to start a fire at Woodhurst Manor, which would finish with you becoming a thief and the biggest criminal in the forest. He sent me to stop you, hoping it might repay the debt he felt he owed your father." I took a breath. "Which means, I'm only here because of Jerimiah Woodhurst."

Rob shook his head. "I won't be grateful to that man for a single thing. Maybe it's your father who is the reason you came back here. If he hadn't run that night, he'd have died too, and you..."

"Would never have been born." That was the exact reason Avery had told Dad to run. So he could have a life.

"He was right. I told you I'd been on my way to kill Gisborne the day you interrupted me."

I nodded. He'd wanted to take back his home, but I'd ruined that for him by shooting a deer.

"Lucky your dad sent you here, or I'd either be dead, or a criminal with no morals. Either way, I'd never have had the pleasure of knowing you." His voice softened with his last words.

"Or me you," I said, just as quietly.

There was silence between us and immediately Rob's thoughts returned to Tuck. I saw it in the way his shoulders stiffened and his jaw tightened.

"Rob, Tuck's sorry—"

"I don't want to talk about it. Him. Don't want to talk about him." He stood up and started to pace along the edge of the river. "How could he do it? I was only a child."

I moved in front of him, forcing him to stop walking. "Not now. You can't be angry over this now. We have to leave in a few minutes to go get

Alan back, and you need to be totally focused while we're there. The Sheriff—"

"I couldn't care less about the Sheriff," he spat. "My own life is falling apart at the seams. The one person I thought I could rely on above any other has just stabbed me in the back like everyone else I ever loved. For once, I just want a few minutes to wallow. Is that too much to ask?" His nostrils flared.

It wasn't. It totally wasn't.

I wrapped my arms around his neck and pulled him into a hug. He resisted for a moment then put his arms around me and tucked his head into the crook of my neck. When he pulled away, his face was wet with tears I hadn't known he'd shed.

He fisted them away and straightened his back.

I forced light into my voice. "You know you're being a baby about all this, right?" He did this so easily when it was me who was upset. I never realized how much it might have cost him or how difficult it was to try, until I wanted to do the same for him.

"A baby?" His eyebrows shot up to his hairline.

"Yeah. I mean, it might have been the first time Gisborne shot you with an arrow, but I don't imagine it was or will be the last. Tuck did manage to save your life which meant you have a scar you can show off to anyone who might—or might not—want to see."

The confusion left his eyes, replaced by something lighter. Something that said he remembered another day and another serious conversation. And scars. "It *is* a good scar," he said quietly.

This was why I'd fallen so hard for him, even if I might never get to tell him so. He was trying. He was far from in the mood for games, but still, he was trying. I gave a dismissive shrug of one shoulder. "How bad can it be? It's just an arrow. Being sliced by a sword through an arm is a much better scar."

He smiled now. Just a small one, but a smile all the same. "What, exactly, are you trying to say?"

"Just that I have a scar that almost killed me, made by a sword. And it's got to be far worse than the little arrow scar you're crying over." God, I hoped I hadn't pushed him too far.

His eyebrows rose again, and light danced in his eyes. "So, you're saying if I show you mine, you'll show me yours?" Mission accomplished. Not the showing of scars part, the light in his eyes was what I'd been looking for.

I shrugged and started for the clearing, dragging him by the hand. "I'm saying, this is a conversation for after we've rescued your brother."

Sixteen

Tuck had run off somewhere by the time Rob and I returned to the cottage. We left for Bestwood without him, and I hadn't stopped worrying since. For Tuck. For us. For Alan. I hoped Tuck was all right, wherever he was, but I wished he'd come with us. We needed him.

The soldiers at Bestwood stood lined up exactly as they had yesterday, their bows in hand, staring straight ahead across the field toward the forest.

Gisborne, the Sheriff and Alan stood on a raised platform—newly built for the occasion—behind the soldiers. We could only see them from the waist up.

Rob came to a dead stop when he saw his brothers, one older, one younger, standing side-by-side. We waited again hidden in the forest, giving Rob a few moments to get himself together. I touched his arm. "Alan looks well." He did. He was standing tall today, no chair needed, and the bruises on his face had faded to almost nothing.

He nodded, not taking his eyes off Alan. "He'll look even better when he's standing at my side." He took his bow from his shoulder, stringing it before pulling an arrow from his quiver. "Get ready. Maryanne, you stand at that end of us." He nodded to his right. "Keep your arrow on the Sheriff. John, you're at the other end, arrow on Gisborne. Miller, you keep an eye on Eliza in case she does anything stupid. I'll watch them all. And please, only shoot if something goes wrong. We don't want to give them any reason not to return Alan to us."

We all nodded. This was going to be fine. Everyone wanted something. Everyone would do exactly what we needed to make it happen. John caught my eye and pointed to the left with his head.

Tuck was here. Some of the tension left my shoulders. John had barely used his bow since Gisborne took his fingers. He would have tried for Rob's sake, but it was better that Tuck was here.

He took John's place at the opposite end of our row, ready to step out of the forest with us, with Gisborne as his target. I glanced at Rob to see if he'd seen Tuck. Now would not be the time for another brawl.

Rob's eyes were fixed on his older brother, and maybe his younger one, too. The stiff set of his shoulders could have had something to do with standing this close to his greatest enemy, but I thought it had more to do with knowing the friend who'd once betrayed him had come to help when Rob needed him most.

"Ready?" he asked, stepping forward. "Eliza's not to come out until I say."

Miller was overseeing her for the moment. There were tied together with a length of rope. He would stay behind us when we stepped out of the forest to let the Sheriff know we'd arrived. Only once Rob said the word would he let Eliza go and point his arrow at her as she left.

Rob moved about half a step before the rest of us. He didn't go far, maybe ten paces. The field was flat where the Sheriff and his men stood. It was plowed and, in some places, tiny green shoots were beginning to show themselves.

I risked taking my eyes off the Sheriff for a moment to properly look at Alan. When I'd told Rob he looked well, I'd meant he seemed healthy. He was also petrified, but I knew the moment he saw us. His chin lifted, then he ducked his head and his eyes went to the ground.

"Sheriff," Rob called. "We did as you asked yesterday. We have Eliza Thatcher with us today. Hand over Alan of Woodhurst and you can have her back."

A slow smile crossed the Sheriff's face. "You must think me very foolish, Robin of Woodhurst, if you think I'm simply going to hand him over without first seeing Lady Thatcher is unharmed. Send her to us. Once we are certain she is well, you'll get your brother back. Your older brother." He smiled at his own joke.

Rob shook his head. The Sheriff had made new rules yesterday, we weren't allowing him to do the same today. "That's not the way this is going to work." He turned and called quietly over his shoulder. "Miller, bring me Eliza."

Miller untied the rope binding the two of them. He spoke a few quiet words to her, gave her a hug—which Eliza returned—then brought her to Rob. Eliza was quiet, her eyes downcast. I'd caught her looking at Gisborne through the trees when we arrived, but she now seemed nervous. Did she expect something to go wrong? An arrow in her back, perhaps? Or Gisborne to ride away laughing as he left her with us?

I felt sorry for her. There were moments when she was easy to hate, lots of moments. But I was beginning to understand why she was the way she was.

Rob gripped Eliza's wrist so she couldn't run. "You see, Sheriff. Eliza Thatcher has been well looked after. She bears no injury from her time with us." Rob clearly had some sort of plan to get past this stand-off. I guessed he'd been thinking about all the ways it might go wrong after the Sheriff changed the rules yesterday.

The Sheriff crossed his hands over his fat gut.

"Bring Alan down off the platform. We will let Eliza go and she can start walking toward you at the same time as you let Alan walk toward us."

The Sheriff was silent as he weighed up that option. To my surprise, he said, "Seems like a fair deal. Gisborne, take him from the platform."

Gisborne spoke in a low voice to Alan. With a glance at Rob, Alan lifted his hood over his head, and followed Gisborne down the two steps at the back of the platform. I lost sight of them both for about twenty seconds behind the wall of soldiers. My heart skipped, but they appeared a moment later, walking side-by-side. The soldiers moved to let Alan through, and head bowed, he began to walk slowly toward the forest.

The two couldn't have contrasted more. Eliza in her pale yellow and slightly worse for wear dress, walking away from us with measured paces and a high chin. Alan, shuffling toward us, head down and hidden inside his cloak.

Their progress seemed painfully slow. I wanted them to run, sprint even. I wanted Alan to be back here so we could melt into the forest and this could all be over. Yet, it felt as if a single step took a full minute, like an entire hour passed before they met each other in the middle.

I took my eyes from the Sheriff to check on Gisborne. I wanted to see how much he was going to hurt when the girl he claimed to love left him next month once I freed Tabitha. He deserved every piece of pain he felt, especially after everything he'd done to Rob and me. He wasn't watching Eliza, though. He was watching me. Even after all the ways I'd proved I wasn't her, he still thought I was Maud. He still wanted her. Still thought she…I…would come back to him. He was here to rescue one girl, but he wanted another. I couldn't find a single redeeming feature about that man. He did at least smile when Eliza reached him, before directing her toward a waiting carriage.

Finally, Alan reached us. He stumbled, falling on his knees in front of Rob. Rob dropped down beside him. "Alan. Are you all right? Did they hurt you?"

Alan didn't speak. I flexed my fingers on the bow I still had pointed at the Sheriff's chest. If they'd done anything to hurt him, they would pay. Right here. Right now.

"Alan?" Rob moved to pull his brother's hood back, but Alan flinched away with a whimper, eyes on the ground. "Alan. It's me. Rob. You recognize me, don't you?"

Alan nodded.

"Then let me help you. Tell me what's wrong. Where do you hurt?" Rob moved slowly forward, like he was dealing with a spooked horse and not wanting to frighten it further.

"Rob. The Sheriff is moving." I still had a clear shot if he wanted me to take it. Somehow, the Sheriff had come out a winner today. By brokering this exchange, a large sum of gold was heading his way, thanks to Carston Sutherland. Not that I cared what the Sheriff received. We had Alan back. We could get on with our lives.

"No. Let's get Alan out of here. We'll deal with whoever hurt him later." He crouched in front of his brother, and I pulled my arrow from my bow.

"Rob!" The yell was a male's voice that came from down in the village. A voice that was painfully familiar.

I looked up.

So did Rob.

Gisborne and the Sheriff walked briskly away from us, their burgundy cloaks flaring out after them.

Beside Gisborne, almost running to keep up, was Alan. His hands were tied, and he wore a burgundy cloak rather than the one that matched Rob's. Gisborne gripped his arm. "Rob!" Alan yelled again, trying to wriggle free.

Gisborne turned, said something through gritted teeth, then backhanded him across the face.

Rob pulled the hood roughly from the figure at his feet. It was a man, pale and already bloodied. Someone had hurt him badly. The man's eyes rolled up into his head and he fell forward onto the ground, no longer breathing.

Whoever he was, he wasn't Alan.

Anger heated my blood. Gisborne was a dead man. I took aim at the center of his back and pulled my arrow back until the fletching brushed my cheek. Four soldiers walked briskly up behind Gisborne and the Sheriff, blocking my shot. I cursed under my breath and ran along the edge of the forest in the same direction as Gisborne, searching for a clear shot.

Rob ran, too. Down toward the village, toward his brother.

A shout came from somewhere among the soldiers and a hail of arrows fell in front of Rob. He stopped dead and raised his own bow, pointing at Gisborne.

"Rob," I screamed. He needed to get back here. Out there in the open, he was going to get himself killed. "Rob! Come back!"

I couldn't get a good shot on Gisborne. His long strides had him moving faster than I could target him. His soldiers surrounded him, shielded him from my attack, and from Rob's. Tuck was closer. He'd get him.

I tore my eyes from Gisborne for just a moment, just to check on Tuck. To check he was still on our side. He had the shot lined up. *Take it,* I willed. The feathers in the end of his arrow rested against his cheek. My heart raced in my chest. If he made this shot, if he hit Gisborne, all hell would break loose. We'd have to grab Alan and run, but since Rob was halfway there and hadn't listened when I'd called him back, we had a chance. We could do this.

Tuck blinked. Then blinked again, before bringing his bow down by his side.

Without shooting.

I twisted around to see the Sheriff and Gisborne climb onto their horses. Gisborne leaned down and grabbed Alan by the arm, pulling him up behind him. With a glance over his shoulder, and perhaps a smirk at Rob, he kicked the horse in the ribs and galloped away.

Gone.

Slipped through our fingers, leaving us with nothing.

Rob was still standing in the open, an easy shot for the Sheriff's archers. If they'd wanted him dead, he would be by now. I was certain he was only alive because of Gisborne's petty need to hurt Rob in every way possible. Watching Gisborne steal Alan away a second time was going to kill Rob.

"Rob!" I screamed his name until he gave in and ran back to the forest.

"Damn, damn, damn!" Rob slammed his fist into the nearest tree. We'd walked back to the stone cottage single file and in deadly silence. Rob was making up for that now. "How did I not see this coming?" He looked at me. "You...you could have shot him." It was a plea rather than an accusation.

I wished I could have, so badly. "There wasn't a clear shot, Rob. There were soldiers in the way. And if I'd shot them, I thought the Sheriff's soldiers would have killed you. I'm so sorry." We'd expected things to go wrong, but somehow, we hadn't expected to come away with all our lives but no Alan. And no bargaining chip.

Rob strode up and down the length of the clearing in front of the cottage with blood dripping from his scraped knuckles. He stopped in front of Tuck, digging a finger into his chest. "You were closer. *You* could have shot him." This was clearly an accusation.

Tuck's eye had swollen shut from Rob's earlier punch. He shook his head. "I couldn't."

John moved to stand near Rob, ready to jump between them if Rob's anger got the better of him.

"Of course you could. If you'd wanted to. It's beginning to look a lot like you're still on Gisborne's payroll." Rob's voice shook with anger.

Low blow, but I couldn't disagree. Tuck had the shot. He'd been the closest of any of us and he hadn't even tried. Why was that? We all wanted to know.

Tuck let out a growl and shook his head. "You're out of your mind."

"Am I? Because I'm not the one who dragged a child out to the forest to die. And I'm not the one who could have taken a friend back from the enemy but couldn't be bothered to fire an arrow."

John shuffled closer to Rob but kept any warnings to himself, while Miller stopped pacing to watch, his face sullen. I guess it felt a lot like seeing his parents fight. Tuck had been responsible for him for years, but it had always been Rob he'd wanted to emulate.

"How was I supposed to do it, Rob? My good eye is almost shut, I can't see well out of the other, and I didn't want to miss and hit Alan." He jutted his chin. "I want that bastard dead almost as much as you, but what was I supposed to do?"

"You were supposed to..." Rob's voice petered out to nothing. He glared at Tuck, his face set.

Tuck stepped toward him. "Shoot anyway and hurt Alan? Put my own life in danger by running down and tackling Gisborne? Believe me, if I thought either of those would have gotten Alan back, I'd have done it without a second thought." He swallowed. His next words were quieter than the rest. "I'll always have your back. The same way I have every day for the past six years. The same as I'll continue to do for as long as you want me around."

There was an opening there for Rob to shoot him down, to tell him he was no longer wanted. We all heard it in the silence that followed. Instead, Rob shook his head. "You should have told me. Before today." He walked off into the forest without another word.

I watched for a moment, caught between going after him and giving him space.

John put a hand on my shoulder. "Leave him. He needs time to work through all of this on his own."

"And us? What do we do now?" Alan was again out of our reach. We were back to square one and I had no clue how to move past it, or what to do next.

John gestured to the center of the clearing. "We eat."

That seemed rather myopic. We needed to look at the big picture. Find a way to move forward, rather than sitting on our butts and stuffing our faces.

John gave a slight nod as if agreeing with himself. "We eat. We talk. We come up with a new plan. Come on," he said, beckoning with his head. "The best plans are made over good food."

John was wrong. His food was amazing—as always—but it was no help in coming up with a plan. We were in the same position we'd been in the day Gisborne stole Alan away almost a month ago. Worse, because even if we wanted to continue with life as it had been before Alan was taken— which we didn't—we couldn't rob any carriages to help the poor because Alan would hang.

We were all sitting silently around the outside firepit, relying on Rob to return with an idea we could work on. So, when we heard footsteps approaching our clearing, we turned toward them with muted anticipation. It wasn't Rob that pushed through the bracken.

It was Eliza.

She'd changed into a new dress. It was far simpler than her yellow one; a deep green color with a matching cloak. Her hair was pulled into a bun at the back of her neck. She wore no jewelry and had no adornments in her hair.

Tuck, John and Miller all jumped up, drawing their weapons.

Eliza put her hands in the air. "Relax. It's only me. I made sure of it."

The open-mouthed disbelief on each of the boys' faces said they didn't trust her. A look that was probably echoed on mine.

John gripped his staff tightly. "Miller, stay here with Maryanne. Tuck and I will go and check things out. Make sure she's not lying."

Eliza gave a suit-yourself shrug and watched Tuck and John walk away.

"You've got a lot of nerve." I folded my arms over my chest. "After what happened today..." I shook my head. "You can forget about my offer to release Tabitha." That might happen whether I wanted it to or not, but I was angry and needed to take it out on someone.

Eliza licked her lips. "I understand why you won't help me. I would feel the same way in your shoes."

We stared at each other in silence. I wanted to ask why she was here, but she seemed uncomfortable and I got a perverse sense of pleasure from it, so kept quiet.

Tuck and John returned a few minutes later. "There's no one else out there," said Tuck, resting one end of his bow on the ground. His face was hard, anger sitting just below the surface. "So why is it you're here?"

Eliza took a deep breath. "Alan is to be hanged. Tomorrow morning. For your crimes against Lady Sutherland and myself."

"What?" Miller jumped to his feet. He'd been glaring silently at Eliza since she arrived. "Our crimes? We never hurt you. We fed you. We looked after you. You even had fun with us." He pointed a finger at her across the fire, his face rigid. With good reason. Miller had gone out of his way to make both women feel comfortable, but especially Eliza.

"I told him that. Begged him to reconsider." Her bottom lip wobbled, and she looked between John and Miller. "Please Miller, John. You must believe me. Surely, you know I wouldn't want you to get hurt. Bridgette said the same. She was very vocal, but they didn't believe her either." She turned in the firelight.

I gasped and stepped toward her. Her top lip was split and there was a purple bruise high on her cheek. "Gisborne did this?"

She nodded.

"Did he hurt Bridgette, too?"

She gave a sour little laugh. "That's not his job, though if her husband is anything like Gisborne, I imagine he'll find a way to keep her from speaking out again."

My dinner grew heavy in my stomach. Another black mark against Gisborne.

"Thank you for letting us know," I said as politely as I could. I was grateful to her for taking the risk to tell us what we might never have known otherwise.

"There's more," she said.

John sat on the log and patted the empty space beside him with a grim smile. I hadn't realized how much both he and Miller seemed to have enjoyed Eliza's company. "Come. Sit. Eat."

Eliza looked at me, asking without speaking if she could sit a while. I nodded and let her pass. I couldn't send her straight back to the man who'd beaten her for standing up for us.

We watched in silence as she ate. I listened to the forest around us, just in case Gisborne was out there somewhere. And also for Rob. He'd been gone for hours.

"What else?" Tuck asked the moment she swallowed her final mouthful. He'd beaten me to the same question by mere seconds.

"Alan's chamber is only being guarded on the outside, tonight."

"Meaning?" asked John.

"Meaning Gisborne has expected you to come for him since the moment he took him. He placed guards inside and outside his chamber every night so they could stop you. Tonight, they're celebrating their win and they've left only two guards stationed outside the door."

"I fail to see how this is a good thing given there are still soldiers guarding his chamber." John leaned his elbows on his knees, watching Eliza. I failed to see it, too.

"Gisborne chose his chamber carefully when Alan first came to us. It's up on the second level. And there's an oak tree with very large branches right outside his window." She glanced at me. "It's almost next door to the chamber you stayed in. Gisborne thought the tree would make it more appealing to break into Alan's room."

"You're saying there are no guards in his room tonight? And we can use the tree to get inside?" I eyed her warily, surprised she'd tell us any of this.

She nodded.

Okay. Now it sounded somewhat better, assuming we could trust her. "But getting through the castle gates at night? How would we do that?" Because I didn't imagine the guards would happily allow Robin Hood and four of his armed associates to wander in without a fight.

"The tunnels." She almost smiled. "The one we used last time will take you inside near the dungeon. From there, you can climb the stairs and find his chamber from the inside. Or you can go outside and use the tree to get to his room, which would be my suggestion."

I glanced at Tuck. We'd considered the tunnels already, but they were a no-go. "The doors on the tunnels are bolted. We can't get through."

She shrugged. "I can help with that. But we have to leave now."

"How do we know this isn't a trap?" asked Miller, arms folded over his chest and voice hostile.

"You don't. And if you have a better idea, go with that. Or if you've decided not to rescue Alan, go with that. I'm simply offering you another option."

We couldn't leave yet. Rob wasn't here. But if there was even the slightest chance of this being a possibility, we needed to work out all the details before he got back so we could leave at a moment's notice. "Why?" My voice was even. I wasn't sure how I felt about Eliza. Mostly I disliked her intensely. Occasionally, I felt the opposite. "Why would you help us?"

Her laugh was humorless. "I never intended to leave Gisborne, despite what I told you. I was going to go with you to the tree and get Tabitha back, then have her come to live under the same roof as us. Until today. Do you know he barely looked at me as I walked toward him at Bestwood?"

I did. I'd watched him, the same way she had. "But he did smile when you reached him."

She shook her head and gave a dismissive roll of her eyes. "Barely. He was too focused on Rob. And you." She glanced at me then dropped her eyes to the ground. "He doesn't love me. He loves you. Or her, I guess, since after living with you for a week I'm certain you aren't her, no matter that you somehow have her ring." She shrugged, looking at me. "I saw how you fought Rob so he would treat you like he treats the others. How you did everything you could to stop him putting a metaphorical chain around your waist. I've never seen a woman fight for what she wanted that way. So, I'm doing the same thing. I can't leave him. There's nowhere else for me to go. But I can fight for the friends I made here." She glanced at John, then Miller. "You both treated me better than anyone I've ever known."

There was so much sorrow in that statement. She'd been our prisoner—in a fairly relaxed prison, but still. It said something about her life that telling jokes and playing games with Miller and John was the best she'd ever been treated.

She pulled something from the folds of her dress and held it out to me.

I took it. "Gisborne's ring." Or Maud's. The price Eliza had asked for her to get Tuck, Rob and I out of the castle a month ago. The knot in my chest eased a little. She wasn't expecting anything of us tonight, and she was handing me a peace offering. I slipped the ring on my finger. "We need to talk to Rob. See if he wants to..."

"I do." Rob stepped into the light of the fire and stood behind me. "I heard it all, and I want to do it. The tunnels. The tree. Everything Eliza suggested. I want to get Alan back."

SEVENTEEN

OUR weapons were ready from earlier in the evening, so we were trekking toward the tunnel entrance within half an hour. I carried a knife in each of my boots, the sword I'd been practicing with constantly since Bridgette had started teaching me—I still couldn't use it well, but I was better than I had been—and my bow. And that was only about half the number of weapons each of the boys carried.

The tunnel, at the bottom of the hill on which the castle sat, was a damp and dirty hole in the stone only wide enough to crawl through. It was covered by a grate, locked in place with a heavy chain bolted into the stone. Eliza had the key.

I crawled inside, my heart racing. Part of me wondered at the sense in trusting Eliza. The rest of me said we had to try something. It could very well be the last something any of us ever did. I gave Miller a quick hug, then inched through the tunnel until it widened enough to stand, waiting while Rob lit the two candles we'd brought with us. Miller stayed at the entrance, guarding it should Gisborne ambush us from behind. At the very least, he'd be able to yell and warn us of trouble, at best he might kill anyone coming our way.

A shallow stream of water ran through the bottom of the tunnel. Animals—probably rats—splashed through it ahead of us. Our candles were next to useless in the pitch black, so I ran my fingers against the damp stone wall to find my way.

The walk was long and uphill, zig-zagging toward the castle. No one talked. The only sound was heavy breathing and footfalls. If everyone else was like me, then we were all worried about what was to come.

At the heavy wooden door into the castle, Eliza stopped. She looked at Rob. "Do you remember the way from here?"

He nodded. She'd brought us this way when she helped us escape, but I was too worried about someone catching us to remember every turn, and since I wanted to make sure nothing went wrong, I said, "Remind us."

"Out this door and up the corridor. Just around the first corner you'll have to pass the dungeon guards—hopefully they'll be sleeping—then go past the staircase and keep walking until you find a large door on your left. It will take you out of the castle. When you're outside, keep heading right and you'll find the tree. Remember, once you're out in the open, watch for guards up on the inner wall." She'd told us that already. She'd also said she didn't think they'd be much of a threat, since they would be looking out, not in, but if we looked suspicious, they would act.

Eliza handed Rob a large and heavy-looking ring with two big keys on it; the two keys we'd need to lock the door and the grate behind us as we left.

"Thank you. For your help." Rob nodded to her.

I stepped up to her. "If everything goes wrong in here and I don't make it out, I think you might find Tabitha waiting for you at the Big Tree at the next full moon. No guarantees. I don't know if she'll be able to leave the portal, but I'm almost certain she'll be there either way." Eliza had helped us, it was only fair that I gave her what she desired.

"Thank you," she whispered. "And good luck."

John stayed behind to guard this end of the tunnel for the same reason we'd left Miller at the other end, while Tuck, Rob and I went in search of the oak tree and Alan's chamber. Rob hadn't spoken a word to Tuck since we left the cottage, and I got the feeling he'd rather not head into the castle grounds with Tuck beside him. But at least if Tuck was beside him—rather than guarding one of our entrances like John or Miller—Rob would know straight away if Tuck betrayed us. It was better than being ambushed because he'd trusted Tuck with a different role. There were still things to be said between the two of them, but they kept those to themselves as we tiptoed in the direction Eliza sent us.

The guards were dozing in front of the dungeon entrance like Eliza hoped they would be, their snoring loud as we drew closer. Their inattention made getting past simple. The corridor was empty and, in the silence, our careful footfalls seemed to echo for miles. But the guards didn't wake and the door we were searching for was exactly where Eliza said it would be.

Outside, the full moon cast long shadows and a lot of light across the grounds—good for seeing, not so good for hiding—and I barely breathed as we edged our way around the outside of the castle, our backs against the stone, and one eye on the inner wall. The guest wing—where Gisborne was keeping Alan—looked out over the castle walls toward the forest. The chamber I'd used here at the castle had the very same outlook and I'd even considered using the tree to make my escape. My room hadn't been close enough to the tree to put that plan into action, though. Unlike Alan's.

"How are you at climbing trees?" Rob asked, looking up at the huge oak.

As a kid, it was my favorite pastime. Carrie and I often competed to see who could climb the highest, usually as Mom called us down while trying not to hyperventilate at our height. A fall and a broken wrist put a stop to my tree climbing career and my love of heights, and apart from the cage Gisborne had kept me in high in Sherwood Forest, I hadn't been in a tree in years. But tonight, I'd do whatever was necessary. "I'm all right."

"Good. Tuck, you stay down here. Warn us if you see anything out of the ordinary. Maryanne, come with me. Alan likes you. It'll be good for him to have people he trusts rescue him."

Tuck shifted uncomfortably. I wasn't sure if Rob meant that as a dig at him or not. It sure sounded like one. He nodded at Rob's instruction before helping me onto the bottom branch.

After that, the climb was easy, and the limbs were large and strong.

"Almost there," I whispered.

Rob leaned out to reach the latch on the shutter, while holding a branch with his other hand. I may have been dreaming, but it seemed as if Rob's hands were shaking. If I looked at my own too closely, I was sure they'd be doing the same thing.

Even when he got the shutter open, my heart didn't still. A hundred *what if*'s ran through my mind: What if Eliza had lied to us? What if there were guards waiting inside? What if this wasn't Alan's chamber but was instead Gisborne's? What if we were about to die?

Rob peered through the open window before taking hold of the shutter and jumping across to the windowsill. Then he reached out to offer me his hand and help me inside.

Alan's chamber—or whoever the sleeping form in the bed belonged to—was larger than the one I'd been allocated for the two nights I'd stayed here. This room was on the corner and had windows looking out over top of the inner wall to the stables and over the outer wall toward the forest. There were burgundy and gold tapestries laid over the floor and walls, and the fire was burning in the hearth, despite it not being particularly cold tonight.

With a deep breath, Rob walked over to the bed, leaned over the sleeping form and put a hand across his mouth. A pair of eyes snapped open, and Rob put his finger to his lips. The eyes widened.

"Alan. It's me, Rob. You need to be very quiet. We're going to get you out of here." He lifted his hand from his brother's face.

Alan sat up and grabbed hold of Rob's wrists. Then he wrapped his arms tightly around Rob's neck. They whispered words to each other that I couldn't hear.

I tiptoed over to the chest at the end of the bed. I pulled out some clothing and laid the items on the bed. "Rob. We need Alan to get dressed so we can leave." As nice as their reunion was, we didn't have time.

Alan opened his eyes, still gripping Rob tight. "Maryanne?"

I put a finger to my lips and nodded.

Alan's face creased into the hugest grin I'd ever seen. "I saw you. At Bestwood. I wanted you to shoot Gisborne."

My heart broke, and I touched his hand. "I wanted to shoot him, too."

Rob extracted himself from Alan's grip, but left one hand on his brother's shoulder a moment longer. "We're getting you out of here." He untied his cloak and placed it on the bed, then pulled off his tunic. "You're going to have to be very quiet. And listen to Maryanne. She'll keep you safe, okay?"

He nodded, eyes wide.

"Get dressed into my clothes."

"Rob? What are you doing?" I whispered. I could see no benefit to this change in clothing. If anything, it would slow us down.

His back was to me as he removed his sword belt. He took a deep breath as he turned around bare chested. "Staying."

I tilted my head to one side. "What do you mean *staying?*" We hadn't discussed this. Our plan was to get in, get Alan and get out. All as fast as possible. There had been no talk of staying. No one was staying. We were all leaving. Right now.

Panic rose inside me. Rob couldn't do this. Gisborne would kill him. He had unlimited soldiers and weapons at his disposal here in the castle.

Rob turned away, stepped out of his pants and pulled on the pair belonging to Alan that I'd left on the bed. "I'm going to kill him, Maryanne. I'm finished with always looking over my shoulder, always wondering what Gisborne's going to throw at us next."

"If you kill him, Gisborne's soldiers will kill you."

He refused to look at me as he spoke. "Not if I can help it."

"Do you have a plan?" Because this all seemed very rushed, and we both knew rushed ideas never went well.

He turned back to me, tightening his sword belt around his waist, his bare chest all planes and hollows in the moonlight. "I'm going to dress as Alan, pretend I'm him. They won't expect me to be carrying a sword. The moment I get the opportunity, I'll kill Gisborne. Then I'll run like the wind, back to the forest."

I shook my head. "That's a bad plan." Terrible, actually. "You do realize the Sheriff plans to hang Alan tomorrow. Take his place and it might be you in the gallows."

He lifted one shoulder, like he was beyond caring. "I'm fast. I think I can get away." I didn't believe him. I don't think he believed himself, either.

"Don't do this." I'd beg if I had to. "Please." It was a suicide mission. If we left now, we might actually make it out of here. We could come back tomorrow, all of us, or any other day, and kill Gisborne.

"Rob?" asked Alan. "You're not coming?"

"I'll follow later. Get dressed now, so Maryanne can take you home."

Rob and I moved to the corner of the room and turned away to give Alan privacy while he dressed.

Rob reached into the purse on his belt. "I went to see Lizzie yesterday. That's where I was all day. Got my ring back, like you suggested." He held it up in the moonlight for me to see. "I'm not engaged any longer, which means we can work on us."

"That's great," I whispered, wondering if my sarcasm would translate in such hushed tones. "But there can't be any 'us' if you're hanging by your neck." Right now, I couldn't even consider us. Not when he was about to do something so stupid.

"There will always be an us. You'll never escape me." He brushed a strand of hair from my face. His touch sent a shiver up my back. It felt like a long time since we'd stood this close. "If I don't come home today, I'll wait for you wherever I am until the day you die."

I shook my head. That painted far too graphic an image of what might happen once it was light, and I couldn't deal. "Don't."

He misunderstood me and one side of his mouth rose. "Oh, I'll be waiting. You can count on it." His face grew serious. "Will you wear this?" He held up a ring—his mother's ring, not the one

Lizzie had worn. "I had it made smaller so it would fit you."

Was that an engagement ring? "Do you think giving me a ring will solve everything that's been wrong between us?" Things between us had been better lately, but I'd refused to let our relationship advance until Lizzie was gone. I didn't want to be engaged yet, and I especially didn't want it to happen the day he died.

He shrugged, light dancing in his eyes. "Maybe I think you'll let me kiss you if you're wearing it."

I shook my head, unable to speak. I knew very well that wasn't the reason he was giving it to me now.

He let out a deep sigh. "Honestly, I hope giving it to you will stop you forgetting me."

As if I could ever. Tears filled my eyes. He was really doing this. How dare he. And how dare he tell me about it here, when I couldn't yell and scream and try to stop him. And doubly so because I couldn't stay to help. He'd brought me so I would take Alan to safety. And he was saying his goodbyes now because he expected to die.

"You know I did it this way on purpose. So you had no time to find a way to stop me." He cupped my face in his palm, talking as if he could read my mind. "So you'd have no choice but to leave with Alan."

I glanced at his brother, struggling to pull his undershirt on, then leaned into Rob's touch. His thumb caressed my cheek and I closed my eyes. "I hate you," I whispered. "For doing this. For leaving. For thinking you're never coming back."

"I know. But maybe in time...?" He bent his head, hopeful eyes meeting mine.

I shook my head. "I'll hate you forever if you die today."

"I know." His words were whispered, and he let out a hushed sigh, still watching me. "So, will you wear it? To remember me?"

Of course, I'd wear the bloody thing. He could ask almost anything of me and I'd probably agree, no matter how much I didn't want to. I nodded.

He took my right hand and slipped the ring on my middle finger. "It suits you." He closed his hand around mine.

I wished I hadn't been so stupid. I wished I'd listened when he said his engagement to Lizzie wasn't real, that we'd had a proper relationship before he ran off to die. Our time together had been too short, with too many interruptions.

I cast another quick glance at Alan. His back was to us has he laced up his pants. Rob and I didn't have time for this conversation. "Alan, are you nearly ready?"

"Just need to lace up my boots and pull on my tunic." He spoke in a low whisper.

My eyes found Rob again. Alan and I had to go, but I had another moment or two before Alan was ready. "You know, you didn't need to put a ring on my finger to be able to kiss me." Of course, he knew. He'd done it twice before. It was the fact the ring was on someone else's finger that had stopped him lately. That, and all the arguments we'd had.

He grinned, his eyes going to my lips. "I know." He leaned forward. "But I wanted you to have it anyway."

His kiss was slow and gentle, filled with promises that would never be. I kissed him back the same way, hoping he saw what might be between us if he gave up his revenge on his little brother and stayed with me. I was glad to have known him. But we could have been so much more than what we'd been in the short time we'd had. I wanted him to see that. I wanted him to change his mind and I wanted to tell him all of that with that final kiss.

"Ready." Alan whispered.

Rob pulled away. His breathing was heavy, pupils dilated.

"Don't do this." I clamped my hands around Rob's, wishing we could stay like this forever.

"I have to." He'd told me something with that kiss, too, because I understood. He wanted this to end, one way or the other, no matter what that meant.

Rob turned to Alan. "Maryanne will go first. She'll show you where to put your feet and your hands. Be brave and by morning you'll be back in the forest."

He gave Alan a quick hug. He lifted me onto the windowsill and squeezed my hand. "See you soon."

I don't think he believed his words any more than I believed mine. "You better."

Eighteen

"WHAT'S your plan, Maryanne?" I'd told John the details of Rob's whereabouts once Tuck, Alan and I met him at the end of the tunnel. We stood on the tunnel side of the closed door, the candle in John's hand casting moving shadows across our faces.

I was torn. On one hand, I wanted to do what Rob asked and get Alan back to the safety of the forest. On the other, I didn't want to leave Rob to whatever awaited him once the sun rose over the city of Nottingham.

"To go back to the forest, I guess." Keep Alan safe like Rob asked.

Tuck shook his head. "No. You're quiet. You do that when you're working something out in your mind. Share it with us."

That was the problem. Had I been able to come up with some way of ensuring Rob's safety, I would have shared, but I was blank. I had nothing. Not a single idea. "I'm trying, but I don't know what to do." We *should* take Alan back. We should also save Rob's neck, the same way he would save ours.

"I hate Gisborne." It was the first thing Alan had said since leaving Rob, and he said it with such venom, I had no doubt how much he meant it.

"We all do." Even at a whisper, my voice still seemed too loud in this silent place.

"He said he would see me at lunch, right before they tied a rope around my neck." Alan glanced uncertainly at me. "That means they're going to hang me, doesn't it?"

I put a hand on his shoulder refusing to answer. "You're safe now. Try not to worry about Gisborne anymore."

Tuck stepped toward Alan, his face ghostly in the candlelight. "After lunch? Are you sure?"

Alan nodded, wrapping his arms around himself against the chill of the tunnel. "They're having a party. Gisborne said I would be the entertainment." He shook his head. "I don't want to be the entertainment, don't even want to go, but he doesn't care. He never listens to what I want. Not like Rob. He wouldn't make me do it."

"Lunch." Tuck started pacing. "We can come up with a way to help Rob before then."

We could. It was more time than I thought we had. "Alan, what were you supposed to do this morning? If you were still in the castle?"

He shrugged. "Nothing. I had to stay in my chamber and wait. Nothing to do in there. Gisborne said he'd send someone to get me when it was time to go to the party."

"And you're sure Gisborne wouldn't have come to see you before then?" I asked.

"He never came to my chamber. And he had too much to do today, told me so all yesterday as we rode back to the castle."

So, no chance for Rob to kill Gisborne undetected. Pity.

"Do you know anything about the party they're having?" asked Tuck.

All our voices had grown in volume, and I put my finger to my lips to remind them all to speak quietly.

Alan's eyes lit. "I do! Xanthe said—she's your friend, too, isn't she Maryanne?" I nodded. "Xanthe told me all about it. They're celebrating the start of spring. Eating outdoors. Xanthe will be there. She has to serve the food." He let out a small sigh. "She said she wouldn't be able to look out for me anymore. Even she couldn't save me from being dead." His voice wobbled.

I put an arm around his waist and drew him into a hug, wishing Rob were here. What did I say to that? I settled for rubbing his back and murmuring a few useless words. "It's okay, Alan. We've got your back."

"What about Rob, though?" He pulled out of my hug. "Is he going to die instead of me? Because I don't want him to. Rob loves me. And I love him, too." The emotion choking his voice made tears spring to my eyes.

"We don't want him to die, either." Tuck put a hand on Alan's shoulder, his voice losing some of its usual gruffness. He turned away from Alan and his face grew hard. "Why was he so stupid? We could have done this together. Made a proper plan."

John ran his hand through his hair. "Why are you even surprised? This is what he does."

It was. He'd come for me when Gisborne took me to Nottingham, on his own and with only a basic plan. It wasn't that he didn't think things through. He knew the risks and likely outcomes better than anyone. It was that he didn't want to put anyone who might help him at risk. Pity he hadn't learned that all of us wanted the same things as him and were willing to take the same risks. "Alan, are you certain Xanthe is still in the castle? When was the last time you saw her?" I'd given her gold for helping us. She should be long gone.

"She's here. She came to my room last night to set the fire."

I couldn't believe she hadn't left, but her still being here could work in our favor. "Do you know where in the castle they're holding the luncheon?"

"In the courtyard, of course."

I tried to work out where that was in relation to where we'd been tonight.

Tuck nodded like that was the obvious place for the party. "It's a little farther around than where we went into Alan's room."

Of course. I'd walked across it the night Gisborne brought me here. "Is there any way we could..." My voice trailed off. As I heard myself speaking, it seemed like a stupid idea.

"What?" Tuck paced back and forth across the dark tunnel. Each time he passed the candle John held, the light flickered and threatened to die. He glanced at me as he spoke, and I realized they expected I would come up with a way to save Rob. That was a lot of pressure. Almost as much as I was putting on myself to come up with the same thing.

What the hell. Any and all suggestions wanted, right? "Could we go to the luncheon as servants?"

Tuck's pacing stopped and he looked my way. The candle didn't cast enough light to properly see his expression, but the fact he'd stopped walking made me think he was a step further ahead than me with a possible plan. "All the invited nobles would recognize you as Maud Fitzwalter, so you can't go. But the rest of us, if we could get hold of some servants clothing...maybe."

No. No way. They were not leaving me behind if we were going back to save Rob. "I'll wear my hair up inside a bonnet and no one will give me a second glance." Maybe I could pull it low on my forehead for a little more disguise.

"Then what do we do?" asked John. "Poison them all with the food we serve?"

"If you think we can pull that off, it could be a solid plan." I tried to smile. Poison would certainly be the easiest way of getting rid of our enemies. Pity none of us had access to any.

"Perhaps with more time..." John's smile didn't reach his eyes. Mine probably hadn't, either.

I waited for Tuck to jump in with an answer. When he didn't, I spoke the idea that was rolling around in my head. "We back Rob up. The moment he kills Gisborne, we pull out weapons we've hidden beneath our clothing and cover him. We run back here to the tunnels. Lock the door once we're through, and don't stop running until we reach the forest."

"And Alan?" John asked, far more practical than I was today.

"I'm coming, too. I can help. I can...throw rocks."

We couldn't leave him alone here in the tunnel to wait, and, I imagined he'd be easily recognizable to anyone who'd come across him while he was at the castle. "Do you like Xanthe, Alan?"

He nodded. "She's nice, like you. She looks out for me."

I glanced John's way. "Could we leave him in the kitchens with Xanthe?" Assuming she'd take care of him. It was a long shot, but so was the entire plan.

Alan clapped his hands together. "I get to see Xanthe *and* Rob?"

I couldn't answer. He might see them both.

Or he might see neither.

John and I left Tuck and Alan in the tunnel. They were going to bring Miller through to help us. Since I was the only one who knew Xanthe, John and I were sneaking into the castle to speak with her, and hopefully find some servants clothes at the same time. And since Eliza's chamber wasn't far out of our way, we were stopping there, too. I had something to ask her.

To reach the staircase up to Eliza's chamber, we had to pass the dozing guards at the dungeon entrance. John pulled a long knife from the inside of his boot, carrying it in his fist as we sneaked by. I did the same with my tiny dagger, cringing every time my feet tapped on the stone floor. I had a sword with me. It was petite and light, but I still didn't feel confident enough to use it. The dagger in my hand was much more comforting.

Neither of them woke, and we hurried to the staircase. It was dark but deserted. Just a thin wedge of light came through a narrow window high above.

The corridor leading to Eliza's chamber was deserted, as always. I knocked on her door, and she opened it immediately. She was fully dressed, still in the plain clothing we'd last seen her wearing. Her eyebrows lifted when she saw us and she opened the door fully, inviting us in without a word. As she pressed the door closed, she said, "What's happened?"

"Nothing. Yet," said John.

That earned another raised brow from Eliza.

Her chamber was a mess. Before we kidnapped her in the forest, she'd been heading home to Woodhurst. It looked as though someone had stood at the door to her chamber and emptied the trunks she carried with her that day onto the floor.

She folded her arms. "I'm listening."

I told her of Rob's plan for Gisborne and how we were trying to help him. It was a risk. Despite the beating he'd given her, she was probably still in love with him, and she'd always be his cousin.

She shook her head. "I won't help you kill him. And I won't explain why. Just know, I will not do it."

"I'm not asking you to. We just want you to know what we're planning, because we want you to come with us. After." She needed to get away from the man who would only ever hurt her.

She shook her head. "I could never leave him." But as she said it, something lit behind her eyes. I hoped it was her realizing Gisborne wasn't her only option. "What do you need?" she asked, her voice small.

I shrugged. Nothing from her today, except a promise she'd at least think about leaving Gisborne. "To find Xanthe Mason. And we need some servants' clothing."

"Xanthe Mason, the servant?" Eliza never lost the stillness I'd noticed about her the first time we met. Even now, in the middle of the night while knowing we planned to kill one of the most powerful men in the castle, her movements were considered and regal.

I nodded. "We need a favor from her, too."

Eliza lifted her brows again. "You're going to pretend to be servants?" She held up a hand. "Wait. Don't tell me. The less I know, the less I can tell anyone if this all goes wrong. Because, it's probably going to go wrong." She eyed me sideways, then stepped over the mess of jars and papers on the floor to the trunk at the end of her bed.

There was a high chance she was right. What we were planning bordered on impossible, but I wasn't considering outcomes at the moment and I refused to think about all the ways this could go wrong.

Eliza dug around inside the trunk and pulled out a burgundy dress with gold piping running around the sleeves and hem. "This is what the servants like Xanthe will be wearing. It's the only one I have. I don't have any men's tunics." She glanced apologetically at John, then her eyes moved back to me. "But this should fit you." She held it out to me with one hand, digging about in the chest with the other. "And, you'll need a bonnet." She handed me one of those, too. Exactly what I needed. "Put it on now. You won't look so out of place wandering the halls at this hour of the day."

While Eliza gave John directions to the kitchens and hopefully to Xanthe, I changed into Eliza's clothes and strapped the little sword I was carrying around my waist, beneath my dress. It wasn't easy to get to, but it was with me should I need it. John took my old clothes, bundling them up beneath one arm. We'd leave them in the tunnel and collect them on the way back through.

John stepped up to Eliza and bent so he was in her line of vision. "Maryanne's offer was genuine, Eliza. Come with us. You know we'll keep you safe." His voice was firm, like he wanted her to understand she had options. "When things start to happen at lunch, go to the tunnel. We'll meet you there, by the door."

"I couldn't." She shook her head, then added, "How will I even know when to go?"

"You'll know." John ducked further until he caught her eye. "Okay?"

She nodded.

"Thank you, Eliza," said John.

She smiled at him. Eliza Thatcher rarely smiled at anyone.

The kitchen was hot. And busy. And loud. Four cooks worked over two different fires, preparing food and throwing instructions out to whoever was listening. No one else in the kitchen stood still. There were people carrying sacks of flour, rolling out dough on huge tables in the center of the room, placing fruit and biscuits and anything else that wouldn't spoil onto platters, and washing dishes. Everyone had a job.

Xanthe was easy to find. As she rushed from the kitchen carrying a tray piled high with food, we pulled her into the same alcove John and I hid in when we came to find her last time.

"Xanthe, don't scream. It's me." I pulled the bonnet up on my forehead.

"Milady?" She took my arm and turned me slightly, so our backs were to anyone passing. John stood on my other side, making sure no one overheard our whispered conversation. "What are you doing here? Dressed like...me?"

"Long story. More to the point, what are you doing here? Didn't you use my gold?"

"Gave it to Ma. She needed it more than me." She glanced over her shoulder as two servants rushed past us and into the kitchens. "Was there something you wanted?"

Her tone made it clear that standing here was a fast way to get caught. There was no time for pleasantries. "I was wondering if I could ask for your help again? I have no gold to pay you today, but I can get you more." And I would. Once this was over, and so long as I walked out of here.

She shook her head and my heart fell. I was barely listening when she started talking again, already working out what else we could do with Alan while we helped Rob. She raised her hand to brush a piece of hair back beneath her bonnet and the sleeve of her dress fell back, revealing black bruises on the inside of her wrists.

"Xanthe, who did this?" I took hold of her wrist.

She pulled away. "No one. I'm just too clumsy for my own good."

Bruises like this didn't happen by accident. "Was it Gisborne? Because you don't need to put up with that."

She pulled herself up and raised her chin. "And what, exactly, would you have me do? I'm a serv-ant, not a lady like yourself. Working for Gisborne gives me a better wage than any other job I could take." She waved her bruised arm in my face. "This is a small price to pay."

"Leave," I hissed. "Go to your ma. The gold I gave you should be enough to get you on your feet. I'll give you more if you need it. Just...don't stay where he can hurt you."

"I don't need any more gold. You gave me too much last time. And I will go and live with Ma. In fact, I plan to go next week." She smiled tightly. "So, don't you worry about me. And, I will help you. If I can."

"You will?" John's voice was hopeful, almost pleading.

She nodded. "What do you need?"

"I have Alan," I whispered. "We took him from his room in the early hours of this morning, and we will take him back to the forest. We'll leave the castle after the luncheon, but we need to hide him somewhere until then. I was hoping you might keep him with you in the kitchen. He really likes you. And he's a quick learner if there's any work that needs to be done."

"You have him? But...I saw him not ten minutes ago. When I went to his room to stoke up the fire for the morning. He was lying in his bed, snoring."

My heart lifted. Rob was still okay. "We have him now. He's safe with us. Can we count on you to keep him safe for an hour or two? I'm sure he could help you with some work." I really hoped

Alan had read her correctly, and that she liked him as much as he liked her.

She nodded, a slight smile forming on her face. "I'll look after him. He's such a good man. Gentle. Doesn't deserve the way Gisborne tore him away from the family who loved him. Is there anything else you need?"

I drew a deep breath, knowing we were asking a lot of her. "Is there any chance you can get us three of the Sheriff's serving uniforms? For men."

She glanced at John. "I might be able to find something large enough. Do you want them all the size of him?" She motioned to John.

"Two that size. One smaller." Tuck and John were of similar size, although sometime recently, John had eclipsed Tuck in height. Miller was smaller but if she could only find large, we'd make it work.

"And a set for Alan. No one will notice him if he's dressed like me." She nodded as if she was having some sort of conversation to herself. "Wait here." She raced away, along the corridor. In less than three minutes, she was back, a pile of clothing in her arms.

"Thank you, Xanthe," I said.

She gripped my hand. "No, thank you. The gold you gave me helped Ma get out of debt. For the first time in her life, she's learning to weave like she always wanted to. Even making some money from it. She'll have her own place to live soon. I'm truly grateful."

"As am I, to you."

She nodded and turned back toward the kitchen. We slipped through the darkened castle halls to the tunnel where the others waited.

The morning passed quickly as we blended in with the servants preparing for the luncheon. I found a job bringing the tableware outside. It was perfect because it didn't show anyone what I didn't know how to do, which was almost everything else. Tuck and Miller were out here, too, constructing tables, while John was inside getting as close to the cooking as he could. As promised, Xanthe took Alan under her wing and had him polishing silverware.

I'd never seen Tuck wear anything but a monk's robe, and I'd wondered if he'd even wear the clothing we brought back to the tunnel for him. But he pulled the tunic and pants on without a word of complaint, and even looked quite dashing in the Sheriff's burgundy and gold.

The courtyard was beautifully decorated. Banners in the Sheriff's colors hung from the walls. Round tables were laid out on the cobblestones, then covered in burgundy tablecloths, and topped with silver cutlery and plates. Someone had even located spring flowers, which sat proudly in vases as the centerpiece of each table. The matching chairs were covered in gold fabric that draped to the ground and would require a good wash once the day was over. The only eyesores, in my opinion, were the soldiers stationed at regular intervals around the outside of the courtyard, and the large set of gallows that stood ominously at the far end. Every guest had to walk past them as they arrived, and every table had a direct view facing them.

The guests arrived slowly at first, just two couples initially, dressed in their best with jewels dripping from their fingers and necks. Someone pressed a jug of wine into my hands and I had a new job—filling glasses; something else I could actually do. After the first couples, the rest of the guests arrived in a rush, about fifty people in total. There were dresses of all colors; navy, green, lilac, purple and even a rather revolting lime green ensemble. Husbands dressed just as bold and colorfully as their wives, many of them matching each other's color choice.

The Sheriff and Gisborne were in their best, too. The Sheriff wore a long burgundy tunic with gold pants, and a burgundy brimmed hat on his head. Gisborne was in royal blue, and also wore a hat. The Sheriff mingled with his guests, laughing and talking, occasionally slapping someone on the back and moving from chair to chair. Gisborne was more subdued, watching from his own seat with a full glass of wine in one hand and a frown marring his forehead.

I tried not to look at the gallows. Every time my glance caught on them, I felt sick to my stomach. It was too easy to think about who might end up hanging from them in an hour or two. I'd come back in time to help make a legend, not to have front row seats at his execution.

I was just beginning to relax into my work, fairly certain Rob wouldn't be led out until after the meal was served, when Bridgette Sutherland arrived. As she took her seat, wrapped tightly in a thick emerald cloak even though the day was warm, I turned away, taking my jug to another table, but her husband called me back.

"Girl!" He clicked his fingers. "My mug is empty." His voice was raspy with age, but hard with authority.

I kept my eyes down as I filled his mug, but glanced at him as I was done, curious what Bridgette's husband looked like. He was older than I'd imagined, even after Bridgette had told me his age. His hair was white-grey, and his face was lined and marked with age spots. His keen eyes skipped from one couple to the next, and I had the feeling his hearing was good too, as he turned his head slightly as if listening to the surrounding conversations.

"Is there something you want, girl?"

I jumped and shook my head catching Bridgette rolling her eyes behind his back. Hiding my smile, I dropped my gaze and moved away. I risked a quick glance back as I filled another mug to find Bridgette watching me with a furrowed brow. I nodded to her, wishing I could ask if her husband had hurt her for standing up for us, the way Gisborne had with Eliza. Before I could think any further about how I might speak with her, someone pounded their glass on the table, expecting me to fill it and when I looked back again, she was deep in conversation with her ancient husband.

I knew the moment Rob was led out. Much earlier than expected; the food wasn't yet served. But a muted hush fell over the tables, followed by a loud cheer. Steeling myself, I looked up. He could have been Alan.

Flanked by two soldiers, he was wearing a cloak that clearly belonged to the Sheriff. It was burgundy; duller than that of the soldiers and trimmed in fur. His hood was up, head down, a lock of blond hair visible beneath the hood.

This was it. Whatever was going to happen to-day, was going to happen any moment. I searched for John, Tuck and Miller, and found them all serving tables with one eye on Rob.

Gisborne stood and wandered over to the Sheriff. He spoke in his ear, and when the Sheriff nodded, he strode over to stand next to Rob, turning to his audience and clapping his hands three times, the sound bouncing off the surrounding castle walls. The silence that followed was almost immediate.

"I hope you're all enjoying your drinks." he called. "The meal will be served shortly."

There was a chorus of cheers, the loudest coming from those whose mugs I'd filled most often.

"As you all know, our Sheriff is a very just man." He waited for the clapping that followed to die down. "He's never tolerated the bandits that hide in the forest and steal your hard-earned gold." Some booing came from the crowd. "He's worked hard to rid the forest of them. So, when we caught their leader—when we caught Robin Hood—and discovered he was in fact my long-lost brother, he allowed a truce, so the two of us might be reunited." The clapping that followed came mostly from the women in the crowd. Gisborne smiled, and a few of them tittered. When I'd first met him, I'd seen how his black hair and blue eyes could have been attractive, but in the time since, his personality had eclipsed any attraction I might ever have felt. There were plenty of women in this crowd who'd either never seen that side to him or didn't care.

"It seems his followers have little concern for his life and the deal we offered, because they broke our truce when they captured my cousin." He nodded to a soldier standing in a doorway. The soldier stepped aside, and Eliza walked out. She moved slowly toward Gisborne, head high, the bruise on her face hidden by a sheen of powder. Her dress was a lighter shade of the blue Gisborne wore, and although she smiled, it was plain to see she'd rather be anywhere else but where she was right now. Plain to me, at any rate.

"I'm pleased to announce we were able to retrieve her yesterday and she is quite well, as you can see." The crowd clapped. "It does mean that along with the wonderful food you are all about to partake in, we will have some entertainment. As some of you may have guessed from the gallows, today we shall also have a hanging, because the Sheriff is not one to go back on his word. It's what we all respect most about him." He raised his glass to the Sheriff.

"Brother." He indicated to the steps up to the gallows.

I put the wine I was holding on the nearest table. My hands had started to shake, and I had no wish to spill it and draw attention to myself. Plus, I wanted both hands free for when I needed them. Which, I imagined, would be any second.

Rob moved so fast, I barely saw it happen. One moment he was shuffling toward the gallows, and the next, he threw his hood back, drew his sword and thrust it at Gisborne.

NINETEEN

GISBORNE was just as fast. He jumped out of the way and drew his own sword. Using his other hand, he dragged Eliza in front of him. "Would you hurt a woman just to get to me, Woodhurst?" His snarling voice echoed across the silent courtyard.

Rob lifted his sword, raising it like he was about to do exactly that. The soldiers who'd been watching from beside the castle walls, sprang into action and sprinted toward them, drawing their weapons. Rob pulled out of his attack and whirled around, blocking a thrust from one soldier then swinging at a different soldier and slicing into his arm.

With Rob's attention diverted, Gisborne stepped around Eliza, and took aim, striking again and again. Rob parried while I stood glued in place, helplessly watching. Rob whirled, blocking an attack by one of the soldiers, then spinning back to block Gisborne's advance. But he was too slow, Gisborne too fast. He flicked Rob's sword from his grasp, and it clattered loudly against the cobblestones and skidded out of reach.

The nobles, still seated around their tables, clearly thought this was part of the planned festivities, because they clapped politely at Gisborne's swordsmanship.

I don't recall beginning to run, but I found I was already moving toward Rob when he lost his sword. I reached under my borrowed dress for the sword I'd strapped to my waist. I didn't care who saw the long underwear I wore as I lifted the folds and clumsily pulled my sword from the scabbard. "Rob!" He met my eyes with an open mouth. I threw my sword to him and he reached out and plucked it from the air. Thank the lord for Bridgette. I'd never have brought that thing with me had she not convinced me I needed to learn to use it.

Gisborne dragged Eliza in front of himself again, smirking at Rob. "You can't win. You won't kill her, and you're outnumbered and in an enclosed space."

"Just watch me," said Rob, through clenched teeth.

Six more soldiers ran into the courtyard from somewhere inside the castle. They paused a moment as they stepped through the door, assessing the commotion before running toward Rob and Gisborne. From the other direction Miller, Tuck and John ran toward him, too. They pushed people who stood in their way, clambering over tables or chairs, and drawing their weapons as they ran.

The clapping of the crowd turned to stunned screams, as they realized this wasn't a show.

"Arrest her!" The Sheriff pointed at me, his voice booming over the clashing of swords.

A soldier peeled off from the group running at Rob and came charging at me. I turned to sprint from him to find another soldier coming from the other direction. I'd been so caught up watching Rob that I hadn't thought to pull my dagger from my boot. I bent now, my heart pounding as I fiddled with the lacing that secured it in place. I couldn't release it while I moved. If I stopped, they'd surround me, and one little knife was no match against two swords. I gave up on my dagger, straightening and searching the courtyard for a place to hide.

"Maryanne!" Bridgette's voice came to me over the panicked yells of the Sheriff's guests. She ran toward me, something about her gait seeming wrong. As she reached me, she stopped, untied her cloak and let it fall to the ground, then she unstrapped a small bow and quiver from her back and threw it to me. From the scabbard strapped to her waist overtop her beautiful silver dress, she pulled her own sword. "They're all the arrows I could bring. Use them wisely." She hooked her hand through my arm and dragged me over to the wall of the castle. At least no one could attack us from behind here.

The two soldiers came to a laughing halt in front of us.

"Nice try, girlies," said one. "Time to stop playing with the men's toys and hand them over."

"Men's toys?" asked Bridgette, all innocence and light. "Oh, you mean this?" She held up her sword as if she was going to hand it over. The soldier who'd spoken reached for it, but he was slow and unprepared for Bridgette's attack. Quicker than I thought possible, she buried her sword in his gut. Grunting, she pulled her sword free and swung at the soldier next to him, blood dripping from the shaft.

Around us, women screamed. Chairs fell backward, crashing against the cobblestones as people ran for the nearest exit. Plates, mugs and cutlery clattered to the ground, no one caring what they knocked over in their rush to safety.

The soldier blocked Bridgette's blow with the slightest effort, snarling at her. "Best say goodbye to Lord Sutherland, because you're about to die for killing my brother."

Bridgette ducked and danced in that elegant style of hers, and sliced into the soldier's arm, then brought a second swing down onto his neck. She turned to me, blood spattered over her face. "Run."

I couldn't. I had to help Rob. I glanced his way. He was still battling soldiers where I'd left him, the clashing of their swords adding to the commotion in the courtyard.

Bridgette grabbed my arm and pulled me away, weaving through the upturned chairs and tables. "Up there." She pointed to a set of steps that led to a closed door into the castle. When I hesitated, she dragged me up. She stopped before entering the castle, turning me by my shoulders to look out across the courtyard. "Use your bow."

I stared at her. "How did you know? To bring weapons, I mean?" It was a huge risk on her part, and whatever happened now, she would be implicated right along with us.

"Eliza. She came to me just after dawn. Said you were planning something, and that she recommended I bring my sword." She shrugged. "Had a feeling you might not be able to bring a bow inside the castle. Guess I was right."

I shook my head. If she hadn't been here, if Eliza hadn't told her, I'd have been captured by now. "Thank you. For helping me."

"You're welcome. Now don't let it go to waste." She indicated at the courtyard in front of us.

The steps we stood on looked out over the heads of the few guests who hadn't yet fled to safety. A group of soldiers jogged toward us. I pulled an arrow from my quiver and shot, hitting a shoulder, a chest, a neck, while Bridgette handed me arrows. "How's Rob doing?" I asked, aiming at another soldier, the last for the moment. The rest were approaching Rob, moving away from us.

"Fine, I think. There are soldiers on the ground at his feet. Bleeding."

"Gisborne?" I fired my arrow then followed her gaze.

Gisborne was still gripping Eliza to his chest. He'd gauged his brother correctly. Rob wouldn't hurt her. And given the bond between her, Miller and John, they wouldn't either. It meant Gisborne wouldn't die today. But we would if something didn't change. There were more soldiers on the way. I could see them in the distance, all the way down by the stables. They still had a decent distance to cover to get to us—up the cobbled street and through the inner gates then up another street to the courtyard—but we needed to leave now if we wanted to live.

"Can you hit Gisborne?" Bridgette asked.

I shook my head. Eliza was in my way, and the range of the small bow likely wouldn't reach. Plus, I was getting low on arrows. I didn't want to waste one on a shot that wouldn't help anyone.

A crack sounded louder than the clashing of blades, the noise different from the sound of metal hitting metal. More like something hard ricocheting off wood. I looked around to see where it had come from but couldn't find a source.

Another thud registered above the clashing of blades and Eliza crumpled in Gisborne's arms. Her sudden weight overwhelmed him, and he dropped her, before stumbling over her lifeless body.

There was a shout from the opposite side of the courtyard, and I turned. Alan stood on a set of steps identical to the ones we were on with his hands in the air, the way I'd seen him do when he won a game in the village of Oxley. In his hand was a stone, and on the ground in front of him, at least three more. The first crack had been him hitting the wooden railing of the gallows with a rock.

The second had been his stone hitting Eliza's head. I hoped she was all right.

I now had a clear shot at Gisborne. Whether my bow was up to the job was another question we were about to get an answer to. I focused on him. With his sword drawn, he approached Rob. I would kill the bastard before he got close enough to do any damage.

"Soldiers, Maryanne."

Ignoring Bridgette, I drew the bowstring back to my cheek. Then I pulled it back further, making sure I got the extra distance.

"Maryanne." Bridgette's voice was high-pitched and panicked.

I dragged my eyes from Gisborne to find three soldiers running toward us. They must have come from inside the castle, because the large group from the stables was yet to enter the inner walls. Three quick shots and they were no longer a threat.

I turned back to Gisborne.

John approached a soldier from behind, swinging the leg of one of the tables at him. Another soldier jumped between them and took the full force of John's blow. He hadn't even hit the ground before John was searching for his next victim. Miller held his own against a different soldier with a sword. Tuck dispatched yet another soldier with a stab to his gut. He ran to fight back-to-back with Rob, who had three soldiers surrounding him, including Gisborne.

With Gisborne now in the middle of the fighting, my chance was gone. There was too much movement, too many people in the way for a clear shot. And I now only had one arrow left.

"We have to move." I pulled my arrow from the bow and started down the steps. I needed a better vantage point. Somewhere closer to aim my arrow at Gisborne.

Gisborne was strong. He'd trained all his life with a sword. He lined Rob up and brought his sword down toward him. Rob blocked, but the blow knocked Rob off balance. He stepped back, stumbling on a soldier lying prone and losing his footing to land on the ground. Gisborne loomed over him, his sword pulled back ready to strike.

Halfway down the steps, I stopped, raised and nocked my bow and drew the string back.

Gisborne's sword started to come down.

Rob scrambled to stand. He was too slow, wasn't ready, couldn't block.

He was going to die.

I let my arrow loose, talking to Rob beneath my breath as it flew.

Get up, Rob. Raise your sword.

Everything was happening too quickly. And too slow at the same time. Gisborne was going to win. There was nothing else I could do to stop him. I was out of arrows.

Get up!

Gisborne's sword came down. I braced to watch it bite into Rob, and take off his head, or arm or leg.

My arrow hit.

It plowed into Gisborne's shoulder, through the beautiful royal blue material of his tunic. It felt good to see his body jerk as the arrow connected. It felt better to see his sword stutter in its arc. I hoped he was hurting. I hoped he felt more pain than he'd ever inflicted on anyone else.

But what should have stopped Gisborne's swing, didn't. His sword continued its motion, Gisborne too stubborn to give in to an arrow in his shoulder. With his eyes fixed on his brother, his sword came down toward Rob.

There was a blur of movement.

A scream curdled my blood.

Guests yelled. Blood sprayed.

Gisborne's sword had found a home. In Tuck's arm, near his shoulder.

Tuck stumbled and his knees gave out. He toppled over at Gisborne's feet.

Gisborne bent, pulling his sword from Tuck's body, leaving a spurting wound at the top of Tuck's arm.

I didn't see Rob move. One moment he was on the ground. The next he was on his feet, sword raised above Gisborne as he leaned over Tuck removing his weapon. Rob's sword sank into Gisborne's back like a knife through butter.

Gisborne hit the cobblestones face first and silent. Rob reared back and hit him again. And a third time.

Bridgette grabbed my arm. "Come on. Time to go."

Gisborne was dead. There was no doubt this time.

Soon, the soldiers from the stables would be here. Someone would step into Gisborne's shoes as commander, and the soldiers would attack us in force. Right now, though, we had a few stunned moments to retreat.

Rob bent beside Tuck, pressed his lips together and flung him over his shoulder. He called for John and Miller, but there was no need. They were already following.

Miller took a couple of steps then crouched beside Eliza, who was still flat on her back.

"Miller!" Rob screamed at him, his voice the only thing I could hear above the rapid thud of my heart.

With just a moment's pause, Miller lifted Eliza over his shoulder and followed Rob, John and Tuck. They reached the side of the castle, heading for the dungeon entrance. In less than a minute, they'd ducked out of sight.

"You need to go." Bridgette tugged at me.

"I know." I hurried down the rest of the steps. Everyone else was closer to the dungeon entrance than me. I had to run across the courtyard before I could follow them around the side of the castle. First though, I had to find Alan. Rob must not have seen him. There was no way he'd have left without him if he knew he was here. Already backing away, I glanced at Bridgette. "What about you?"

She shrugged, a soft smile creeping onto her face. "Whatever happens, it was worth it to wipe the smug look off those soldier's faces."

"Come with us." I saw her ancient husband in my mind as I spoke. And the way she only ever truly lit up when she was using her sword. She'd get no chance of that again if she stayed here, assuming they didn't take her to the gallows for treason because of what she'd done today.

She shook her head, uncertainly. "I couldn't."

"Of course you could." I took another step away. I needed to go. "But you have to decide now."

She stood on the bottom step, glancing around.

"I can't wait here. I have to find Alan. If you want to come with us, meet us at the dungeon entrance. We're leaving now."

She nodded and ran forward to give me a firm hug. Not coming then. I hugged her back. "It's been good to know you, Lady Sutherland."

"You, too, Lady Fitzwalter."

I ran then, sprinting the width of the empty courtyard, dodging chairs and tables while trying not to trip on walking sticks, flower vases, tankards and anything else that had sprawled onto the cobblestones as guests rushed to safety.

The pounding of hundreds of feet told me the huge group of soldiers were approaching the inner wall. There wasn't much time, but we'd come for Alan. He was the whole reason we were here. I couldn't leave until I had him with me.

I ran toward the place I'd last seen him, the steps on the opposite side of the courtyard like the ones I'd used. They weren't there now, I could see that, but I hoped they were nearby and waiting for me.

As I drew closer, they scrambled from their hiding place behind an overturned table.

"Come on, Alan. Let's go." I barely stopped running to take his hand. "Thanks, Xanthe. If we get out of here, we'll repay you with more gold than you've ever seen for what you did today."

I'm not sure if she spoke, because I was still running, this time with Alan's hand in mine. He gripped me tightly, putting his head down and sprinting beside me.

We rounded the corner where I'd last seen the boys, passing the oak tree Alan and I had climbed down just a few hours earlier. An arrow whistled between our heads, missing us both by millimeters. A soldier up on the inner wall pulled another arrow from his quiver. I pulled on Alan's hand, desperate to get away. Other than the oak, there was nothing for us to hide behind. We just had to keep running.

"Maryanne!" I turned at the sound of my name.

Hiding behind the oak, was Miller. He was bent in half, breathing heavily. An arrow jutted from his shoulder, and a groggy-looking-but-alive Eliza sat at his feet. "Miller! What happened? Are you okay?"

He nodded, wincing from that small movement. "I'm fine. Bastard up on the wall got me as I rounded the corner. I can't carry Eliza, though. Makes it hard to breathe."

"Go. Take Alan. I've got her." I turned to Alan. "Can you look after Miller for me? Take him through that door up there." I pointed to the place we were heading. We'd get there in less than a minute at a sprint. Slower with our injured. "I'll be there in a moment." I gave Alan's shoulder a squeeze. His brow furrowed, and his hands shook, but he nodded anyway. "Be brave a little longer. We're nearly safe."

He threw his arms around me, squeezed once, then pulled away. Taking hold of Miller's hand, the two of them ran toward the dungeon entrance, staying as close to the side of the castle as they could.

Eliza got to her feet, swaying. "You should run." Her words slurred and she bent over and rested her hands on her knees.

An arrow hit with a thunk, lodging into the trunk of the tree. I glanced at the inner wall in the distance. The Sheriff's archers were good shots, and they owned the best possible bows. We were very likely on the edge of their range. And there must be only one archer, or more arrows would be raining down on us.

"Gisborne's dead." I had no time to bundle it up any sweeter. And this time he was dead for real. Tabitha couldn't do a thing to save him today. "Do you want to come with us? You know you're welcome."

Eliza's shoulders fell. "I have nowhere else to go."

I took that as a yes. "Put your arm over my shoulder." I placed my hand around her waist. "We have to run. There are soldiers coming, and arrows. Can you do that?"

She nodded, but her knees buckled.

"Come on, Eliza." I held her up, taking her weight on my shoulders and hoping she was with it enough to help even a little. "I can't do this on my own." I glanced over my shoulder. No one was following. Yet.

This time I received a single nod. "I'm ready."

I steeled myself. The door to the dungeon wasn't too far. If we stayed close to the castle wall, we'd be as far from the arrows as possible. But we were still out in the open. There was nothing else to hide behind. "Let's go."

Eliza tried. She tried so hard to get to that door. But each time she got her legs under her, they buckled, and she stumbled. Every time, she hauled herself up, trying again and again as sweat dripped from her forehead.

It was no good. We were getting nowhere. The soldiers were coming. They might even be waiting on the other side of the door into the castle. Eliza and I making it to the dungeon was looking like a long shot.

"Here. Let me help." Xanthe ran up to us from behind, lifting Eliza's other arm and sliding it around her neck. "Let's go."

We were running before I had the chance to thank her. "Xanthe. You shouldn't be here. I'm going to get caught." And you will, too, was what I meant but couldn't voice.

"Not if I can help it." She stopped, forcing me to stop, too. Shuffling sideways, she pushed her back into Eliza's body, hoisting her into a piggy-back. She was small but so much stronger than me. I guess that's what years of hard labor did to a body. "Let's go," she said.

I ran beside them, a hand on Eliza's back, hoping she wouldn't fall. Xanthe was fast and fit, and we were almost at the door. Just a few more steps and we'd be inside. Then it was just the corridor to navigate before we were free. Maybe we would do this after all. Maybe we weren't going to die.

There was a soft thunk, and Xanthe let out a cry of pain before stumbling onto her knees. She teetered there a moment, still gripping tight to Eliza on her back, then she fell forward onto the ground. I dragged Eliza off her back. "Xanthe? Are you all right?" I held out my hand to help her.

She lifted her head and met my eyes, her face creased in pain. Her breathing was rapid, and she shook her head. "Arrow," she wheezed.

TWENTY

IT wasn't possible, not with Eliza on her back and the arrows coming from behind.

She made a motion with her right arm.

I bent and gingerly pulled back her cloak from where it had landed draped over her. She was right. There was an arrow embedded in her side, between her ribs. I'd heard it hit a moment ago. I just hadn't realized what the sound was.

I could have cried. We couldn't catch a break. "Can you get up?"

She shook her head, her breath coming in tiny gasps. "You go. Don't let...me slow...you down."

I wanted to leave. So much. I didn't want to die. I didn't want an arrow in my back or a sword through my neck. I wasn't brave. I was terrified. All I wanted was to be in the forest and away from this place. But I couldn't leave her. She'd helped us so many times. She deserved better than to be left on the ground to die.

I glanced from her to Eliza. Eliza seemed least injured, so I helped her to her feet, then pressed her hands against the outside of the castle. "Lean on the wall to hold yourself up. Get to that door over there. I'll help Xanthe then come back for you."

I didn't wait to see if she did as I asked, just raced over to Xanthe. She was smaller than me, and heavier than she looked. No matter how hard I tried, I couldn't lift her onto my back. I especially couldn't when she cried out in pain every time I moved her. I stared down at her, on her knees on the ground, wondering how I would get her to the dungeon.

"Just...do it." Xanthe clenched her jaw. I considered for a moment, before ignoring her cries and dragging her onto my back.

We reached the door into the castle dungeon to footsteps slapping against the stone floor. I stopped, feeling like a deer caught in headlights. After everything, all the fighting, I was done. I had nowhere to hide. No weapon to fight with. No idea how to escape. The soldiers guarding the dungeon were dead—I guessed the boys had taken care of them already—but even without them to contend with, I still didn't have enough time to get all of us around the corner to the tunnel door safely before those running feet found us.

It was over.

I'd tried.

I'd failed.

I laid Xanthe on the stone floor. I wanted to curl into a ball and cry.

"Maryanne?" Rob appeared around the corner in the corridor, with John close behind. I let out my breath. It was their footsteps, not the soldiers.

"Eliza," I panted, turning and running back out the door. Rob caught up to me, then sprinted ahead when he spotted Eliza. With one of us on each side, we guided her through the castle door.

"You're all right." Rob breathed the words out, like they were a relief to say as I slammed the castle door shut and pulled down the wooden bar that would keep it that way. Hopefully the lock would slow the soldiers who were coming for us— I could hear their shouts as they neared.

I had no time for relief. Or joy. Or any of the hundred other emotions I should be feeling to see him alive. We weren't safe yet. "I am. Are you?"

He picked Eliza up and started down the corridor behind John, who was already carrying Xanthe. He nodded. "I'm fine." The outside door rattled as someone tried to open it. When it wouldn't move, there was a string of curses followed by the banging of weapons against the wood. The security bar wouldn't hold them out for long.

"Let's go!" Rob called.

No corridor had ever felt so long. For every step I ran, it seemed like the door into the tunnel moved two steps farther away.

Behind us, the door into the castle rattled and banged again. From somewhere inside, voices called, searching for us. They were close.

We were closer.

I burst through the final door, the one that would give us our freedom, and, once Rob and John followed, Alan slammed the door shut. With Miller holding a candle for him to see, he put the key in the lock, twisting until the bolt slid into place. Eliza said there was only one key to that door. And we had it.

For a second, everyone was silent. I drew in a deep breath, and I heard the others do the same. I felt as if I hadn't breathed in the longest time, like I'd been holding it, waiting for an arrow to bury into my body.

I leaned against the damp wall, letting the bite of coldness sink into my sweat-soaked back.

We'd done it.

Alan was free.

Rob was free.

The price to get them back, however, was high.

Eliza was probably concussed. Xanthe and Miller had arrows sticking from their bodies and Tuck had a deep gash in his arm. He lay silently on the cold ground. Even by the dim light of Miller's candle, I could see the dark outline of blood on his tunic. What I hadn't expected to see was Bridgette, leaning over him and pushing a cloth against the wound.

"Bridgette?"

She gave a half-shrug. "I took a short-cut through the castle. Does that offer to come with you still stand?"

Of course it did, though I wasn't sure how we'd come for one person and brought out four.

Footsteps and voices sounded on the other side of the door. Someone rattled the handle. I wanted to run, but Eliza put her hand up to stop me. We were safe. The door was too heavy to break down. They couldn't get through.

"How's Tuck?" I asked, still trying to catch my breath.

Rob shook his head, holding a candle up.

What did that mean? That he was...dead? I crouched next to him. His chest rose and fell. Not dead then. Judging by the stickiness of the ground where I knelt, he'd lost a lot of blood. Tourniquet. That's what we needed, so we could move him. "I need more cloth. And a stick." I took over from Bridgette, holding the cloth to his wound.

Tuck reached up and grabbed my arm. "Forget it. I'm a goner, anyway." His voice was a whisper between breaths.

Rob crouched on Tuck's other side. "Not happening. You're coming with us and you're going to make it. No excuses." He ripped a strip of cloth from the bottom of his tunic. "Will this do?"

I nodded. There was no wood in here to wind the tourniquet, except the piece John had used for a staff, and that was too big. "Alan, can I have the keys, please?"

He handed them over and I wrapped the cloth around both Tuck's arm and the key ring then twisted the ring to tighten the band.

"I'm sorry," Tuck whispered. I thought he meant about getting hurt, until I looked up to find him watching Rob.

"Nothing to be sorry for. Unless you die." Rob tried to smile but it was hollow and lifeless.

"You know there is. I'm sorry, Rob. For what I did that night. I'm not sorry about after. The last six years have been the best of my life."

Rob shook his head, lifting his eyes to look past Tuck and into the darkness of the tunnel. "Don't talk like this, Tuck. Maryanne's going to fix you up, and we're going to get you out of here." He looked at me, his eyes shining. "Right?"

I couldn't answer that because he wouldn't want to hear what I had to say. Even if I could get the tourniquet to stop the bleeding, what did we do with him after? He'd lost so much blood already. And then there was the risk of infection since he was currently lying on the floor of a rat-infested tunnel.

"Right?" he asked again.

I half-raised my hands. Probably not. But I wouldn't say it. Not in front of Tuck.

Rob got to his feet, strode two paces away, then let out a loud growl. A moment later he was back, kneeling on the ground beside Tuck. "Maryanne will fix you. But in the meantime, you should know I'm sorry, too. For hitting you. I never should have done it. It's the whole reason we're here right now."

Perhaps. Perhaps not. If Tuck's eye hadn't been half-closed from that punch, he might have been able to make the shot that would have stopped Gisborne taking Alan back to the castle, and we'd never have had to return here today. Then again, he might have missed. Or perhaps he'd only have wounded Gisborne, who then would have killed Alan and set thirty soldiers on us. The possibilities were endless, and none of them mattered.

"But you need to know something, too. I knew you'd worked for him, for Gisborne's father. Or suspected, anyway. I don't remember you dragging me out to the Big Tree, but I'd often wondered how you found me in the forest if you didn't already know where to look. Plus, why else did you have a pile of coins hidden in the base of the tree when I was younger? It never mattered to me because you more than made up for it every single day since. I wouldn't be here without you." He paused, looking out over Tuck's head again and drawing a deep breath. "But I'm not ready to forgive you yet. I'm going to need you to hold on just a little longer."

Tuck reached up and gripped Rob's hand. "Thank you, Robbie. Your forgiveness means everything."

Rob shook his head, his eyes finally meeting Tuck's. "Didn't you hear me? You're only forgiven if you hold on. Don't die, Tuck. Don't you dare die." His voice was rough.

"I'll try."

"You better. Because me and my sword are dying to kick your butt for getting yourself injured today." He put his other hand around Tuck's and squeezed it tight.

"You and your sword won't ever be good enough to kick my butt." Tuck's voice shrank to a whisper, while the banging against the door grew louder.

"Stick around. Find out." Rob's voice wobbled this time. The lightness was there, but he'd figured out what Tuck knew already. What I knew, too, even though I kept tightening the tourniquet just in case it helped.

"Miller?" Tuck breathed.

Miller moved out of the shadows to stand beside Tuck. Tears stained his face. I didn't think they were because of the arrow no one had thought to remove from his shoulder.

"I'm so proud of the man you're growing into, Miller. You've come so far from the boy I found lost in the forest almost four years ago. I'm going to need you to do something for me."

Miller nodded, moving toward his friend with slow feet and crouching next to him. Rob shuffled to the side, and Miller took Tuck's hand.

"Look after Rob for me. He's prone to getting himself into trouble. Does stupid things. Doesn't think anything through."

Miller barked out a laugh. It was the saddest sound I'd ever heard.

"I need you to keep him in check. Make sure he doesn't get himself killed. Can you do that?"

Miller nodded, wiping his face with the sleeve of his tunic. "I can. But I'd rather you did it. Please, Tuck."

Tears sprang to my eyes. Tuck was the reason this group was here. The only reason. He'd kept them alive. Taught them how to live in the forest, helped them become friends with each other. He'd been the parent none of them had, even though he wasn't much older than John and Rob. He was the glue that bound them together.

"You'll do a better job than I ever did." He twisted his head, stopping when his eyes landed on John behind me. I started to stand, to get out of his way, but Tuck shook his head. "Wait," he said quietly to me, his eyes moving to John. "John. Make sure Miller remembers to eat. And don't let him near the whiskey ever again, no matter what. And no matter how old he is."

"No problem there," mumbled Miller. "I'm never touching that stuff again."

John's laugh was thin as he bent to listen to Tuck's fading voice.

"Talk to Rob. And make sure he talks to you. Like always." Tuck didn't want them to stop being the friends they'd always been once he was gone.

John nodded. In the dim light, his bottom lip wobbled, and I wondered if he didn't trust himself to speak, because he said nothing.

There was silence, just the sound of Tuck's labored breathing and the rest of us trying to keep our tears inside, all punctuated by the banging at the door.

"Rob," Tuck said. "You have to let it go. All of it. You've got a better family here than the one of your own blood. You must do what makes you happy. That goes for all of you. Nothing else matters but happiness. And Maryanne." He beckoned me closer. I leaned in for him to whisper in my ear. "Tell him how you feel, and then keep telling him. You're good for him. Don't listen to anyone who disagrees. They're wrong."

He was talking about himself. He'd been the one who never wanted me to go near Rob. I guessed it was a compliment that he was now giving us his blessing.

"Tuck, please." Miller wasn't even attempting to stop the tears streaming down his cheeks now.

"Stop. You're going to be all right. Maryanne's going to make sure..."

Tuck's smile was soft. "I am all right, Miller. Perfectly all right."

TWENTY-ONE

GRIEF is a funny thing. It hits everyone differently, at different times, and we all have different ways of coping. In the weeks after Tuck died, for Rob, coping meant spending hours on his own, hunting, fishing, listening to the forest. For Miller, it meant talking about Tuck. A lot. Something that didn't do any of us any harm at all. For John, well, he hadn't grieved yet. When he did though, we'd be here for him. All of us. As for me, I threw myself into sword lessons. From Miller. From Bridgette. From Rob. Anything to get myself out of my head. To stop replaying that day again and again, and to leave the guilt behind, even just for a minute or two.

I wasn't the only one who felt bad. I'd talked to everyone about that day, including Eliza, Alan and Bridgette, and every one of us felt like we could have done something different, something that might have saved Tuck. I was certain I could have put myself into a better position to fire an arrow into Gisborne's heart before he hurt our friend.

I felt doubly guilty. Xanthe also died that day. Quietly and with only Bridgette by her side, while the rest of us hovered over Tuck. I'd cried so many tears over that. She'd helped us and died for it, and the only person she knew—me—wasn't even with her when she passed. I should never have dragged her into our battle.

Bridgette said Xanthe told her she'd never had as much excitement in her life as she did when I was around. I think she meant it as a compliment, but I couldn't stop seeing another picture. One where she'd given her gold to her mother to get her out of a bad situation while she kept working for a man who hurt her. In another week or two, she planned to get out of there. Now she never would.

The first day I met her, I'd seen a bruise on her cheek, and I'd never given it a second thought until I saw her bruises the night she died. I wished I'd known how badly Gisborne treated her sooner.

I wished I'd tried harder to help her out of that place and away from that man.

Eliza had passed the weeks quietly. She was grieving, too, but not for Tuck. One morning, not long after that day, she'd screamed at Rob for killing Gisborne, had hit him with her fists and called him every name under the sun until she was exhausted. He'd taken her into his arms and cried with her for the little brother he'd never really had.

"You're pretty strong for a girl." Miller's voice pulled me out of my reverie. He sounded so serious as he spoke to Bridgette while they moved a log across the clearing. He didn't even slightly mean it. He and Bridgette acted like brother and sister. He'd do whatever he could to wind her up, looking for any sort of reaction. Usually, a comment like that would do it.

We'd moved back to the sprawling oak—the place Rob carried me to after Gisborne kicked me in the face at Edwinstowe—and we were making a permanent home. That log was going to be part of the framework for the first cottage. One of three we hoped to build here, in the middle of the forest.

"And you're in a good mood," Bridgette shot back with a smile on her face, not taking the bait. "Could it be because of a girl?"

Miller's cheeks colored.

I had no idea where he'd found the time to meet someone new, but according to John and Rob, whenever they went hunting with Miller, he always found a reason to stop in Edwinstowe. He spent half his time talking about how pretty she was, and the other half wandering around with a silly grin on his face. "When do we get to meet the mysterious Molly?" I asked, putting my first aid kit into my pack for later.

"You...want to meet her?" Miller's forehead creased into a frown.

"Of course, we do." Bridgette and I spoke at once. We were both curious about the young lady who'd brought a smile back to Miller's face.

"But..." Miller's frown deepened.

I got to my feet. "What's wrong, Miller? You don't have to bring her to meet us until you're ready. We're just kidding."

He looked at Bridgette. "Why would you care? You'll be going back to Nottingham soon, won't you?" His eyes moved to me. "And you're going to end up back in your own time because you insist on going to the Big Tree tonight. It'll be just like the last time you went there on a full moon." The night after the tournament when Tabitha had taken me home against my will.

I sighed. These past few months had been hard on everyone, but possibly hardest on Miller. He'd felt abandoned when Rob went to live with Alan, and now Tuck was gone and never coming back. It was no wonder he was worried about introducing us to anyone if he thought we were all going to leave anyway. "I'm not going anywhere, Miller."

"You might not have a choice." Miller had told me so many times I shouldn't go to the Big Tree tonight. He'd never said why he didn't want me to go until now.

I walked across the clearing and threw an arm around his waist, looking up at him. "I don't have a choice. Even if Tabitha wanted to take me home tonight, she couldn't. I can't go back. I'm here to stay."

"I can't go back, either. I'll be hanged." Bridgette came to stand on the other side of Miller. "But I don't want to. I love living out here. I want to help you when you get back to stopping carriages. I want to help the poor. I want to be like you." She leaned forward and lowered her voice like she was telling a secret. "Don't tell Rob, but this is what I wanted the very first time you stopped my carriage. I came into the forest that day thinking if I impressed Rob enough with my beauty or my wealth, or if I could get him to like me enough, he might just ask me to stay."

Miller's eyebrows shot up. "You were in love with Rob?"

Bridgette shook her head. "No. I didn't even know him. I just knew I agreed with what he was doing—what you were all doing." She lifted her shoulders. "And that I couldn't stand living in the city another day. Unfortunately, it didn't work out that way. But now you've brought me here, you're not getting rid of me that easily."

I grinned at her. I loved having female companions out here and didn't want her or Eliza to leave.

Miller looked between the two of us before finally nodding. "Okay. If you both degree not to leave, I'll bring her to meet you next week."

I glanced at Bridgette, a grin splitting my face. "What do you say? Can you degree to that?"

She laughed and pulled us both into a hug. "That is most definitely something I can degree with."

"Who's agreeing to what?" Rob spoke from behind us, his hair wet from his recent bath in the river. He'd changed into a clean tunic and pants rather than the ones he'd been working in to build the cottage earlier today.

"None of your business." I grinned.

"Ready to go?" he asked, picking up my pack from the ground and holding it out to me.

I nodded. Tonight, I was acting on a promise it seemed I'd given in another life. Rob, John, Eliza and I were going to the Big Tree for the full moon.

"Let's go, then. We're already ten minutes behind the others."

I smiled again. "Because you had to have a bath before we left."

He put his hand on my back and directed me toward the trail. "I know how much you like it when I smell good."

I was too nervous to speak as we pushed our way along the narrow path drawing closer to the Big Tree. Ever since Eliza came back to tell us about Alan, maybe even before that, I'd begun to like her. My initial promise to help her had been to get myself out of a hole. Tonight, I wanted everything to go the way Eliza wanted, because she deserved this.

Three months. That was the time frame Tabitha and I had agreed on as she sent me back here a second time. If she came to the Big Tree tonight, it would be because my family had helped her, and she was free of the portal. It was a big *if*.

"Can you feel it yet?" Eliza asked from up front. She turned as she spoke, walking backward. Bouncing, actually. She was trying hard—and failing—to keep her excitement inside. John walked beside her, watching with a bemused smile, the way he always watched her these days.

We were close. The air was growing cooler, the way it did when the portal opened. That was what Eliza was asking about. I nodded and watched a smile light up her face. "Eliza, you do understand, she might not be free?" Maybe Tabitha wouldn't be here at all. Maybe the chill I felt was just a change in the weather.

Eliza let out a loud sigh, turning to walk forward again. "I *know*. You've told me. At least a hundred times." She strode away ahead of us, speaking in a muted voice to John.

I had told her. Because I didn't want to disappoint her.

Rob put his arm over my shoulder. "Relax. You've done all you can."

I hadn't actually done anything except act on a hunch. I nodded toward the two of them. "Those two spend more time together every day."

A slow smile spread across Rob's face as he watched his friend. "They do. They're good for each other."

"Do you think there's something between them?" They were friends. I wasn't sure if they were anything more. Or if either of them even wanted that.

Rob shook his head. "Not yet." His sentence sounded unfinished. Like he wanted to add *but soon*.

A few months ago, I would have laughed at the idea of John and Eliza being friends, let alone something more. Now, it felt right. I hoped their friendship would grow. Watching them together made me smile.

I drew in a breath. Both Rob and Eliza turned to look at me. I nodded to the question in their eyes. It wasn't a change in the weather. The air had just shifted. The portal was open.

Eliza broke into a run with John just a pace behind. I followed, but they were fast, especially Eliza, now she'd given up her beautiful castle dresses and boots for a simpler wardrobe that worked better in the forest.

By the time I got to the tree, Eliza was in her sister's arms, hugging and laughing like a child on Christmas morning. John stood at the edge of the bracken, watching with a soft smile on his face.

The clearing glowed, the way it did when the portal was open. I turned in a circle and sighed, my shoulders drooping. Tabitha was here, but she was alone. It could only mean one thing.

"What?" asked Rob, standing beside me.

"I don't think it worked. There's no one here to take Tabitha's place in the portal. My family mustn't have been able to help her."

Tabitha looked up, releasing her sister. "Hello, Maryanne." Her movements were regal and considered. She smoothed her red dress. It touched the leaf-strewn ground and had long, wide sleeves; more fashionable in the twelfth century than the twenty-first. "I spoke to your family."

I nodded. I hadn't tapped on the tree to summon her—the way I did when I wanted to travel through time—which meant she was here of her own free will. Was she here to tell us my family couldn't help? "And?" Because the dress made me wonder. If she didn't intend to stay here, why bother dressing this way?

"Yes," she breathed, her smile as wide as her sister's.

"You're free?" Eliza asked.

Tabitha nodded. "Thanks to Maryanne. And Maud."

She stepped aside and the girl who looked just like me was there, in blue jeans and a cropped T-shirt, with a leather jacket thrown over top. Slung over one shoulder was a small blue backpack.

Rob drew in a breath.

I broke into a grin. "Maud!"

"Maryanne." She ran across the uneven ground and wrapped me in a hug.

"Was I right? Is Keeper of the Portal your dream job?" Maud once told me she didn't want a boring life. She wanted to see, do and experience all the things she would never have had the chance to do in her own time. Plus, she never again wanted to live in the time she was born. The portal seemed like the perfect place for her, especially because she'd made a home with my family, and she could go back to see them any time she wanted.

She nodded, her face split with a beaming smile.

" *You're* the new Keeper of the Portal?" Rob's eyebrows shot up to his hairline. I hadn't given anyone any details of what I hoped would happen tonight. Mostly because I wasn't certain there was anything to tell.

She nodded again, her face glowing as if she'd won the lottery. "When Tabitha knocked on our door a month after you left, I almost slammed it in her face."

"Almost?" Tabitha's eyebrows rose.

Maud shrugged. "Okay. I did slam the door in her face. Tried to, at least, but she shoved one of her Doc Martens in the way and wouldn't move until I promised to let her talk to your dad."

"And he figured out a way to swap you for Maud?" Rob frowned as he tried to work out how they'd all come to be here.

"He tried." Tabitha glanced at Eliza quickly, as if she couldn't quite believe she was here, before continuing to speak. "He tried so hard to help, especially once he knew it was Maryanne who suggested I come to him. He spent a month researching and I went back after the next full moon, but he still had no idea."

I shook my head. "So, how are you both here?" I'd thought Maud would be the perfect candidate for the job, and that Dad would know how to make it happen.

Maud gave a wry smile. "Your dad kept inviting Tabitha for dinner."

"I think he has a soft spot for us orphans," Tabitha interrupted.

Maud was shaking her head before Tabitha had even finished talking. "I think anything to do with time travel makes him feel closer to Maryanne." Tabitha tilted her head slightly, agreeing, and Maud continued. "Once I got over myself and forgave her for sending me back through time, we got to talking, and I realized the job Tabitha hated more than anything was the job I'd been searching to find."

Tabitha grinned at her. "Your dad kept looking for information, and one night just over a week ago while Maud and I sat outside talking, he came racing out trying to hide his smile. He suggested

Maud think about the thing she wanted most while saying aloud she'd help me with the thing I most wanted."

I raised my eyebrows. "It was that easy?"

Eliza frowned, shaking her head like she couldn't believe it was that simple either. "But...you're not a witch."

Tabitha gave her sister a raised-brow look. "She's not. And neither am I."

"Then how...?" Eliza shook her head.

Maud slipped the backpack off her shoulder, placing it on the ground at her feet. "The Keeper can only be someone who already has the ability to time travel. And someone who wants the job."

Eliza shook her head, her eyes going between Maud and Tabitha. "But you never wanted the job. You got it anyway."

Tabitha shrugged. "I was tricked. The witch who was here before me wanted infamy. The tithe she demanded when people traveled wasn't gold or riches. It was that they spread her name. She wanted everyone to know her, and I believe many people did. At least within the community of time travelers anyway—they all knew who she was." Tabitha leaned forward as if she was sharing a secret. "I think she also wanted to terrify people, but when you're linked to a portal that travels through time, there's often far scarier things awaiting travelers at their destination than a witch who can manage a few party tricks."

Eliza shook her head. "I still don't understand."

I did. At least, I thought I did. "By telling ten people at once about that witch, the magic saw you helping her get what she most desired. You are lucky enough—or unlucky, I guess—to have the ability to time travel. Both those things together told the magic in the portal you wanted the job and led to you becoming the Keeper of the Portal." I glanced at Maud. "And now, by helping Tabitha get what she desired—back here to Eliza—you can take her place."

Maud and Tabitha nodded. "How did you know?"

I lifted my shoulder. "I wasn't certain I knew anything at all, but when I was in the portal with Tabitha—awake, instead of whatever she did to me the other times—the magic nudged me in the right direction. I never had any plans to mention Maud that day, but the magic kept nudging me to do it until I was certain it was the right thing to do. And that Dad would help with the rest."

"How could you not hate this job?" Eliza looked at Maud. "I don't want to talk you out of this, but are you sure you've even thought this through?"

"I have. It's what I want." Maud's tone was measured, and she watched Eliza carefully, her happiness disappearing the moment their eyes met.

"You know you'll be trapped in the job for the foreseeable future. Tabitha isn't coming back when you decide you've had enough." The snap in Eliza's voice spoke volumes about the bad blood between the two of them.

I couldn't imagine Maud ever being sick of the portal. But then, Eliza barely knew that side of her. I didn't want them to fight. In fact, I was certain if they got to know each other, they'd become friends. "I think it's more a matter of perspective, Eliza. Tabitha wanted to be where you were more than anything else."

"And I said goodbye to my family long ago. They didn't care about me. Just ask Maryanne. They never came searching once they heard I was back, did they?" Maud raised her eyebrows as she looked at me.

I shook my head. I had doubts the Sheriff had even told Maud's father she was back. He'd told me he was going to send a letter. The next day, I'd ruined his tournament, and I'd never set eyes on the man. As far as I knew, he was still in France.

Maud shrugged. "Gisborne was the only one who cared about me, and he screwed that up by kissing Eliza. Nothing is holding me to the time I was born in. And being the Keeper of the Portal means I get to visit different times, and see all the places I've read about in the history books. And I can still go back to Maryanne's family whenever I want to. Which reminds me..." She picked the backpack up from the ground and threw it to me. "Josh sends his love."

I caught the bag and opened the zip. It was filled to the brim with king-sized blocks of chocolate.

I laughed, and Eliza let out a whoop.

"He thought you might be missing your favorite food."

"We all are," said Eliza, with a grin.

"Tell him thanks." Miller would be set for a hundred breakups now, with that amount of chocolate. Or maybe we'd down the whole lot tonight when we got to talking about Tuck again.

"I probably won't see them for a while." Maud's gaze was apologetic. "There are so many things I want to do and see, and the portal can take me to all those places. I did promise to be back for Josh's birthday, though. I'll tell him then. And maybe you could leave me notes here at the tree? When there's something you need?" She glanced at Tabitha for guidance. Tabitha had once left a note for Eliza. There was no reason Maud and I couldn't do the same. Tabitha nodded. "Do it, if you need me. I've got your back. All of your backs." She looked at each of us.

"I have a gift for you, too." I slipped her engagement ring off my finger. I'd been wearing it since the night Tuck died. The night Eliza returned it to me. "So you don't forget your past."

She took it gently from me. "I was so in love when he gave me this. Then he…" Cheated on her with Eliza Thatcher. And the rest was history.

"Wear it anyway," I said. "And remember the good times."

The moon lit up the forest floor, bathing the trail in light. Maud, John and Tabitha had already returned to our camp. Tabitha had plenty of gold from the tithes she'd collected in the portal, but before she started spending any of it, she wanted to get to know Eliza again. And the people who were important to her. Us. It suited me because Eliza would be staying around for a while. I was fairly sure it suited John, too. All three of them had left with huge grins on their faces.

Rob refused to travel back with them. He was taking me somewhere, and it was a secret. I didn't ask where we were going, instead enjoyed the feel of his hand wrapped around mine as we wandered slowly through the dark forest rather than running for our lives.

Rob talked for our entire journey, about the trees we were passing and how he'd climbed them as a kid, about Woodhurst Manor, about his friends, even about Tuck. Aside from the gaping hole Tuck's death had left in his life—in all our lives—he seemed happy. And it made me happy, too.

Finally, we stopped at the edge of the forest, looking down over a little village lit up in the darkness by the silvery light of the full moon.

"Do you recognize this place?" he asked.

Of course, I did. This was where I'd come on that first day, where I'd found the baby and where I'd met Rob. And where, on a different day, I'd first met Eliza and Gisborne, too. It was the village of Edwinstowe. Tonight, it wasn't deserted, or terrorized. There weren't people lying on the ground dying, and others running for their lives. There were three newly built huts with smoke pouring from the chimneys, and timber lying on the ground for a fourth. "Why are we here?"

"Do you remember getting angry with me?"

I raised my eyebrows. "Once or twice. Can you be more specific?"

His lips twisted as he tried not to smile. "The first day we stopped Bridgette's carriage. When I took her ring."

My cheeks heated. Of course, I recalled that day. I'd fired an arrow because I'd been jealous of her. Not my proudest moment. "Oh, that day," I said casually. "I think I remember."

He pressed his lips together trying to hide another smile. No fooling him. "I wanted to show you where it went."

I frowned. "Where what went?"

"Her ring. It was too dangerous to give it away as it was, so we kept it until we found someone who could melt it down. Then we found someone else willing to swap gold for the jewels. This is where the gold went. I've wanted to show you ever since you came back, but..." He shrugged. It wasn't like we'd had a lot of down time since I returned.

"I thought they all died, the people who lived here." There hadn't been any sign of survivors that day, or the day we returned to find Eliza. And the one time I'd been back since, I'd only seen a few men in the fields.

"They were hiding in the forest. There are only four families here now, and life isn't easy, but still." He pulled a small pouch out from beneath his cloak. Opening it, he dipped his hand inside and drew out some coins, offering a few to me.

"Where did you get that?" It seemed like an age since we'd stopped any carriages for gold.

"Miller talked me into it the day the rest of you went to Nottingham. Haven't had a chance to hand out the gold until now. Tomorrow, we'll get ourselves some more. I've got a legend to uphold, right?"

I nodded, smiling.

"Now, pull your hood up."

When we reached the huts, people came cautiously from their homes, the words *Robin Hood* quietly on their lips. The full moon lit the town like it was midday. Rob handed a coin to each person, nudging me to do the same. In all the villages we'd visited doing this exact thing, I'd never seen such gratitude—life was clearly still difficult here, and probably would be for some time to come.

A baby sitting on a woman's hip caught my eye. I turned to Rob. "Is that...?"

"The baby you rescued? Yes. Edwina—the woman you left her with—brought her back here to bury the girl's mother. And never went home. I believe she's fallen in love with a man who lives here."

I walked over to Edwina and handed her a coin. She bowed her head in thanks, not seeming to recognize me. But the little girl squealed then giggled, reaching her arms out, and I told myself she remembered me. Giving her hand a squeeze, I returned to Rob, and the two of us started back up the hill toward the darkness of the forest.

"Thank you." I felt lighter than I had in weeks. Years. "For showing me."

Rob swallowed. "I didn't want you to be angry with me. For letting someone we didn't know see my face. Especially since that's what caused all that trouble at the tournament, which led to Tabitha taking you back home. I wanted you to know that to me, it was worth it. I'd show everyone my face as many times as it took, if it meant these people and the others trying to get by in the forest would have a proper village to live in."

I shook my head. "I'm not angry with you, Rob. What happened that night, happened. It's worked out for the best." We'd been through so much since that day.

Rob let out a breath. "Good." He was silent for a moment, our footsteps in the long grass the only sound. "You're not wearing the ring I gave you." It was more of a question than an accusation.

I hadn't worn it since the night he gave it to me. I wasn't sure if Rob really wanted me to have it, or if he'd just handed it to me because he expected to die in a few hours. A less cowardly person would have talked to him about it, but I told myself he wouldn't want to be bothered by such things so soon after his friend's death. "I thought you might have changed your mind about giving it to me."

He took a deep breath. "Do you remember asking me why I came out of the forest to help you with Gisborne that day at Edwinstowe?"

I nodded.

"I told you there was another reason, too. I...think...I want to tell you that reason now."

I already knew this. "You told me once before. You said it was because I made you care about something other than revenge."

"That's true. But there was another reason, too." The moonlight caught on his beautiful face, forming a mask of dips and hollows. "The other reason I came out of the forest that day was because I already liked you. I liked you from the moment I saw you fire my bow at the deer. Years before I met you, I had a dream about you. I saw you, not your face, just you, using your bow." He shrugged as if that was the best he could explain it. "I knew back then that if you ever came into my life, you'd be the only woman for me."

We'd managed to skirt around this conversation for months. If we were doing it tonight, then I had some things to say, too. I'd promised Tuck I would. "I fell for you the day you followed me to the Big Tree then bandaged my hands and wiped my tears, even though you didn't understand anything I was saying."

His grin grew wide and wicked. "I think you're lying."

I tried not to smile and failed. Wherever this was about to go, I had a feeling I wasn't going to like it.

"I think, Lady Maryanne, you fell for me the day we swam together at Frog Rock."

I choked out a laugh. I'd certainly seen more of him that day than I'd planned. He'd seen more of me than he should have, too.

"You haven't called me that for a long time." I'd been Lady Maud to him when we met. Once he knew I wasn't her, it had taken a while for him to drop the formality of her title. Now he rarely used it.

The wickedness on his face was replaced with a lazy grin that lit me from the inside. "You like it when I call you that. Your cheeks go pink and your eyes light up. And it makes you want to kiss me."

I put my hands to my warm cheeks. "Are you sure you're not talking about yourself?"

He pressed his lips together, a smile in his eyes. "You call me by my name all the time. Like when you're angry with me, or when you're telling me to run from soldiers. I don't believe I've wanted to kiss you *every* time you've said my name."

I stepped toward him, happy to play this game. There had been bursts of this playfulness since Tuck's death, but they were always short lived. "I beg to differ. But if that doesn't do it for you, perhaps another name will. A name that, under different circumstances would have been yours." Had his brother not been such a bastard. And had the Sheriff not seized Woodhurst as the King's property the moment Gisborne died a month ago. Maybe one day Rob would get it back again. We were certainly planning to fight for it, but that was a fight for another day. "My lord."

He sucked in a breath and his eyes went to my lips.

I giggled because I loved the effect those words had on him. "Told you so."

He met my eyes, a wolf finding his prey. "You told me once you didn't think you were the one for me, that my legend said there was someone else. Do you still think that?"

It felt like a long time since I'd worried whether I was Rob's Marian or not. It had seemed so important when I first arrived, like I'd needed to know where I fit in. It didn't matter now, though. I was here. I was part of his legend and I wasn't *Rob's* anything. I was here in my own right. Maryanne Warren. Part of his legend because of the things I'd done to help, not because of how he might or might not feel about me. I was proud of that. As for whether I was the one for him, I didn't know. It wasn't like we'd had time to work that out. I shrugged. "Maybe."

"What's her name? This woman that's supposedly going to mean more to me than you do?"

He didn't need to kiss me to get my heart racing. He could do that just as easily with words. And he did. Often. I didn't want to think about what might be in my future anymore. I just wanted to take the days as they came. "Marian. Her name is Lady Marian."

"Huh." Rob stopped at the edge of the forest, took my hands and pulled me toward him. For a moment, he stared at me, those eyes that reminded me of summer in Sherwood Forest searching my face. My heart hammered again, the way it always did when he was near.

Rob shook his head. "You're a funny little thing sometimes, Maryanne Warren."

As he spoke, the magic that let me understand his twelfth century English wavered and I heard the way he said my name.

Marian.

For all the months we'd known each other, he'd called me Marian. It was the way the magic made him hear my name. I just hadn't known.

"It's a good thing I don't need to go out searching for her." Rob leaned in and pressed his lips to mine. "My Lady Marian is standing right in front of me."

GET THE SHERWOOD OUTLAWS
PREQUEL NOVELLA FOR FREE

Thanks for reading Outlasted.

I really enjoy getting to know my readers, it's one of the best things about being a writer. I send a newsletter to my readers group once a month, and that group is the first to find out about new releases and special offers.

If you sign up to my readers group, I'll send you a copy of Outcast for free. Outcast is a novella narrated by Rob, set before he met Maryanne. And, for now, my readers group is the only place it's available.

Just use the link below, then complete your email address. I'm looking forward to meeting you.

www.hayleyosborn.com/outcast

Enjoy this Book?

You can make a difference.

Honest reviews are an important part of a book's success as they help new readers discover new stories to enjoy. They are the most powerful thing for getting attention for my books.

If you enjoyed this book, I'd be forever grateful if you could take five minutes to leave a review on the book's Amazon page—it can be as short as you like.

Thank you!

Also by Hayley Osborn

The Sherwood Outlaws series

Outlawed
Outplayed
Outlasted
Outcast

Go to www.hayleyosborn.com to find out more.

Acknowledgments

At the start of this year, I decided I wanted to write an entire series before the end of the year, then publish the three main books a month apart. I was under no illusions about how much work was involved. At least, I didn't think I was. I knew writing 250,000 words would take some time, but I was up for the challenge. Turned out, writing the words was the easy part. Getting those words ready to publish—starting with editing and followed up by formatting (so it looks pretty), getting reviews (so readers know what to expect), and figuring out how to work a website—and finally pushing publish was infinitely more difficult. The payoff has been watching my thirteen and fifteen year old read and enjoy these books.

Melissa, thanks again for editing. And for making me laugh with your comments.

Kat, thanks for reading this whole series in its raw form, offering suggestions to make it better and being such a great support at the other end of my emails.

To Hayden, Jacob, Ashleigh, Zach, Mum, Dad and Kelly, thanks for your support. It means a lot.

And to everyone who read the entire series, thank you. You guys rock.

ABOUT THE AUTHOR

Hayley Osborn lives in Christchurch, New Zealand, with her husband and three children, cat and dog.

Online, you can find her at:

www.hayleyosborn.com.

To connect with her on social media, you can find her on Facebook at HayleyOsbornAuthor, or on Twitter at @Hayley____Osborn. Or if you prefer to make contact via email, you can contact her at hayley@hayleyosborn.com.